Grateful acknowledgement is made to *MCA Records, Inc.*, and *The Tragically Hip* for permission to reprint previously published material from the song *50 Mission Cap*. Copyright, 1992, MCA Records, Inc.

Cover design and concept by Julia Pelish.

Printed in Victoria, Canada

National Library of Canada Cataloguing in Publication Data

Brijbassi, Adrian, 1971-
  50 mission cap

ISBN 1-55212-616-1

  I. Title. II. Title: Fifty mission cap.
PS8553.R47F53 2001   jC813'.6   C2001-910075-2
PZ7.B7655Fi 2001

TRAFFORD

This book was published *on-demand* in cooperation with Trafford Publishing.
On-demand publishing is a unique process and service of making a book available for retail sale to the public taking advantage of on-demand manufacturing and Internet marketing. **On-demand publishing** includes promotions, retail sales, manufacturing, order fulfilment, accounting and collecting royalties on behalf of the author.

Suite 6E, 2333 Government St., Victoria, B.C. V8T 4P4, CANADA
Phone   250-383-6864   Toll-free   1-888-232-4444 (Canada & US)
Fax   250-383-6804   E-mail   sales@trafford.com
Web site   www.trafford.com   TRAFFORD PUBLISHING IS A DIVISION OF TRAFFORD HOLDINGS LTD.
Trafford Catalogue #01-0018   www.trafford.com/robots/01-0018.html

10   9   8   7   6   5   4   3

50

Mission Cap

Adrian Brijbassi

50 Mission Cap

T he saviour was supposed to come in the form of a skinny kid from a town with a long French name. That's what I had been told. After three seasons so miserable 2-1 defeats became bearable and shootout losses downright success stories, it was also what I needed to hear. Not only had the Kildare Kougars obtained a supreme talent, but we were going to win because of it. Make the playoffs, get on a roll, maybe even, you know, catch a break here or there, and, who knows after that, right?

Okay, so I was getting ahead of myself, but who wouldn't have?

"Scott, things are going to be different now," said the team's new owners. "We can finally get this town a winner and you that scholarship."

And there was more. No more month-long losing streaks, they had sold me. No more getting used to teammates only to see them traded away. No more disrespect. And I bought into it, all of it, no matter if it was true; it was the hope I was after. That's what I told Grandpa Joe, and he understood. I knew he would. For both of us, the truth could wait. In tiny

Kildare, Ontario, life, as my teammates and I knew it, was about to change.

The previous year we had won just ten of fifty-six games. Think of that: ten of fifty-six. So many players came and went, and the losing streaks dragged on so long that by the end of it I felt I had endured a career. Still, after three humiliating seasons as a Kougar, I returned for more; in uniform again, preparing for a new season. Lured back, with hope and promise as the bait, to that parochial little town in the heart of the Ottawa Valley.

But I felt conned when Dion Marcelle, the keeper of much of that promise, arrived at training camp. Swiftly, like a slap, the phenom managed to sully expectations before even one practice. He had no confidence, much less an aura of greatness. Tall and gangly, he kept his head hung low, hiding his pimply face, acting more like a nerd than a talent. On the ice, he would stumble when he tried to turn a corner and was so slow he barely stayed ahead of the fully equipped goaltenders, limited because they strained to contain their laughter. It wasn't long before he began to pant, taking deep, heaving breaths and blowing out frosty air as if allergic to it. A supposedly speedy centre with a wicked shot, Marcelle had moved to Kildare with his family from rural Quebec because "of undisclosed personal reasons," as the paper reported. The Kougars, believing the scouting reports that oozed with praise for him, immediately brought him in to foster change on our Junior A team that needed lots of it. Unfortunately, Marcelle displayed no traces of being a star, let alone a salve. After finishing my laps, I brushed my black hair out of my eyes, wiped sweat from my face and leaned against the boards, shaking my head at the sight of him lagging behind the other players, only a handful of whom showed signs of skill themselves. It wasn't long before I had company.

In my daze, I didn't notice Brendan Kowalczek, my best friend and our best player, gliding toward me. He was bent over with his stick resting across his knees until he whacked me on the shin with it: a hockey player's hello.

"That there's the future of Kildare hockey, my man," he said and lifted his chin to gesture toward Marcelle.

"Then I can't wait to be in its past," I replied.

He laughed. "One more season, bud," he said. "Just one more and it's welcome to the USA."

"Yeah, I wish," I said. "Looks like just another long year to me."

"No worries," he said. "We get that first win, things'll be lookin' good." He then jabbed my belly with the end of his stick, glanced up and said, "Gotta get rid of this, though."

"That's what camp's for."

I pushed his stick away and gave him a playful smack on the helmet. But he was right. Not into weights, I had gained a few too many pounds during what was a downer of a summer. Brendan, on the other hand, was in the finest shape of his life. His future was waiting to be seized and he was already putting a vice on it. Entering his final season of junior, Brendan, tall and blonde, built like a sword's blade, was being recruited by several schools from the States and was guaranteed a scholarship. He just had to decide where he wanted to go. Most of the rest of us — the less apt — had much more tenuous offers, if any at all. A couple of scouts had told me that — maybe — if I continued to show improvement, and stayed healthy, I would have a good shot at getting an offer for a full ride. Although that possibility was the main reason for my return to Kildare, I had never been totally convinced it would come true. Besides, I was too concerned about the present to ponder my future.

"How's Gramps?" Brendan asked. The coach's whistle had blown and he quickly skated to centre ice, looking away from me like he didn't want to see a wound.

"Doin' good, doin' good. He's hangin' in there," I said.

I followed him to the redline, where all the players were gathering. We lined up in front of Tyler Raycliffe, our new coach, who was eyeing us like a judge ready to pass sentence.

"Okay, lads, we're gonna keep it simple today," he said in a bellowing voice. "Just some easy drills — some up-and-backs, some breakouts — so we can see what you can do. But don't get used to it, we're going to be working here from now on."

He skated back and forth in front of us like a general marching before troops. His bushy brown eyebrows were furrowed and looked like a baby squirrel's tail. Hidden under his vinyl track pants was a brace that bulged around his left knee like a disfigurement. "I know this team has had a couple of tough years, but we're gonna turn it around. And we're gonna do it with hard work. So, let's get to it."

He blew hard into his whistle, smacked his stick on the ice a couple of times and his two aides took over. They separated the forwards from the defencemen, sent the goalies to the nets and readied us for a two-on-one drill. Assistant coach Clyde Parker, a fat, volatile man, was charged with instructing the defence. He demonstrated proper positioning by holding his hands out as if he wanted to be hugged and skating backwards, head constantly swivelling. "Take away the pass!" he yelled, his green eyes intense. The defencemen nodded, when they weren't wiping snot from their noses.

In the mean time, Peter Jones, the equipment manager and volunteer coach for the day, was dividing up the rest of us: eighteen forwards, six each at centre and on the two wings.

Once everyone was in position, Raycliffe's whistle chimed and the first pair of forwards darted off from the redline, their skates scribbling the ice like dried-up pens as they rushed ahead. The awaiting defenceman turned to his side, took a couple of strides toward the goal then began to glide backwards, his knees bent, head up and rear end stuck out. He kept his stick low and outstretched, and his body between the puck and open man. Clyde Parker had a hopeful look, but only for an instant. The assistant coach was soon left swearing under his breath, and turning red, just like he had done so many times the season before.

Turns out, the defenceman was slowing down too fast and once he realized the forwards were going to get past him, tried to swing himself around to stay in the play. He went toward the puckcarrier, who rushed a pass to his partner, leaving the defenceman with nothing to do but watch. But his play was not the only poor one in the sequence. The centre's pass was errant, the winger stretched out to get his blade on it and inadvertently threw his stick, which followed the puck into the boards and made a heavy thud that sounded like a head smacking against a wall. Raycliffe wiped a hand over his eyes. He was struggling, but managed to stay composed. "Go! Go! Go!" he shouted and the next duo was sent to attack like infantry men. After a few rushes, the forwards would change positions so everyone got turns playing centre and off-wing, and with different partners.

The defencemen, though, had no such variety. They had a steadfast task: deny the pass. While each centre and winger brought an individuality that was encouraged to flourish, defencemen were supposed to be as interchangeable as the pistons of a motor. The forwards dipped and dangled, spun and stuttered, but the backliners had to be stoic. Keep the play in front, don't get turned around, be patient. And when they were none of those things, that's when they were punished, as Johnny Carruthers, a quiet, unassuming kid, found out that first practice. Johnny was a good defenceman, but had a lot more potential than he showed. (The scouts loved him because he could skate and pass, and, though thin, was tall.) On that day, it was just bad luck for him that he happened to be the defender when Brendan was teamed with me for our only rush. As soon as Brendan took the puck, I knew what he was going to try. We had developed a play the previous season that called for him to cut to his right as soon as he crossed the blueline and immediately float the puck softly, like a water balloon, in the opposite direction, back toward the top of the left faceoff circle. Defencemen were usually caught going backwards or toward Brendan, not expecting him to release the puck so quickly. They would be out of position to defend the pass and too far away to block my shot as I strode into it.

Johnny must have been paying attention to us, however, because instead of dropping back, he charged at the blueline. But Brendan Kowalczek wasn't considered one of the two or three best players in the league for nothing. He read Johnny's eyes, stepping away from the check as if he expected it. While the defenceman was left to bat at air, we suddenly had a two-on-none. I got the pass and immediately returned it, getting the goalie to flop helplessly as Brendan snapped the puck in. We high-fived and a couple of guys banged their sticks in approval, but the blast of Tyler Raycliffe's whistle startled us into silence.

"You can't do that!" the coach screamed as he skated over to Johnny. "Never get caught like that!" Raycliffe was inches shorter than Johnny, but as he glowered he appeared to tower over the poor kid, who tried to shrink away while moving to the rear of the defence line. Brendan and I were already back in our queues, looking away from him.

We all got focused again when Raycliffe's whistle sounded once more, restarting the routine. It wasn't long, though, before the coach was again left to shake his head as he had to endure the sight of Dion Marcelle fanning on a shot while desperately trying to catch his breath. Raycliffe, it seemed, got a good sense of what he was in for and already needed a break from it. He stopped the drill short, gave himself — and us — a five-minute rest, and told his helpers to ready the puck-control test. Clyde Parker grabbed a stack of bright orange road cones and began depositing them on the ice.

While heading to the bench, I glanced back at Raycliffe and whispered to Brendan: "Think he'll last the season?"

After looking at the coach, who seemed as if he should be perpetually scratching the thinning hair on his head, Brendan said, "Don't think he'll last the day."

We laughed and skated over to meet our teammates. Brendan knocked gloves with Jesse Sullivan, our hulking defenceman.

"Scotty Mac, good to see ya back," Jesse said and smacked my shoulder. "Ready to kick some ass, or what?"

"You bet," I said. "I hear we're a shoe-in for the playoffs."

"Yeah," Jesse said with a snort, "and I'll see you on Team Canada." He leaned over the boards to grab a squeeze bottle from the bench and began squirting water on his face.

"MacGregor, you fuck," goalie Chris Cooper said as he skated over to shake hands. "No give-and-gos on the first day, eh."

"Sorry, man," I said. "Just reflex you know."

He rubbed the back of his shoulder, winced and said, "Man, I think I pulled a muscle on that play."

"He's always pullin' his muscle," Brendan joked.

"Fuck you, Gretzky," Cooper snapped back. "And why'd you have to pick on Johnny C. for anyway?"

"Yeah, man," Jesse said. "Some friend you are."

Coop and Sully winked at each other, they knew how to get to Brendan, who shrugged and looked apologetic while watching, with the rest of us, as Johnny got more from the coaches. To be fair, Raycliffe wasn't being a hardass. He probably noticed he was too tough on Johnny right off, so he kept his distance, spoke slowly, waved his stick in the direction of the blue-line and acted out some of his own instructions. When Johnny nodded and said okay, Raycliffe patted him on the shoulder and was off. Clyde Parker, who had been paying careful attention, stayed, apparently to advise the kid further. He, too, made a few hand gestures and waited patiently until his point was across. Parker, who also billetted Johnny, got the requisite nod, then gripped his pupil's shoulder with one meaty hand. When he let go, Johnny lowered his head and skated to the bench to join us, sort of. After reaching down for a water bottle, he slouched along the boards several feet away.

"Hey, Johnny. How ya doin'?" I asked, knowing it sounded ignorant.

"Hey," he said. "Okay."

Brendan went over to him and said, "Sorry about that, J.C."

Johnny said not to worry about it, forced a smile and stood where he was, silently, while the rest of us continued conversing. And there we were, more than five years ago. Five teammates, the veterans of the Kildare Kougars. We thought we were readying for hockey, we would get a heavy dose of life.

"This is the beginning of the new Kildare Kougars, lads," Tyler Raycliffe said before wrapping up practice. "This town wants a winner. It deserves a winner. And you can give it to them. Each and every one of you."

But what would Kildare give us? Indeed, what would it take?

Raycliffe blew his whistle and we filed off the ice. One by one, our group of teenaged boys disappeared into the dark of Leroux Arena, some of us innocent. Each of us full of hope.

Thus began my final season of junior hockey and the most tumultuous year of my life.

2

"S o much for the hype, eh, Scotty?" my dad said after taking in that uninspiring practice.

"Yeah, I guess so. Grandpa Joe's got better legs than most of these kids."

"You bet. The old fart may be laid up, but he can still throw a mean cross-check," Dad said and chuckled.

The equipment bag Grandpa Joe had bought me was stuffed with all my gear, including a couple of sticks whose ends were stuck out of it. The bag was hanging off my shoulder and I looked like an archer carrying an over-stuffed quiver as I lugged it to Dad's BMW. "Tell him, next time he sees me, I'll have my backhander down," I said. I put my gear in the trunk and slammed it shut.

"It better be, or he'll make you skate until it is."

Laughing, I got in. We were silent for a moment. Dad was concentrating on where to turn and it gave me time to word my question. "He's gonna make it, right, Dad?"

"Sure, sure," he answered. "He'll pull through. He always does. He does this every couple years just to get your mother and me anxious."

That certainty was in his voice. The nurturing tone he had used to teach me how to fish and drive. The voice that told me not to worry about school or girls or moving to Kildare.

"So, where to?" he asked.

"How 'bout food."

Somehow, I needed to extend that moment. With Grandpa Joe sick, Dad would have to be around home and wouldn't be able to come up to see many of my games. Plus, he was going back to the law firm and Mom was teaching seventh grade for the first time and was already busy with school. We knew the only way we would see each other before Christmas was if Grandpa Joe took a turn for the worse. And although we never expressed it, my father and I shared a keen sense that change was marching on us.

It was a hot September afternoon and a warm breeze swirled, lingering in the heat like a bear might before hibernating. Turning onto Main Street, we saw a flat road lined with neglected parking meters that looked like passengers waiting to be picked up; regulars at the used records store came in and out, same went for the Salvation Army thrift shop across the road; a few kids hung around outside the McDonald's. Otherwise, the downtown streets were empty. It was before supper time, but most of the store lots that weren't vacant were already about to close. Looking in the windows, I could see shopkeepers pulling down blinds or carefully counting cash. With most business moving to the malls, the few old shops that could afford to stay open couldn't afford a late staff. So by nightfall, Main Street was desolate.

We passed the *Chronicle* building as a reporter exited. He waved. "You know him?" Dad asked.

"Yeah, he covers the games." I waved back to Randy Delisle.

"You're a regular celebrity, eh?"

"Not really. Around here I'm just Brendan's buddy from the Hill," I said then indicated for him to go left.

We passed the usual sites. First was Kildare High, where some students were still idling after the first day of school. On the right, came the old Williams house and its pond, where people said the Mahovliches played shinny. Like he always does when he sees the town's tiny courthouse, which is smaller than some school portables, Dad laughed and made a quip. Then in quick succession, we drove by the Leroux Refinery, Leroux Lumber Yard and Mill, Leroux Hotel, and, of course, palatial Leroux mansion.

"Geez," Dad said, this time shaking his head, "that Leroux's still hangin' around, eh?"

"Yep," I answered. "But he sold the team, and that's all that matters to me."

"Oh, I know. What a relief that is!" he said. "You boys won't have to put up with him anymore."

I nodded in agreement as we drove on, passing the town's other hockey rink, next to a large church. Then came the edge of Kildare, where Leroux Avenue intersects the Trans-Canada. A huge truck stop indicates the city limits like a beacon, or smoke signal. Dad stopped for gas and we grabbed a couple of sandwiches.

"Wha'doya think?" Dad asked as we ate. "Still glad you came back?"

"Yeah, well, I didn't have much choice, eh," I answered.

"Scotty, if your heart's not into it . . ."

"No, nothing like that. I wanna play. I'm just sick of losin', that's all." I took a bite of my chicken club, chewing quickly so I could finish my thought. "Besides, I can't quit. What would Grandpa Joe think?"

"Believe me, the old man wouldn't want to see you punish yourself." He paused, looked out the window, then added, "Just do what's best for you, son."

Playing hockey was the best thing for me. That meant, like it or not, Kildare was the only place for me. Moving to another team, especially in that region, was nearly impossible because the Kougars wouldn't trade me unless they got something good and wouldn't trade me to a division rival at all. Also, changing teams, especially in my last year of junior, would have been detrimental. It would have looked like I gave up on my teammates. No one would get anywhere with that rep. Sure, I thought about quitting once or twice, but not seriously, not after seeing what Grandpa Joe was going through. I watched him fight his disease every day; going for his pre-scribed walk, taking his pills and vitamins at precisely the right time, eating even if he didn't feel like it. He was determined, especially then, when things didn't look so good. So, no way was I going to quit, not after all he had done for me. Not after all he had taught me.

I finished my snack, looked up at Dad and shrugged. "It's just one more year. Can't leave the guys now," I said. "Who knows? Maybe I'll get a scholarship out of it."

"That's true," he said. "But you can always go to school in Canada."

"C'mon, Dad, no one from school here makes it to the pros."

His forehead crinkled as if what I had said didn't make sense, but he didn't question it, saying instead, "This is a big year for you, eh?"

"The biggest."

"Make sure you keep your head, now."

"I know."

"You gonna score fifty goals?"

"Count on it."

"Better lose fifty pounds first."

"Oh, ho, wise guy."

He laughed and settled the bill.

When we were back in the car, Dad, who seemed to be taking in the whole day's proceedings like he would a case before summation, turned to me and said, "Who knows, son? Hockey's a strange game. The town's really gonna be behind you this year. You fellas might be able to put somethin' together yet."

That's my dad, a forever optimist. But it wasn't so easy believing the old man this time; the Kougars were no easy fix and neither was Kildare. A lumber town, Kildare had long ago chopped away its main resource, leaving it barren and too many of its 18,000 residents searching for work. The Lerouxes contributed a lot for a while, but even that changed. Now, the town struggles to bring in cash, trying manconcocted solutions like conventions and snowmobile races, and always being left with the only reliable commodity Kildare has always had: hockey.

The game is imprinted everywhere, from street games to the Pepsi dealer that doubles as puck manufacturer to the men who still play in the senior league long after their dreams of glory have faded. Every year, minor hockey tournaments attract teams from all over, even the Maritimes and the States, bringing in thousands in tourist dollars. And then there are the Kougars, the pride of Kildare. When I got drafted, I was excited, thoughts of adventures away from home swept me up, but after all the disappointment — three years worth — I needed things to change and so did the town.

"It'll turn around, son," Dad said after he stopped the car.

I swung my head like I wasn't sure and continued to sit.

He shook my shoulder. "You really want to make it to the pros, don't you?"

I nodded.

"Good for you, son," he said then smiled and patted the back of my neck twice. "Good for you."

We got up to get my bags out of the trunk. "Give us a call," he said.

"Sure, sure," I replied. "Let me know about Grandpa."

"Will do."

We shook hands on the sidewalk outside the Kowalczeks. "Say hi to Mom for me."

He said okay and looked at me with love in his eyes. "Take care, Scotty," he said. I looked down to get a grip.

Just then we heard the screen door behind us rattle and a female voice rang. "John, come in for dinner," Mrs. Kowalczek called.

"Sorry, Pam, gotta get home," Dad said. "Lois made plans."

"Oh, you MacGregors. Always up to somethin'," she said. "Next time then. You and her both." Dad waved to her. He then put his hand on my shoulder, looked at me again and pursed his lips. I watched him until his BMW made a turn and all I was left to stare at was the horizon.

"C'mon, Scotty, room's all ready for ya," Mrs. Kowalczek said. She was at the top of the steps, holding the door open for me, her warm, motherly grin making it easier. I picked up my things and headed in.

3

Tyler Raycliffe stopped practice. The whistle dropped from his mouth and his eyes led all others upward. What we saw was a sight we all had believed — hoped — forever banished from our eyes: Lannie Leroux in the presence of the Kildare Kougars. Yet there he was, the team's former owner, standing on the top step between the last row of seats, in his normal attire: a loose-fitting, conservatively coloured, ankle-length dress. He held his big-boned arms akimbo, fists on hips, and his feet were spread apart. His makeup and eyeliner were meticulous, as usual. He seemed ready for business. And he wasn't alone. With him was a man in a three-piece who walked around with a carpenter's measuring tape and surveyed the building like a tailor about to fit a suit. Of course, we might not have noticed either of them if Lannie was not so maddeningly loud. When he walked into Leroux Arena, his whistling caused an echo that prompted Raycliffe, and all the players and few onlookers in the stands, to turn our heads.

"Oh, it's so-ooo delightful to be in this building again," Lannie crowed. "Thank goodness I didn't sell it, too."

Lannie was the keeper of a tiny empire. During the Twenties, the Lerouxes made a name in Central Ontario with their lumber manufactur-

ing business. They rolled over the profits into real estate and stock invest-
ments, and after a couple of generations they were worth millions. The
Lerouxes also had a history of philanthropy, especially in Kildare. They
created children's charities, donated funds to local hospitals, founded the
Kougars in 1933, and built parks and a library. Their grandest creation
was the family mansion, a four-storey, forty-room dwelling that overlooks
the Ottawa River on Kildare's westernmost border.

Its only current resident is Lannie Leroux — also known as "Lady
Lannie," "Loopy Leroux" and "Raggedy Lann" —, a middle-aged man
whose crisis became Kildare's. More specifically, the hockey team's.

The Kougars were a good franchise that used to play in front of more
than two-thousand people every Thursday night, but Lannie's antics
changed that. First, he started to attend games in his most outlandish out-
fits, even wearing shoulderpads underneath a ballgown once. His mere
presence caused the team's general manager at the time to quit, saying,
"No twenty-five-thousand-dollar-a-year job is worth this kind of humiliation." During my tenure, Lannie fired coaches at whim, traded players if
they didn't score when he wanted them to, even instructed the sound
operator to play "In the Navy" by the Village People during the opening
skate. Through it all, Lannie danced in the press box like Nero fiddled as
the Kougars sank to the depths of the Central Ontario Hockey League.

As if losing wasn't enough, we were adorned with the nickname
"Lannie's Ladies" — or some variation thereof — by our legions of heck-
lers. In every rink, we were pelted with insults and cackles. Even at
home, some of our fans got on us; calling us names, booing all the time,
even cheering for the other team! Life as a hockey player in Kildare was
truly miserable. In the summer of 1995, however, the town finally man-

aged to convince Lannie — or got the Leroux family lawyer to convince him — to sell the team and not disturb it in any way. That pact, we all believed, freed the Kildare Kougars of our greatest hindrance. Obviously, we were wrong.

Lannie's presence at practice caused Tyler Raycliffe to scoot over to the glass. He waved a hand to Randy Delisle. "What's he doing here?" the coach asked when the *Chronicle* writer, a bearded man with keen eyes, was within earshot.

"Hell, I was wondering the same thing," Randy answered.

Tyler hung his head. "Let me know when you find out, would ya?"

The scribe nodded and said, "Oh, believe me, I will."

While our practice was on hold, Lannie took the time to greet us. "Hi there, boys. I can't tell you just how much I miss seeing you all," he said with a lisp and blew us a kiss.

A lot of us turned our backs on him, but that didn't solve anything.

"Oh, look," he said. "I think they're showing me their bums. That's so-ooo cute."

Brendan looked at me and we sank our shoulders. Raycliffe had Clyde Parker refocus our attention. Parker dumped out a bucket of pucks and like kids gathering Easter eggs, we all swept up one or more with our sticks. Some guys practiced their stickhandling, others sent passes back and forth to a partner, most peppered the goalies. Brendan wanted to practice new plays with me. He set up behind the endline and delivered passes out front as I cut to the net, but I had trouble settling pucks and my shots were off. My mind wasn't into it. Seeing Lannie, and knowing he was up to no good, had me rattled.

4

All us out-of-towners had to be put up with families when we were in Kildare, and I got lucky when the team paired me with the Kowalczeks. They were the perfect family to billet with, always with food on the table and not afraid to let you have it if you skipped school. Plus, I hit it off with Brendan right away. His sister had gone to school in B.C. before my first season and he was happy for the company. During my time with them, I got to feel like family. Of course, they expected me to chip in with chores and clean up after myself, but that was no problem; I knew I had it good.

"Is that you, boys?" Mrs. Kowalczek asked.

"Yeah, Mom," Brendan answered after we walked through the front door. We quickly slipped off our shoes and headed into the living room to collapse. Tyler Raycliffe, to our dismay, had proven true to his word. He made each practice more trying than the last, working us until our bodies ached and minds went numb. (Yeah, we saw improvement, but when you're complaining or looking for sympathy, you don't emphasize that.)

"Dinner'll be ready at six, fellas," Mrs. Kowalczek said in her happy tone.

"Sure, Mrs. K. Thanks," I replied.

Brendan rolled his eyes at me. His mother's voice was too cheery for him, especially when he was exhausted. I may not have felt completely alive myself, but I didn't need to in that house. The usual cacophony was coming from the kitchen: a thud, thud, thud while Mrs. Kowalczek chopped vegetables, a sizzle from the frying pan and a glub, glub, glub of boiling rice about to overflow, all just below the chatter of CBC Radio. It wasn't long before I heard an "Oh, shoot," when Mrs. K realized the rice was boiling over.

She caught it in time to avert a disaster, then walked into the living room, wiping her hands on her apron. When she found us fizzling on the couch, she said, "Oh, you boys are absolutely being worked to death. I hope you're not getting sick." She touched Brendan's forehead with the back of her hand and he promptly pushed it away. Then she sat on the armrest next to him, but stopped short of mussing his hair. "I better get you two something before dinner."

"No, Mom," Brendan said, almost whining. "Don't worry about it." He was slouched on the couch with his head thrown back and his mouth agape like he was asleep.

"You boys just catch your breath. I'll be back soon." She tapped a hand on Brendan's knee before returning to the kitchen.

Mrs. Kowalczek, a short, stout woman, often resembled a waddling penguin when she hurried about the house. There was always a matter that needed tending to, always something that she had to do right away for someone. And she did it so genuinely, and with such mixed results, it was hard not to smile. Even in my weary state, I grinned easily when I heard an "Oh, dear," from the kitchen when she discovered the chicken overcooking.

"What're you so happy about?" Brendan said and flung a throw pillow at me.

I was too beat to flinch, let alone retaliate, so I simply brushed the pillow away and said, "Just thinking about the look on your face when he said, 'Gimme five more laps, lads.' "

"Yeah, like you weren't ready to puke." He groaned and moved forward. Holding his breath, he pressed his palms down and propelled himself up, wincing as he stood.

"Jesus, how can you even move?" I asked.

"Aah, man. I just remembered I gotta get that stuff for Johnny C. He'll be over any minute."

As Brendan was walking out of the room, his mother was walking in with two glasses of iced tea. "Can I get you something, dear?" she asked.

"Nah, Johnny's coming over to pick up my old gear," he said. "I gotta find the stuff."

"Oh, good. Maybe he'll stay for dinner."

"Believe me, if we ask, he'll stay," Brendan said, and his mom quickly went to make sure she had enough for one more.

Johnny arrived before too long with an empty hockey bag and stomach. He wore his usual attire: blue jeans with a burgeoning rip around a knee and a Nirvana T-shirt. He walked hunched over, with his head down and off to the side. His hair was black and long, its bangs hanging over his forehead and down to his eyebrows, shrouding his pimples. He threw a palm up and said hi as he walked by, following Brendan to the basement. I strained to get up, too, then sat on one of the steps as Johnny sorted through Brendan's old equipment. In one pile, Johnny picked out the items he didn't need — skates and socks — and everything that was obviously too small. In another pile, he put the things he wanted: shin guards, gloves and shoulderpads. Then he tried them on. The gloves didn't cover his entire wrists, but Johnny had small hands and was able to squeeze into them, so they went in his bag. The shin guards fit fine and were stuffed in, too. Next, he picked up the shoulderpads and started to put them on. "Johnny, you sure you want those? You'll have to work 'em in pretty good," I said. "They never threw a check, ya know."

Brendan looked up from his pile and hurled a sock at me. "Shut up, dough boy," he said.

Johnny grinned and laced up the pads. They looked awkward on him. He had laced them too tight, pulling the shoulders down to his chest. His black T-shirt got tugged along and bundled up around his collarbone.

After walking behind him, I said, "Come on, let's get those on right." When I grabbed the pads and pulled them back onto his shoulders, he winced. "You, okay?"

"Yeah, yeah," he said. "Just took a puck there."

"Oh, yeah. When?"

"Ah, the other day," he answered. "Went off some kid and nailed me."

"Never saw it coming, eh?"

He shook his head as I loosened the laces around his chest and realized I could smell alcohol on him. After pulling his shirttail down, he adjusted the pads until they were comfortable.

"Better?" I asked.

"Oh, yeah."

"Won't have these problems next year at State, I bet."

"Hope not."

"So you gonna take 'em?" Brendan asked.

"Sure," Johnny said. He removed the pads by pulling them over his head. "I got nothing else."

"Old stuff got rotten on you, eh?" Brendan said.

"Yeah, it reeks." Johnny pushed the pads into the bag and said thanks.

"No worries. Believe me, my mom's gonna love ya for getting that shit outta here."

"She might even feed ya," I said, winking at Johnny.

"Oh, yeah," he replied, with rare inflection in his voice.

"You hungry?" Brendan asked.

"Man, I'm always hungry." Johnny arranged the equipment in his bag then zipped it shut.

He followed us to the kitchen, where Mrs. Kowalczek was bringing the last of the dishes to the table. Her husband, just home, had already taken his place.

"So nice that you could join us, Johnny," Mrs. K said.

"Thanks, Mrs. Kwal, Mrs. Ko-walczek," he replied.

"Oh, you're welcome. All you boys from the team are like family."

"You're the best, Mrs. K," I said.

"Hush." She flung a handful of air at me. "Everyone help themselves, now."

Mr. Kowalczek looked at us after our plates were full and asked, "So you read the paper today?"

Brendan and I sighed, then nodded.

"What did it say?" Mrs. Kowalczek asked. "Anything wrong?"

"Just Lannie again," Brendan answered.

The *Chronicle* reported that the man Lannie was with was Sinclair Lougheed, a hot shot architect from Ottawa. Lannie told the paper Lougheed was building a rink down south and wanted to use Leroux Arena, a dark, bland-looking place, as the model. No one believed the lie, but no one had a clue of what the truth was either.

"What'd the team say?" Brendan's dad asked.

I shook my head and said, "Nothing."

"Oh, how I wish Lannie would just leave you boys alone," Mrs. Kowalczek said. It was a sentence everyone close to the team had probably uttered at some point. But with Lannie you had to wait and see, and try to go about your life until he decided to interfere with it.

"Did the practice go okay at least?" Mr. Kowalczek asked.

This time, Brendan shook his head emphatically. "The worst one yet."

"Oh, yeah?"

Brendan, who had managed to speak between bites, nodded.

"Yeah," I said. "We must've done thirty laps then breakouts, then puck control, then more breakouts. My legs are killing me."

"Scott, I know it seems like you boys are being punished, but he sounds like a winner to me," Mrs. Kowalczek said of Raycliffe. "You boys'll see. All this hard work's gonna pay off."

Brendan's head was down, buried in his plate, but I still thought I could see his eyes roll.

"What do you think, honey?" Mrs. Kowalczek asked her husband.

"Sounds like a sadistic son of a bitch to me," he answered.

Brendan and I tried to stifle our giggles under a "Murray, please!" from Mrs. K.

"Hey, that's a good thing. Nothing's better for this team than a tough coach, as long as he's fair," Mr. Kowalczek said. "From what I've heard about Raycliffe, he's that."

Mrs. Kowalczek smiled, I said, "I guess," Brendan shrugged and Johnny ate. And he seemed satisfied just eating while we talked. He would chuckle when Mr. Kowalczek uttered hyperbole, sometimes throw in a "Yeah," or "Right," when we were talking hockey. He was there, but not. Lingering. That is, until he became the focus.

Mrs. K looked around the table and saw Johnny scraping up the last grains of rice from his meal. "Heavens, Johnny did you inhale that plate? You must be starving, take some more, dear," she said.

Johnny did. He scooped up another serving and quickly got to work on it.

"Clyde must not feed you, lad," Mr. Kowalczek said jokingly.

Johnny shook his head and grinned. "Nah, he does," he said of our assistant coach who housed him.

"Oh, Murray, don't embarrass him," Mrs. Kowalczek said. She looked worried as she watched Johnny gobbling down his food. "He's just a hungry boy."

"I'm not embarrassing the lad," Mr. Kowalczek said. He took a bite of chicken before looking up to Johnny again. "How's Clyde doing these days anyway?"

I was sitting next to Johnny and could sense his discomfort from having to talk. He sat still while beads of sweat started to appear on his forehead as if speaking was a chore. "He's all right," Johnny answered tersely before continuing with his seconds.

"Heard he was real p.o.'ed about not getting the head coach's job."

Johnny shrugged as if to say, I dunno.

"Where'd you hear that, Dad?" Brendan asked.

"From the guys at the rink."

"Do you believe them?" Mrs. K asked.

"Yeah, sure," her husband said. "I would be pissed, too. Clyde's been helping out the team ever since he got here, but Raycliffe's got Kougar blood in him, so . . ."

"People in this town can be so hard-headed sometimes," Mrs. K said. "How long's Clyde Parker been here now? Five years?"

Mr. Kowalczek nodded.

"That's enough to be Kildarean isn't it?"

Maybe it was, and on top of that Clyde had also set up an electronics shop when he came to town, volunteered with the Kougars and helped out by billeting guys on the team. He was the equipment manager when I started, then he moved up to assistant coach in my third season. Clyde was no Mr. Congeniality, that's for sure, but he always had the defencemen prepared and that's what mattered, I guess.

I wondered if it was true about Clyde feeling resentment and what that might mean to our season. And I wanted to ask Johnny what he thought of all this, but knew he wouldn't say much. He just didn't seem to care about that conversation, or any other. Even when he left, he did it quietly. He kept his head down as he mumbled a thank you to the Kowalczeks, then looked up briefly to Brendan and me, pushed out a chin and said, "Later." Then he was gone. Walking away, his back bent, Johnny looked like he was hauling a much greater weight than that of the gear in his hockey bag.

Johnny was like me, an out-of-towner with not too many friends outside of the guys on the team. He had been traded to Kildare during my second season. Right off, he struck me as a good kid and he would get a good joke

in now and then. All in all, a pretty even-tempered guy with super potential as a hockey player. Everyone figured he had a real future because he
had already accepted a scholarship offer from Minnesota State. All he had
to do was get through one more season with the Kougars and he was set,
we thought.

5

Tim Chaput cupped his hands around his mouth and yelled, "Show me your lutz!" It was a Wednesday afternoon and that meant practice for the senior girls figure skating club. "C'mon, would someone please show me their lutz!" Chaput, our team smartass, said in mock plea. Some of the girls looked up and giggled, others, those who knew him well, tried to ignore anything that came from his lips. Only thing was, Chaput wanted attention from everyone and he wouldn't settle for less. So he continued shouting things such as "Hey Alice, nice ax-le!" and "That's one hot salchow you got!" When he said to one girl, "You can sit spin over here any time you want," he had managed to go too far. The instructor stood glaring at him before she threatened to complain to Tyler Raycliffe if Chaput didn't sit down and shut up.

He sat, with satisfaction.

"You've been a bad boy, Timmy," goalie Chris Cooper said.

"Oooh, think I'll get spanked?"

Chaput leaned back and draped his legs over the seat in front of him while the girls continued to skate. We had been told to show up early for a team meeting, but we would have been at the rink well beforehand anyway. It was the first session of the season for the girls and that was incentive enough. A few of the guys, like Brendan, already had girlfriends on the ice, but the rest of us were scoping for one. We sat in the stands ogling and applauding, checking out the new girls or the ones we could never get enough of.

"Is that who I think it is?" Chaput asked, whispering. Most of us looked around, but couldn't tell who he was talking about. Then he pointed to the far corner of the ice and said, "Over there. Grey sweater."

We turned our heads and saw a blonde ponytail whipping around like a tether. The head it was attached to was twirling and swirling like a loose scarf in the wind while the body spun on one long, stiff, stockinged leg. Wide-eyed, we watched like we were being hypnotized, and were startled when everything came to a sudden stop. The ponytail dropped quickly and Brigitte Chouinard came out of her toe loop with arms raised. She was panting and her breasts were heaving, which caused Manny Rivers to say, "Man, I bet I could break a finger on those."

Johnny Carruthers chuckled and Jesse Sullivan said, "They don't fill out like that down south, eh?"

"Uh-uh," answered Manny, the only American on our team.

"Just remember: You can look, but you can't feel."

And that was no joke. Brigitte Chouinard may have been the most beautiful girl in Kildare, but because of an overprotective father she was the most untouchable, too.

"I know, I know," Manny said to Jesse, "ain't worth the trouble."

Tim Chaput leaned over and put his hand on Manny's shoulder. "But we can still have our wet dreams," he said.

Brigitte and the girls started to do their final laps. One by one, they would pass by us, and each would be greeted by a chorus of hoots and whistles. Some laughed, others pretended not to notice. A cute redhead, unfamiliar to most of us, came by and Cooper asked, "Who's that?"

Shoulders shrugged and a few of the guys said, "I dunno." That made Chaput rub his palms together and say like a glutton, "Looks like fresh meat, boys." Like he often did, he left me shaking my head and wondering why I was hanging out with him. When the girl came by again, Chaput led an unusually loud cheer. The redhead looked up and smiled a little. She skated on before doing a doubletake. When she looked over this time, she smiled a lot, then waved. Because her gesture was directed at me, my teammates shifted their attention immediately.

When I waved back, Cooper slapped me on the shoulder. "Scotty Mac, you fuck, you been holding out on us?"

I shrugged.

"C'mon, man. What's the scoop?"

"No scoop," I said. "Just a chick from English class."

"Oh, fuck. He's boinked her," Chaput said.

"Big time, I'd say," Cooper added.

"I haven't done anything, asshole," I said, more to Chaput than Coop.

"Sounds like you're fuckin' whipped already," Chaput said with more spite than jest.

The next several minutes were spent with me trying to convince them I knew little about Michelle Lessard other than her name. Of course, there was more to it. Brendan came rushing up the stairs and was intercepted by Cooper.

"Hey, has Scotty Mac been nailin' that redhead with the big tits, or what?" asked Cooper, who spoke the way he played goal: by instinct, without thinking about it.

Brendan smiled. "No," he said. He then looked over at me and laughed. "But he wishes he was."

I was pissed and gave him a shove over the whistles of the other guys.

"Just another chick, eh?" Chaput said with a smirk.

"Alright, they want us downstairs," Brendan said. "It's meeting time."

The bunch of us got up like a squadron, and moved one at a time down the steps and toward the locker room. We had to pass by the glass and when I saw Michelle Lessard looking at me, I returned a smile.

Clyde Parker walked into our dressing room and sat, slowly, the way fat men do, putting one half of his body down then the next. He was beside Johnny Carruthers, who scooted over a bit to give Clyde room. "Well, what's the good word, ladies?" Clyde asked and placed a shopping bag he was carrying at his skates.

"Hey, Clyde," a few us said in greeting and after that, no other words were spoken for a few seconds, making some of the guys anxious.

"So what's going on, Clyde?" Jesse asked.

Clyde turned to him and managed to just get out, "After practice . . .," before Tyler Raycliffe flew through the door and stole our attention. He clapped his hands twice, then held them still for a moment before rubbing them together as if he was working in chalk. "Okay, lads, this is it," he said. "We got a good feel for what we want, so final cuts'll be made after tonight."

We responded with a collective look of, *Huh?* We had been under the impression the roster wasn't going to be set for more than a week. Raycliffe looked around the room, and made sure he made eye contact with Brendan and me before he said, "Remember, no one's made it yet, so everyone better be hustling."

He paused for the words to impact then clapped his hands again. "Okay, Clyde's gonna take it from here. See you on the ice." Raycliffe gestured to Clyde then walked out as swiftly as he had come in.

Right away, we started getting into our practice gear. Clyde stayed seated and told us in his Prairie drawl what drills we were going to be run through, then wanted to know if we had questions.

"Yeah, what's the deal?" asked one worried guy who had been on cruise control all camp. "Why's he makin' cuts now?"

Clyde shrugged and said, "Hey, I just work here."

He then patted Johnny on the knee and got up. Before leaving, Clyde took his shopping bag over to Tony Lacroix, a rookie defenceman who had been impressive in camp.

"I thought you could use 'em," Clyde said then turned to walk out.

Lacroix, who was still half-naked, looked inside and excitedly said, "Oh, man, cool." He pulled out a pair of new hockey gloves and hurried to put them on. "Thanks, Clyde."

Clyde waved a hand and was gone. Meanwhile, Johnny Carruthers, who watched the exchange, was beginning to dress, with a frown.

6

D ion Marcelle got his jersey — No. 27 —, checked the spelling of his name on its back then nonchalantly hung it in his stall before heading, in his practice uniform, onto the ice. He had made the team. How and why, we didn't know.

If Tyler Raycliffe instructed him, he would nod politely, maybe even execute his duty effectively for a turn or two before slipping back into his rut. During our scrimmages, he was out of position often and his version of defence was to poke his stick out at the oncoming puckcarrier. Maybe once in every fifteen attempts he would knock the puck free, the rest of the time, he posed no obstacle as the opponent fled down the ice and Dion loped back after his stickcheck failed.

Even the normally cheerleading *Kildare Chronicle* said the only greater conundrum than the centreman's play was that he had managed to make the cut. To that, Tyler Raycliffe said, "Look, he's got a lot of talent. It may not be visible yet, but I'm telling you, it's there." Still, the newspaper surmised: "To the chagrin of the Kildare Kougars and the misfortune of their fans, it appears quite likely that Dion Marcelle is the reverse of Marcel Dionne in more ways than one."

Away from the rink, Dion was not much better, and in some ways worse. He was a loner. Nothing wrong with that, I guess, except he had no reason to be. Being a Kougar meant something in Kildare. (Even Tim Chaput got his share of dates.) But Dion was solitary. It was hard to figure because when he held his head up, he was a pretty good looking kid. His dark hair was thick and his zits were clearing up and he wasn't short, so you figure some girl would take a liking to him. And from what Michelle Lessard told me, some did. Dion just didn't look interested. At least, that's what we assumed.

After practice, he would rush off the ice, get changed as quickly as he could and head out of the locker room to meet his father, a gaunt, expressionless man. Thin, grey hair and a long face made Mr. Marcelle seem even more glum. Yet his attendance would have led anyone to believe he was zealous about his son's life. For every practice, Mr. Marcelle was looking from the stands then waiting outside the dressing room for Dion. He would take the hockey bag from his son's hands, sometimes put an arm around his shoulder. They never really said anything to each other, and somehow it seemed they didn't need to. A month after arriving in town, the Marcelles were still a mystery. No one knew why they had moved, or why Dion had turned down a tryout with a Major Junior team in the Quebec League.

He had talent, Raycliffe assured, but even so, it was no good to us if he didn't have the confidence to use it. That much was obvious, even to people outside the team.

"He needs a girlfriend," Michelle said.

Without thinking, I replied, "No, I don't think he needs that."

"Oh, really!" She spoke in a tone that was half-teasing, but I still felt bad for the way it came out.

"No, I don't mean it like that," I said, defensively. "He's just gotta get accustomed to the team and maybe to the things around here."

"And a girlfriend would help, right?"

"Yeah, maybe," I said faintly, giving in, because the Kowalczeks' driveway was coming up and no way was I going to have the night end on a sour note.

Michelle put the car in park and when she turned to look at me, I leaned over and kissed her, long. I played with her hair with one hand and she didn't resist when I brought the other up to her waist, moving it up and down her left side. When I touched under her breast, she pulled me closer and I cupped my hand there. We kissed more and harder, and eventually I realized I could hear her heart beating. When I started to massage her breast more firmly, she touched my arm and brought it away. "I better get going," she said.

I squeezed her hand and said okay. We made plans then I got out and waved to her before heading in. And I remember thinking that, all of a sudden, things were starting to work out the way I wanted. The Kougars were far from threatening, but at least we had begun to resemble a team. Michelle was great, school was fine and Grandpa Joe said he was doing better. He told me not to worry myself and even kidded about making it to the season-opener. He asked if I was happy and I said I was. He said that was the best news he could have and I joked, "You and me both!"

Yep, for the first time I could remember, everything about life in Kildare was good.

7

Tyler Raycliffe hissed. He blew into his whistle, shooting out a high tweet like venom. "Ten laps now!" he screamed. We moaned and he said, "Make it fifteen! And the first one who pukes gets five more!" And he blew hard with spite into his black whistle. It was the last practice before the season began and he was intent on making it count.

We started to skate like whipped dogs. The faster players sped around the rink confidently with knees bent and arms tugging at the air then pushing it behind us like a loose rope. For the slower skaters, though, it was an anxious time. Hiding like the runts of a litter, they stayed close to the boards. Their heads were down as they pushed themselves, trying desperately to keep up. Of course, they could not. So they hoped that as the rest of us rushed by, they would get lost in our blur and go unnoticed. They did not. The coach would glare at them, his eyes evoking more horror than any bogey-man.

During practice, our new coach was austere, capable of heaping brutal tasks with one tweet. We knew little of him then and what we knew rattled us like a funny sound in our bones after a hard check against the boards. Raycliffe was from Muskegee, the next town up river. He grew up playing with the Curran brothers, Matt and Gary. Matt went on to play for the Maple Leafs and Gary became an NCAA star. Raycliffe did nothing, though it wasn't supposed to be that way. He was the best player on that team, some say the best Kougar ever, but he ripped up his knee in a snowmobiling accident just before the '81 playoffs and never played for the Kougars again.

Worst part was, they didn't seem to miss him. Behind the Curran brothers, the Kougars went on to win the Tremblay Trophy that season. And Tyler had to watch. He then saw the Currans get awarded scholarships to the States while the scouts treated him like a pariah when, just months earlier, Raycliffe was coveted by all.

But he did not go quietly. Off the ice, he fought as hard as he could to get back on it. Comeback attempt after comeback attempt was followed by knee surgery after knee surgery. He would get a tryout then be cut, or have the knee cease on him. At twenty-five, he hung 'em up, finally. Having to deal with the "Now what?" was too much. Drink took him away; we hadn't heard what brought him back. But he came back, bought into a snowmobile dealership and became a volunteer coach with the pee-wee team in Muskegee. They won, he got respect, and when the Currans acquired the Kougars, they hired him.

At last, Tyler Raycliffe was back in the game. Back in it to win. And he wasn't going to let any wise-ass kids mess that up. Employed for his singlemindedness and his unwavering contention that punishment was actually practice, Tyler promised victory. *Or death*, we thought. It was the eve of the regular season and the players on the ice before him were the 1995-96 edition of the Kildare Kougars. His team.

He looked over his charges. His eyes hard and squinting, like he was trying to zap faith into us. Some players were doubled over, trying desperately not to collapse; others had their eyes closed and were wincing, concentrating hard on not throwing up; most of the rest of us had learned to stay quiet and be eager to nod our heads. "This is it lads," Raycliffe commanded before dismissing us. "No more farting around. We got a game tomorrow. You hear that . . .

"A game," he continued. "Competition. For real this time." He pumped a fist in front of his chest. "You're gonna go out there and work. Just like we have all month. Get in there, work the corners, muck it out." He twirled once as if he were looking out for an approaching enemy. "We're gonna lose some games this year, I know that," he said. "But if you work hard, we'll win most of 'em. And that's all I ask: Work hard." He was silent then, for a moment, standing before us, letting his plea settle in. When he was confident it had, he blew his whistle again. "Okay, that's it. Get outta here. Tomorrow's the big day."

He turned and skated away, picking up a couple of loose pucks as he headed off the ice and up the corridor. The players filed off, too, but Brendan Kowalczek, as was his custom, hung around. He was always the last one to leave the ice. Usually, he would skate small, tight circles or just lope back and forth to cool down. On this day, he had the excited look of a prized derby horse at the gate.

I skated alongside him near centre ice. "You pumped?" I asked.

"Big time," he said. "Can't wait."

"Think we can win?"

He smiled. "Better believe it."

Then he took off, swooshing by me and sprinting forty feet to the goal-mouth before turning around and gliding back. I had finally gotten back into game shape, but was in no condition to keep up with Brendan. His faceguard sat on top of his helmet and the chinstrap dangled in front of his fresh face. "I can't wait to score the first one," he said, grinning.

We headed up the runway to the dressing room. Passing Raycliffe's office, Brendan whispered, "This guy's a real hardass. He won't put up with losing."

"Yeah, but what happens when he figures out we got some dead weight here? He can't trade 'em all."

"No, just you," he said and chuckled.

"Oh, ho," I said and bodychecked him into the wall.

"Yeah, maybe we'd get some new pucks for ya." He giggled and threw a glove in my face to push me back. And we laughed as we entered the dressing room to a dreadful sight. Tyler Raycliffe stood, hands at his waist, glaring in the direction of the laughter. "What's so fucking funny?" he yelled.

Brendan and I stood stiff, trying not to look at him, or each other.

He pointed at us, raised his eyebrows and said, "In my office, now!"

We stood in full gear and watched as the coach plopped in his chair and began unlacing his skates. After relieving his ankles, he unbuckled his knee brace, leaned back and lit a cigarette. With the first puff, he sighed an addict's sigh. "No more horsin' around, got it," he said, rather mildly, much more relaxed than we could have hoped for.

"Sure, Coach," Brendan and I said in unison.

"Look, you lads are my best players," he said. He folded his hands on his desk and looked up at us. "I don't want you to be discouraged by what you've seen these last couple a weeks. We got a long way to go to turn this thing around, but we can do it. All right?"

We nodded. Our pupils widened. No coach we had had ever sounded so hopeful.

"I need you two to be my leaders, got it?" He pointed at us with the two fingers that held the smoldering cigarette.

We nodded some more.

"Let me know if I'm screwin' up and I'll let you know if I need you to get on one of your mates' asses," he said. "I been watchin' you boys the last couple of years and know you got talent. We just gotta get the rest of 'em up to your level, that's all." He paused to look at us. "Got any questions?"

We shook our heads.

Raycliffe then threw each of us a patch. "Brendan, here's your 'C', lad," he said. "This is your team now. Don't be afraid to show 'em so."

They shook hands then Raycliffe took mine. He pronounced me the first alternate captain, as my 'A' denoted. Brendan patted me on the back and we returned to the locker room.

"Oh," Raycliffe called, "and would you boys pick a new song to play during the warmup. You know, something that says we got some balls around here now."

As we exited, Brendan and I were giddy. Unfortunately, the joy was fleeting. Change, it turns out, was a deceptive tease, seemingly within reach all the time, but not at all easy to grasp on to.

8

We started on the road. That meant a couple of hours on the bus to remember all the marches to defeat we had had in the past. From my window seat near the back, nothing seemed different. As much as I wanted to believe it all was, there was no fooling my eyes. Too many of our guys were just happy to have made the team and some others were more into the perks of being a hockey player than winning. Before we hit the highway, card games had broken out and Penthouses were being passed around. Tim Chaput found an audience for the same dirty jokes he had been telling for two seasons and got lots of cackles in response. When one kid said, "Alright, another year of missing fourth period. Bring it on, dude," doubt crept up on me like a recurring rash. I tried to block out all of it and think about just going to the net, catching a pass and snapping it up. Lifting my hands, pumping a fist, winning a game. Over and over, that's what I visualized, but at the same time a part of me couldn't help thinking I wouldn't see it. Not often enough, anyway, and certainly not anytime soon.

I wasn't the only skeptic. I heard Brendan sigh a lot and watched Jesse Sullivan knock his head against the window every now and then. We had been there before, many times, with the same insecurities and fears. You

can see, we were beat before we even got to the rink and when I look
back now I realize it shouldn't have been a surprise that we started the
season 0-4. The team had little confidence, some talent and a lot of excuses. Still, it stunk, because, despite all our doubts, we had expectations, too.
For those of us Kougars who had been through the worst of it, it was especially hard to imagine that we could actually be as bad as always.

Tyler's killer training camp, it turns out, was mostly to get us in shape
so we could at least be competitive. (His really tough practices were still to
come.) He put a quick end to the euchre and magazines, demanding discipline whenever he was around, and tried to give us an identity on the ice.
We were going to be a team that emphasized defence. To that end, we
constantly practiced plays to get the puck out of our zone. They worked
pretty well, but that meant we didn't practice much on scoring goals. And
we wanted goals so bad, if just to hear some cheers for a change. Already,
familiar boos and chants of "You're still Lannie's Loser Ladies" were being
hurled — and that was when we were playing at home!

Personally, it was a brutal beginning. I hadn't scored and had taken a
bunch of dumb penalties, including a double-minor for roughing that probably cost us the third game. Sometimes I wondered if we were cursed, or if
I was. Or maybe it was the town. There had to be something; such failure,
for so long, never occurs without an intangible contributing. But how do
you stop such a thing? How do you even find out what it is?

Really, all I knew for sure was we were missing more than just talent on
our hockey team. We were a group that did not believe; we were desperate for faith.

It so happens we found it, unexpectedly. And in grief.

9

The story of Bill Barilko is a numbing one. In the final game of the 1951 Stanley Cup championship series, the unspectacular defenceman for the Maple Leafs charged in for a rebound on the left-wing side of the Montreal net. The score was tied; the game was in overtime. When Barilko got to the loose puck, he immediately swept it to the net with a quick, rising shot. Then the helmetless backliner from Timmins was tripped and sent airborne as the puck sailed to the goal. The occurrance that followed, through the photograph that captured it, has become archived in hockey history books, arenas and sports bars.

The puck found its way to the back of the goal and Barilko, the No. 5 on the back of his jersey rippling like blood from a heartbeat, raised his hands while soaring through the air like a kid bellyflopping into a pool. The last goal he ever scored won the Leafs the Cup. He disappeared that summer — while flying — on a fishing trip in Northern Ontario. The Leafs did not win another championship until 1962, the year his body was discovered. It's as if Barilko was put here to do one thing and just in case anyone wasn't sure of that, God punctuated it.

Bill Barilko's story has become a thing of lore in the hockey world, and the tale took another turn in 1992 as Barilko's heroic act and calamitous end became the focus of a guitar-heavy rock song by The Tragically Hip that is played like an anthem between whistles at rinks across the land. Fans will stand and sing along to "50 Mission Cap," maybe pump a fist, as the DJ turns up the volume only to abruptly kill it when the referee's whistle blows.

Although my grandfather had seen countless games in this modern atmosphere, it wasn't until he died that I found out he was into rock 'n roll.

Before he became bedridden three months before his passing, Grandpa Joe made Dad bring him to all my games. Grandpa Joe said he needed to be there to give me pointers. He was always telling me to skate through my checks and to use my backhand more. "You're a strong boy, Scotty, that backhander'll catch 'em by surprise," he would say.

Yep, my grandfather taught me more about hockey than anyone. When I was three, he got me my first pair of skates. By the time I was five, he had enrolled me in minor hockey and was taking me to the Rideau to skate every winter day. After my first coach said I had promise, he got so excited he had Dad build a rink in the backyard. Grandpa Joe then bought a net and got Dad to break out the old goalie equipment so I could prac-tice on him. One time, when I was barely seven, I skated in on Dad, and deked him out, getting him to flop on his side. "Atta, boy, Scotty!" Grandpa Joe cheered gleefully as I shoveled the puck toward the goal. He was laughing like his heart had risen into his throat and was tickling him on its way back down. But Dad, who usually let me score, ruined the fun when he stuck out a pad by reflex, stopping my shot. Dad looked at me apologetically, like he had just run over one of my toys, but Grandpa Joe didn't buy it. "You knucklehead!" he yelled. "What are you doin'?" He whacked Dad on the helmet and shouted, "The boy makes a move like that and you don't let him score? What's wrong with ya!"

Sometimes, Dad couldn't make it and Grandpa Joe would get on the ice instead. I'd be tagging along as he trudged his bucket of pucks to the backyard. Positioning me at the side of the goal, he would say, "Remember, Scotty, when you're near the net, keep your stick on the ice. You never know when the puck's gonna be comin' at ya." With his stick, he would choose a puck from the pile, move it from backhand to forehand a few times like a pitcher rubbing up a baseball, then snap a pass toward me. The first one would come slow and was usually right on the tape, so I always got it in. Then he would send them faster and faster. A lot of times I ended up whiffing and spinning around. "Don't worry about that one," he would say. "Here comes another." And I'd put my stick back on the ice, lean over it and leer at the next oncoming disc, ready to whack it with all my might.

Once all the pucks were sent, he would ask, "You had enough?" I'd shake my head and say, "Uh-uh," and we would gather them up and go again. He would be out there for an hour or two with me, always giving me tips and never pushing too much.

One time, when I was eleven and playing all-star, I got checked pretty hard from behind. It was a cheapshot. I was along the boards and didn't even have the puck when the other guy rammed me between my shoulderblades, and sent me headfirst into the glass. After falling to the ice, I covered my face and started bawling like a dumb kid. While I got helped off the ice, Grandpa Joe was telling off the other team's coach. He told him he never wanted to see any of his players touch me again, and that I was his only grandkid and he'd do anything to protect me. It was a whole long schpiel.

Man, I loved that old guy, he was always looking out for me. I really think he believed I was going to make it to the top, why else would he have given his own son such aggravation to get to a bunch of Junior A games? When I got drafted by the Kougars, Grandpa Joe was ecstatic. Sure, he wanted me to stay in Ottawa like Mom and Dad, but I wasn't going to get a chance with any of the teams there, so Kildare was a good deal for me. Plus, at the time, the Kougars still had a pretty good tradition and name.

Grandpa Joe was a real maniac when it came to getting to our games. Every Thursday after work, Dad would have to pick him up, then they would drive out to Kildare, watch the game, say hi, maybe we would have dinner afterwards and they would head home. By my third season, though, the Kildare experience had started to grate on both of them, for different reasons.

"Stubborn ol' fool," Dad would say. "He insists on drinkin' at least three beer and then we gotta stop four times on the way back. And the whole time we're there, he bitches about all the noise. Drives me nuts."

And Grandpa Joe used to say, "Why the heck do they gotta play all that loud crap for? It's a freakin' hockey game for Pete's sake! How do you boys even concentrate down there? And why's the gosh darn owner in a dress? My God, we gotta work a trade to get you outta here, Scotty."

Still, without fail, Grandpa Joe would tug at Dad every week so he could come to the rink just to see me play. Yet he was there so often, my grandfather must have taken something else away, I figured. It wasn't until I opened my inheritance gift that I was sure.

We had just lost our fourth game when Dad called. "Scott, I've got bad news." He was in tears. I had never heard or seen Dad cry before. Cancer had finally beaten Grandpa Joe, I was told, after he gave it a beauty of a fight. He died at seventy-four, in his sleep, seven years after he was diagnosed.

As soon as I heard, I rushed home. It hadn't hit me while I was on the Greyhound back to Ottawa. I think my mind must have just been denying it, because I was simply numb. That's what happens, I guess, when things like that occur: you go numb. You try to stay in the present — or the past — for as long as life lets you. Eventually, it catches up and you have to face it, but, for a little while, at least, your mind tries to freeze time, and it can accomplish it, too. I had told Dad not to meet me. He needed his rest, I said, but didn't add that I needed the escape. On the bus, all I did was stare ahead into the back of the seat in front of me, and didn't think of anything but the pattern of its fabric: squares of green and red, with tiny blue dots running around their borders, not at all unlike a large-scale map. I started to count the dots, I remember, until a thought would stray in. When one did, I would take it from the top. I probably got to about thirty or forty each time before losing count and starting over. It wasn't until we got to around Arnprior that my mind started to twinge. Then I had to find something else to occupy it, so I began to make a plan for the station: Walk west to the local platform, check the schedule there, no, no, check the time, as soon as I get off, check the time, then to the platform and schedule; I'm thirsty, I'll get a pop, the snack shop's on the right, below the clock, no, no — no pop. I can't have pop, Grandpa Joe said sugar . . . — first thing is to check the time. Get the time, get to the platform, get to the schedule, get on the bus, get home, get to bed, get to sleep. *"Get your sleep on game days, Scotty."* Iced tea. Or milk. One or the other, after I check the time . . . So, check the time, check the time, *"Check the time, Scott. Remember, you've got to pick up your grandfather at three.";* *"Sure, Mom, I know.";* *"And don't keep him out in the cold too long.";* *"Why not? He loves being down by the ice.";* *"He's old, honey. You don't want anything to happen to him.";* *"To Grandpa Joe? What could happen to Grandpa Joe?"* . . . Shut up, man! Just shut up! . . . Okay, okay, which bus? Which bus do I get on? The local to Rideau, you moron, I told myself. I'm getting on the local to Rideau.

10

I t was late when I got home and Mom was already asleep. Dad was still up, though, and a mess. His eyes were bloodshot, he didn't stand straight and moved around the house in a daze, being deliberate with every task. A snack was in the oven for me, he said, and there was juice in the fridge. He would see me in the morning.

He walked away, but came back before long to hug me again and say, "Here, son, he wanted you to have this," and I was handed a rusted metal box containing my grandfather's last words to me, and the charm I will cherish for a lifetime.

Dad watched my hands shake as I set the box on the kitchen table, then patted me on the shoulder again and went to bed, leaving me with my grandfather. Before picking up the box, I exhaled. Then I carried it into the comfort of the living room and sat on the couch. The box was almost weightless. One side of it was dented and its corner protruded, so the cover fit tighter than intended. I couldn't tell how old it was, just that Grandpa Joe probably had it for decades. Gripping the bottom of it with my left hand, I tried to free the lid by pulling its handle hard with my right. I was wincing because of the effort and didn't see the handle coming free. When it did, it caused my right arm to swing back violently as if I had just pulled a knife in an insane rage. The cover flew off, too, like a trap door. It flung up and landed on the soft carpet. An envelope and a piece of military wear were the sum of the contents. I set both on my lap, then quickly pulled out Grandpa Joe's letter.

"Dear Scotty,

If you're reading this, it means I'm gone. Now I don't want you or your dad or mom feeling sorry for me. I'll be okay. I'm going to be meeting up with your Grandma Helen soon, I figure. Besides, I had a long, full life and a good son in your Dad and a wonderful grandson in you. So no tears.

Now I left you something in this box, and don't worry, I'm not a cheap, old fart. You've got a lot more coming to you, but I've been teaching you about hockey all your life, now I want to make sure you know that there's more to it than that. I know you know I was in the war. Your dad probably told you I don't like to talk about it and he's right. Helen and I lost a lot of friends over there. Some of them died in my arms in the infirmaries. It took me a long time to even be able to discuss it, but I'll do it now because there's something I want you to know.

I was a pilot with the air force and we were in battle with the Germans near the end of the war. Now it was like a hockey team up there. There was about seven of us that day and we were all supposed to look out for each other. I'd been over there for four years and never got my plane hit before, not even a scratch except for a beer bottle I broke over her tail one night. Wouldn't you know, this time a German catches me on one of my engines and I can see him coming around for another pass. Now I know I'm going to have to bail out or else I'm done for, but I don't know if I've got time. Then through my goggles I see my buddy Frank Masters, a good ol' Canadian boy from Kitchener, come flying in to blow that Nazi to smithereens. He even gave me a wave after he did it! I parachuted out and broke my leg on the landing, but thankfully that was all.

Frank wasn't so lucky. He came in to save me with a Nazi on his tail and got shot down from behind, and had to bail in a hurry. His chute got tangled and he landed funny. His spine got crushed and he had to spend the rest of his life in a wheelchair, all because he gave himself up to save me.

Every time I saw Frank or even thought about him, I felt it should have been me sitting there instead of him or that I shouldn't even have been there at all. But he never made me feel bad about it, except when I beat him at poker.

I always tried to be there to help him out with therapy or getting around or just if he needed to talk, and it wasn't because he saved my life. We became real good friends, and all because of that crazy day in the sky.

That was my last flight. Before my leg was all healed, the war ended, and before long Helen and I were married and Frank was my best man. Seeing that that was my 50th Mission, the military gave me a 50 Mission Cap. That's what that song you boys are always playing — that one about Barilko's goal — is talking about, I think.

Anyway, that's what's in this box I gave you. I don't know if it'll help your backhand any, but maybe I'm hoping it'll bring you friendship and the courage to do what's right when the time comes.

Now Scotty you're a real good kid and I'm proud of you, son. I know how bad you want to get to the pros and I think you've got a good a shot at it. Boy wouldn't it be great if you got in with the Habs, would your dad love that or what? You just remember what I told you, and know that I love you like crazy. Make sure you have a good life, Scotty.

Love,

Grandpa Joe"

I squeezed the leather cap he left me, pressing it to my heart, and the more I squeezed, the more I believed I was clutching something magical. Something full of intangibles.

Winning — *winning* — had become mundane to the Coldbury Chevaliers. When they played the Kougars, the Chevaliers often resembled elite figure skaters seeking perfect scores, competing more against themselves than us. At their best, every action was done with such precision and flair it seemed they were after style points as much as goals.

Coldbury's discipline emanated from the coach. Jean Giguere is a strong man with an underslung jaw that is so pronounced it appears he is always sticking his chin out, daring you to hit it. With broad shoulders, forearms thick as goalie pads, and a size forty-two chest, he would have been a line-backer if he were American. Here, though, he is a hockey coach. Giguere has yet to turn forty and often an onlooker gets the impression one or two of his players will reach that age before him. He's a perfectionist, easily incensed by mistakes. Even from the opposing bench, I could see him spitting while screaming at a player for the slightest transgression. The worst offenders were defencemen who played the puck and not the body, and forwards who tried to carry the puck in instead of dumping and chasing. Any guilty bodies usually missed a shift or two and shrunk away on the bench while Giguere shouted in French and English at them.

Giguere is also arrogant and not above embarrassing the opposition. In our last game of the 1994-95 season, we lost 4-3 to the Chevaliers when Giguere, saying he was resting his top players before the playoffs, called up most of the Coldbury midget team to play us in Kildare. He laughed with much delight when we couldn't score the tying goal on the fifteen-year-old goalie playing his first game. Afterwards, my anger peaking, I skated to him and said, "That's low, man."

He smiled wickedly and told me to have fun on the golf course. The Chevaliers went on to win their third championship in a row and I've never been able to forget that game: It was the last time Grandpa Joe saw me on the ice. As I rode from Ottawa to the rink the day after his funeral, I was still overcome with all sorts of emotions, including humiliation. Giguere was probably laughing at us already; another easy two points, is what he was thinking.

But things were going to change. They had to.

I threw open the dressing-room door. "We're not losing tonight!" I said. "I'm sick of losing to these fuckers. They've been pissing me off for three years!" My duffel bag flung out of my hand and skidded across the floor toward my stall. "I've had it!"

Mostly shock, with some fear from a couple of rookies, was the reaction. Then Brendan said, "You heard the man, let's kick some ass." I looked at him and he nodded in a way that said he knew what this meant. I took a breath and felt satisfied I had gotten it out, but I soon realized I wasn't the only one who needed release. From the back of the room, a quiet banging came. I turned to see Manny Rivers hitting his stick on the tiled floor. The thudding was almost hypnotic, and soon Gord Karenzki, sitting next to Manny, joined in, then Gordie Joseph and a couple of others. It sounded like ominous tapping coming from a basement until Gordon Mackilwraith started chanting, "Kougars, Kougars, Kougars." The chant filled the room and we began to sound like impatient fans at a rock concert.

That's when Tyler Raycliffe walked in ready to give his pre-game talk, which I thought he would change to a eulogy like the other coaches had during a losing streak. Instead, he looked like a new father when he came through the door. Some of the voices stopped in his presence and he didn't like that, so he promptly jumped in, pumping his fist: "Kougars, Kougars, Kougars."

"Well, fuck me," Raycliffe said. "You boys don't look like you even need me tonight."

"Kougars, Kougars, Kougars," the cheer rose.

"Who's gonna win this game?" Raycliffe shouted. He then winked at Brendan and me.

"Kougars, Kougars, Kougars!"

"Who's this league gonna be afraid of from now on?"

"Kougars! Kougars! Kougars!"

"All right, boys," he shouted and raised a fist. "Let's whip 'em!" We let out a roar and a few players even charged onto the ice right then, more than an hour before game time.

Tyler, after a few breaths, came over to me and asked if I was okay. I said I was, then he exited into his office, letting out another little chuckle along the way.

I looked at Brendan. He was sitting upright, still sweating from his daily laps around Leroux Arena. He had yet to don his jersey and his grey T-shirt was darkened by perspiration. His short hair was a mess, sticking up like he had just pulled off a toque and his eyes were closed as he began his pregame ritual of focusing on the game. Brendan never wavered in his commitment to his hometown team. The Kougars were his to lead for one year and that sense of ownership brought him enough pride to fill the squad. And sometimes cloud his judgment. As he emerged from his trance, he leaned back and heaved in as much air as his lungs could fill, then tilted his head slightly so he could make eye contact with me, and exhaled. "We can win this game," he said.

I slapped his hand and hung Grandpa Joe's cap on the hook of my stall.

Thirty minutes before warmups, Tyler Raycliffe called the players who had gone for an early skate back in for one last, brief strategy session. "Okay, the scouting report says Coldbury's not as good as last year. They got a new goalie and word is he goes down early, so shoot high. They're still fast up front, so we're going to start off keeping a forward back. Top line starts. Do not pinch on defence," he said. When he was done, he held out his right hand, palm down, in the middle of the room and everyone mimicked him. "On three. One, two, three . . ."

"Kougars!"

"Let's go."

We made our way to the ice, except for the scratches, Dion Marcelle and two other rookies, who all wore plainclothes and were watching from the press box.

The Tragically Hip's "50 Mission Cap" was blaring from the speakers as we went up the walkway to the ice. The lights were on, the crowd was half-capacity and the Chevaliers were already in the midst of their practice routine.

"Don't look at 'em," I whispered to Brendan, who was leading us onto the rink. He bowed his head when he stepped on the ice and took three quick strides away from Coldbury. I was next on and did the same. The others followed.

Coldbury's regimen was efficient, smooth and precise, while our warmup was a work in progress. After all, there were so many other things for us to fix. We wore white jerseys with green trim and a crest that featured a rabid-looking feline. It had yellow eyes and raised hair that made it look like someone had just spun it rapidly by its tail. After several haphazard passes around the goal, we would pepper Chris Cooper with shots from all angles and distances. The goalie was sharp. Coop, too, was in his final year of Junior A and going after a scholarship. Despite our record, he had distinguished himself as a solid netminder. He wasn't big, just amazingly flexible. Doing splits and all kinds of other acrobatic things between the pipes had become routine for him. As performance goes, Coop probably suffered more than any of us from having to play for the Kougars. It was a marvel he wasn't shellshocked since we routinely got outshot by a two-to-one ratio. After the warmups and national anthem, I came over and whacked each of his pads once. "Let's go, Coop," I said before skating to my left-wing spot while Brendan got ready to take the opening draw.

"What's your record, MacGregor?" said Alain Tallard, the impudent Chevalier across the redline from me. "Bet it starts with a zero."

"Fuck you," I said.

He laughed, long and delightfully, his voice turning to a cackle as his pimpled face kept stretching to bare his wretched teeth. With each snort, my ire grew. As I leered at him, his face took on the look of a hissing serpent and he said, "Still Lannie's Loser Ladies, eh?"

The puck dropped. I lunged toward Tallard to cross-check him, he stepped aside like he was expecting me, sped down the wing where he took a pass at our blueline and moved into the slot. With a quick wrist shot, he scored on Cooper's glove side. Ten seconds into the game we were trailing 1-0, and, *Here we go again*, rang through our collective psyche.

"Scott, Scott," Raycliffe called from the bench. He had a vexed look, and his stiff hands were pressed down in front of him and bouncing slightly in the air. Dejectedly, I skated back to centre ice.

Tallard celebrated by tapping gloves with everyone on his bench before heading back to the redline. "Nice check, asshole," he said and put his stick down again. "You guys really suck, ya know?"

The fans were booing me, and all I could do was lower my head and stare in at the faceoff circle, where Brendan won the draw, thankfully. Manny Rivers, our shifty linemate, ducked a check then dumped the puck in as we averted further disaster. When I got to the bench, assistant coach Clyde Parker leaned in my ear and sternly said, "Keep it in check from now on." I turned around, mad, but he was already facing the other way, following the play.

For the next fifteen minutes, I kept my focus and so did my teammates. We denied the Chevaliers chances, a victory in itself. One of our wingers was always back as Tyler had instructed and Coldbury was frustrated, icing the puck and rushing passes that led to turnovers. But the Chevaliers were deep enough to use four lines, we were only using three, and Tyler needed to get at least one shift from our fourth group of forwards; the All-Gord line we called them because it featured Mackilwraith at centre, and rookies Joseph and Karenzki on the wings. Tyler put them on with about four minutes to go before intermission, having them change on the fly. But Giguere coaches like a hunter, eyeing his prey and waiting for an opening.

He saw us bare and began to fire. Right away, he called for a change, getting Tallard and his linemates on the ice.

"Oh, shit," Tyler whispered.

Mackilwraith was carrying the puck toward centre ice when his stick was lifted from behind like a gate by Tallard, who corralled the puck and turned to our goal. His centreman, Sebastien Gendron, joined the attack. They passed the puck back and forth as Jesse Sullivan skated backward with a desperate look before Gendron faked a shot, getting Jesse to sprawl in an attempt to block it, and centered a pass to Tallard, who slapped the puck past our sliding goalie. Coldbury celebrated, the fans booed, and Raycliffe combed a hand through his hair, sighing loudly, like a gambler gone broke. He paced on the bench until period's end, when he led our doleful band into the locker room, down 2-0.

"This fucking sucks," Tim Chaput said and slumped in his stall.

"Shut up, Chaput!" I yelled. "It's not over!"

"Ooooh, what're you gonna do? Cross-check my shadow."

I got up to shove him, but felt the grip of a big hand like a claw around my right shoulder. "None of that!" Clyde Parker shouted and forcefully pulled me back.

I glared at him — no one touches me like that — and he shot back the same angry look. Our eyes locked in a staredown, which he won when I finally hung my head and sat. Clyde, satisfied, moved off.

The tension in the room was thick. "Look, we're in this game," Raycliffe said like a counselor. "We still got two periods to go, the worst thing to do is think we can't win this thing."

But his words had little effect: They had been uttered before by others from where he stood. Sure, we all respected our coach and knew he was better than his predecessors, but one man alone had no chance against the oft-injured pride of twenty-one teenaged boys. If we were to have a change of heart, it would have to come from within. And our leader knew it.

"One shift at a time," Brendan Kowalczek said in a voice so low it sounded like it was coming from inside our own heads. "One shift. We win one shift, then we win the next. Then the next . . ." I looked up, my teeth still clenched, to see him standing in the middle of the room, looking around at each of us. He was speaking louder now and we were hearing clearer. "Don't pay attention to the score, don't pay attention to what they're doin' out there. It's just like practice, work hard, one shift, then the next, then the next. That's all."

He was quiet then, sweat pouring off his face and eyes wandering. I stood for him, put a glove out and he raised his to meet mine. Jesse Sullivan joined in, Johnny Carruthers, Cooper, the Gords, one by one, everyone, even Chaput, and we shouted, "One, two, three! Kougars!"

Re-armed with hope, we flew out the door. On the first shift, Brendan did as he said, working the puck down low, keeping it hemmed in the corner, taking hit after hit in his back, cycling it around to me. Although we didn't get a shot off, we managed to keep the puck. We had won a shift. Our teammates followed the lead, grinding themselves as hard as they could, for as long as they could. Soon, we earned a power play, rankling Giguere. "Hey, ref, that was clean, eh? *Clean!*" he yelled when the referee passed his bench. "You trying to give the home fans a game, now, huh?"

Moving the puck like we would in practice, we got a few shots with the man-advantage, but no goals. Frustrating, yes, but we felt alive, it was only a matter of time.

Or was it?

With less than a minute to play in the period, many of us looked up at the scoreboard and saw what we had when it started. The work wasn't paying off. Again, jeers rang from the crowd after an offside. Our second line joined Carruthers and Sullivan on the ice as the rest of us dropped our heads, fighting doubt, waiting to get away from the impatient fans for another intermission.

The Chevaliers won the ensuing draw and simply slid the puck down the ice like a boxer backing off a fallen opponent. Cooper played the puck to Carruthers, who carried it to our blueline while we watched the seconds tick away. As usual, no one was paying attention to Johnny until he gave us reason to. Like a phantom blow, the defenceman left many disbelieved when he coolly sailed a pass up the middle to Tahani "One-Axe" Kohono, our quick second-year forward. Little Tahani grabbed the perfect feed and raced through the Coldbury defence, catching them off-guard, like he had landed a rabbit punch. He churned his legs as if he were riding a bicycle and before we knew it, found himself on a breakaway. He deked to his left, exaggerating his move with a jerk of his head and shoulders, then pulled the puck back to the right, and raised a backhander over the goalie's glove. The red light went on like a radar blip. Raycliffe threw his hands aloft as if he were ridding himself of something vile. The fans cheered, finally. I looked at Brendan and he looked at me, "Holy, moley," we said with grins before raising our hands and high-fiving. The score was 2-1 with twelve seconds to go before intermission.

Across the ice, Giguere snarled at his defencemen and shouted, "Im-bee-seals! Im-bee-seals!"

Meanwhile, Carruthers, who started the play with the brilliant pass, joined our other four skaters at the Coldbury blueline to rejoice. He rattled Tahani's helmet a little then came to the bench, where we tapped gloves with him if we were close enough, or just said, "Hell of a pass, J.C." Clyde Parker grabbed his shoulders, startling Johnny, and shook them until he finally smiled.

Before the third period, our spirits were high. "We can beat them," somebody said when we entered the dressing room. "Just don't do anything stupid," Brendan said. "Let them make the mistakes."

Raycliffe came in. He looked at Tahani, a short, baby-faced sprite with long black hair and a mischievous grin. "Nice moves, lad," Raycliffe said. "Is that why they call you One-Axe?"

"No. It's 'cause I cross-check more than I score," Tahani, an Algonquin Native, said.

Raycliffe joined the room in a laugh, then said, "I want everyone in here to be proud of yourselves. You lads hung in there tough. We just gotta work hard for another twenty minutes, got it?" We nodded, then obeyed.

Cooper made some terrific saves on Tallard on a Coldbury power play and the rest of us manned our positions well. Tyler did a fine job, too. Instead of putting the Gords on together, he gave them individual shifts on the top three lines, giving us enough rest to skate hard through the end of the game. But we hadn't evened the score. Tyler used our lone timeout with one minute and ten seconds to play in regulation and the faceoff in our end. On his mark, our line took the ice and huddled in front of him. Keeping one foot on the bench, Raycliffe stretched his other onto the boards and leaned forward, his elbow on his knee. "Okay, as soon as we get possession, get the puck to Brendan," he said, then turned toward Chris Cooper. "When we get it to centre, Chris, you head to the bench."

Tyler's eyes then moved back and forth between Brendan and me, knowing strategy alone wasn't going to get it done. "You lads gotta keep the puck down low. Fight for it. Remember, this is what we wanted: a chance. All right, on three . . ."

He stretched his hand out and the rest of us settled our gloved paws in its vicinity. "One, two, three! Kougars!"

The whistle blew. The fans were clapping, whistling and randomly shouting, "C'mon, Kougars! Let's go!"

We got to the circle to the right of Cooper. Brendan skated over to take the faceoff, toes pointed in, body bent over, stick on the ice and both gloves viced around it. The linesman threw down the puck and our captain won the draw cleanly, pushing the disc through his legs and onto Sullivan's stick. Jesse lifted the puck halfway up the boards toward our blueline. Brendan picked it up on the right-wing side and sped to the redline. Through the corner of my eye, I saw Cooper climb onto the bench and Tahani get on the ice. Brendan sent the puck into the Coldbury zone and Manny Rivers took a hit as he pushed it around the Chevaliers' goal. I bumped a Coldbury defenceman slightly at the halfboards, gained control, then took two choppy strides to get out of the corner, but I was at a bad angle and had to pass off. Tahani, who was intimidated by the physical play in the goalmouth, stood awkwardly between Johnny, at the left point, and me. I nodded to Tahani to man my spot on left wing, and after taking a peek at the clock — seventeen seconds to go —, I darted to the goal. Brendan had the puck behind the net and saw me coming. He sent a pass out front, but as I was about to lift it, the netminder's stick smacked it backward while someone knocked me to the ice. What I remember seeing then is clear, but not nearly as vivid as what I felt. Too busy trying to get myself up and my stick in shooting position, I lost sight of the goal — and the puck. After getting to my knees, all I saw was Jesse Sullivan's eyes as he charged in from the right point. Green eyes, bright green eyes, that grew wider and wider like a bubble filling with air. He was looking right behind me and I thought I was about to be whacked across the back or on the head, so I hustled to defend myself. But it was too late, before I could begin to turn around, I felt the hit, the immediate pain and I knew where the wound came from: The stinging sensation of hard, propelled rubber smacking against flesh, bruising and discolouring it, was quite familiar. Feeling it on my ass, was not. That's where I got hit, though, and the puck, as I was often reminded, jumped off my rear end like a pinball and ricocheted past the stunned goalie. The horn sounded, the red light went on, and I leapt up, jumping madly like I was trying to swat a pinata. Brendan put a hand around me, whacked me on the butt with his stick and said, "Now I know where to get it to ya." We hugged and our team-mates swarmed us. Then I happily looked up at the scoreboard: Three seconds to go against the Coldbury Chevaliers and Kildare was abuzz. And in the game.

A five-minute overtime did nothing to settle the outcome and we were guaranteed our first point of the season because of the tie, but Central Ontario Hockey League rules call for a shootout to determine a victor, who is then awarded a second point. "Okay, coach, gimme five numbers," the referee said to Tyler, who had to choose five skaters to shoot.

In order, he gave the first four: No. 9 (Brendan), No. 10 (myself), No. 7 (Tahani) and No. 15 (Manny). But he puzzled for a fifth. He glanced up at the press box, where Dion Marcelle was pining and of no help. Then he raised his eyebrows and said, "Let's go with number three."

That was Jesse Sullivan, the most-experienced player left. But Jesse wasn't great with the puck and Clyde Parker knew it. Although silent, Clyde was visibly unimpressed by the choice, shaking his head vigorously until he caught Tyler looking at him.

After four shooters each, the shootout was tied 2-2. Coldbury's final shooter scored, and it was up to Jesse to even the game. He couldn't, making his deke too late and sliding the puck wide. I banged my fist on the boards as we walked out of the rink, losers again. The rudest fans — those who pay six bucks just to sit and ride us all night — aimed catcalls at us, even urging Tyler to go back to selling snowmobiles. But Tyler didn't respond to them, he just stared up at Marcelle, who was eating popcorn and sharing a laugh with someone in the press box.

Regardless of what moral victory we gained that night, the Coldbury Chevaliers still left Leroux Arena the way they always did, with two more points than they had when they arrived. After the game, some players seemed content with the performance, making Brendan wrathful.

"What the hell are you so happy about?" he asked Tim Chaput, who was caught handslapping a linemate. "We didn't win. We got one freakin' point tonight and they got two. That means we lost and we should feel like shit because of it. I know I do." Brendan slammed his gloves into his stall. "If anyone thinks that team's better than us, I'll quit right here, right now."

The room fell silent and we studied each other. When we looked at Johnny Carruthers, we remembered the excellent pass he made on the first goal. In Tony Lacroix, we saw the check he threw on Tallard to stop a rush. Chaput, the third-line centre, symbolized the harassing forecheck we displayed all night. We glanced around, recognized each other's talents and, somehow, determined we could win.

The moment broke with a knock on the door. "Hey, boys, nice game tonight," said Randy Delisle before pointing at me. "Scott, got time to talk."

"Sure." I left the room anxious to discuss our progress for a change. Randy has been covering the Kougars for more than twenty years. He often interviewed me because he said I gave good quotes.

"That was a heck of a goal," he said, wryly. His notepad was held in front of him, but tilted up so I couldn't see what he was writing.

I laughed and said, "Yeah, I never scored one like that before. I guess that's what they mean by 'Playing from the seat of your pants.' "

He smiled while scribbling, paused and said, "This is the best the team's played against Coldbury maybe since you've been here. Is this the beginning of the new Kougars, or what?"

"Oh, I hope so. You know, we were just working hard and after those first two goals, we just buckled down. When they didn't score again and Tahani did, that gave our confidence a real boost." I looked down the hall and saw Jean Giguere. He was talking to his assistant coaches when he glanced over, looked back at his staff, and quickly turned to face me again. He nodded and turned away. "It just feels real good to know we can play with a team like Coldbury."

"Now, personally, this must have been a hard game for you. I know there was a death in your family, what kind of effect did that have on you out there?"

"I don't know, my grandfather meant a lot to me. He taught me more about the game than anyone. I guess I'm just going to have to work hard to be the player and person he wanted me to be," I said, eyeing my shuffling skates. "It's sure not the same knowing he's not out there watching."

"Hey, he's watching, Scott. Don't you worry," Randy said, knocking me on the arm. He had a smile that seemed fatherly through his greying beard. "But what's this business I hear about a special cap or something you've got?"

"How'd you hear about that?" I said and my eyes lit up.

"Ah, you know, sources?" he said with a wink and sly grin.

"Yeah, right. I think I room with that source. But, yeah, Grandpa Joe left me his 50 Mission Cap from the war. I got it hanging in my locker, there," I said, throwing a thumb back at the dressing room, "so it brought us a little luck tonight, I guess. We even got the sound guy to play that Tragically Hip song for the skate and things worked out. Like you said, maybe he is watching."

The story in the next day's *Chronicle* began:

> Scott MacGregor has been known to use his brain and his brawn to score goals for the Kildare Kougars, last night, he found another part of his body that could do the same trick. Brendan Kowalczek banked a shot off MacGregor's derriere in the final seconds of regulation and, as a result, Kildare can finally say, "Bottoms up!" to its team again. The Kougars came away with their first point of the season in a 2-2 draw against the dastardly Coldbury Chevaliers. Sure, the Kougars lost the shootout, 3-2, but expect one miracle at a time, please.

Whether it was fate or serendipity, the Kildare Kougars did perform what our followers believed were miracles. We went on a winning streak following that Coldbury game, topping Beavers Falls, Timberton, Crowne Place, Salterton and Moosehead. For the first time in nearly a decade the Kougars were owners of a winning record at 5 wins, 4 losses and 1 over-time loss. I carried Grandpa Joe's 50 Mission Cap wherever I went: keeping it in my knapsack at school, on its hook during games and practices, on dates with Michelle, even resting it on my bedside table as I slept. Whenever we had a road game, Brendan would ask, "You got the cap?" before I boarded the bus. After I pulled it out of my jacket and waved it around, he would let out a "Woo-Hoo!" and high-five our nearest team-mate. Indeed, our team believed the cap had powers that were responsible for our sudden success. Thus, slowly, faith in our hockey team was being restored in tiny Kildare, Ontario.

Unfortunately, that wasn't nearly enough for Lannie Leroux. Turns out, he wanted in on all the fuss, too.

12

The Leroux Arena news conference was at 2:30 the afternoon of a road game. Lannie wanted to give the TV station plenty of time to get lots of film for the six o'clock news. Our attendance wasn't required, or requested, but some of us older guys on the team who didn't have a last-period class were curious. Local businessmen, politicians and team alumni also wanted to know what Lannie was up to. So, we all sat in the stands, waiting. Above us, the anxious members of the Kougars hierarchy stood in the press box. When it was quiet, I thought I could hear Tyler Raycliffe pacing. No one knew what was going to happen, the story in that day's paper just said Lannie had "a major announcement" to make about the future of the arena. Everyone perceived it wasn't going to be good news.

To that point, Lannie Leroux had done some obviously rotten things in his life: undermined the team; practiced economic brinkmanship with the community; serviced himself without thought to others. None of it, however, came close to the treachery he displayed when he unveiled plans for "LannieLand."

The lights in Leroux Arena dimmed, a red carpet rolled to centre ice and a lectern was placed on it. Feedback came from the auditorium speakers and the public address announcer, trying his best to sound enthused, announced, "Members of the media and guests, please welcome the soul of Kildare, Mr. Lannie Leroux." A spotlight shone on Lannie as he walked out in a business suit, skirt just below the knees, and blouse buttoned to the top and adorned with a brooch. The announcer had paused, but there was no applause. A few whistles certainly, but no claps. Following Lannie were "Sinclair Lougheed, architect extraordinaire," and "Cameron Frazier, distinguished attorney-at-law." No applause came upon their introductions, either. Lougheed was rolling out a wood-laminated cart with a sizeable, blanketed display on its top.

When all three men were stationed behind the lectern, Lannie stepped to the microphone. He feigned clearing his throat, tapped the mic with an index finger, then checked to find the television camera. A few flashes burst as photographers snapped. Lannie smiled then faced the crowd.

"Ladies and gentlemen, my friends in the media, honoured citizens, thank you all for coming here on this glorious day," he said with a smile so wide he could have been snarling. "I have a grand plan, one I am sure you will all la-la-la-love." He clapped his hands and held them together then turned to smile at Lougheed, who remained expressionless.

"But first," he continued, "let me tell you why I am about to do what I am about to do . . . Ahem . . . Four score and some years ago, my grandfather wanted to be a boy. Well, of course he was a boy. He had to have been a boy if he were a man. But more exactly, he wanted to be like a boy. He wanted to enjoy childhood, play with his sailboats and pet toucans, run around chasing the butler, the normal activities all boys should partake in. But he could not do so. He was not allowed. He was a Leroux. That meant going to opera and travelling to wretched places like Portugal and Japan . . ." Lannie's attorney tapped him on the shoulder, rolled a hand and whispered in his ear. After giving a perturbed look, Lannie faced the anxious audience and said, "Well, nevermind all that. The point is, I, my, my grandfather wanted to join the circus. He just loved clowns, the cute, adorable midgets were his favourites." The lawyer, without pretense, cleared his throat and Lannie hung his head briefly, as if to say, *Oh, all right*, then faced the mic again. He threw up his hands, looked at the ceiling, then plucked the cover off Lougheed's display and yelled, "He-e-e-e-re's LannieLand!"

The arena spotlight and TV camera glare shot over to a large model within a glass case. In the stands, onlookers leaned forward, but still couldn't make out the tiny details. No matter, Lannie was all too happy to fill us in. In his rave, he took the microphone and began walking around the display, spitting out words like an auctioneer. "LannieLand will be the greatest thing to ever happen to Kildare," he said. "Mr. Lougheed, the finest architect in the land, designed it himself. Clowns and elephants and pink carousels, we'll have it all. Rides and games and rides and rides. All right here, where we're standing." He stopped to look at the dumbfounded crowd, held his hands out and asked, "Aren't you happy?"

With that, several members of the town council got up and walked away, cursing under their breaths. They didn't care to be informed of LannieLand's other features: a ferris wheel, mammoth aquarium, retractable roof. And a retractable Lannie.

"What's that in the middle?" a reporter asked.

Sinclair Lougheed stepped forth and sincerely said, "It's a fifteen-foot statue of Mr. Leroux."

"What's it made of?" someone in the audience shouted. "Lard!"

Lannie snarled, for real this time. Lougheed touched his spectacles and answered, "The statue will be made of marble and stand on a hydraulic support, allowing it to be submerged for an hour or two should that space be required for a special event, such as a race or concert."

Of course, everyone thought the whole thing should be sunk, but Lannie, his lawyer or Lougheed had a retort for nearly every criticism. LannieLand would take up Leroux Arena, its parking lot and much of the downtown space vacated by bankrupt businesses. It would vault tourism, they said, revitalize downtown, give Kildare something unique, attract entertainers, and, most importantly, jobs, jobs, jobs. Work would begin in late March. "But what of the Kougars?" Randy Delisle asked.

"Kougars, Schmougars," Lannie said and waved a dismissive hand. "They can play down the road."

The reporter inquired about the team's lease and was told it expired on March 15, just after the end of the regular season. Several heads turned to look up at co-owner Arnold Bramburger, a local businessman, and his partner, general manager Gary Curran, in the press box. Lannie's lawyer said, "According to the lease agreement, the Kougars could rent the arena if they needed it, unless Mr. Leroux had allotted the space for another tenant or for his own use."

"So, would Leroux Arena be available for the COHL playoffs?" Randy asked.

"No," said Frazier, the attorney. "And, quite frankly, if the team was confident about its chances in that regard, it would have booked the space."

More heads looked up to the owners, who by this time had vacated the press box to have a smoke in the men's room. Meanwhile, Brendan, his face red and jaw jutting out, got up to leave, tugging the bill of his baseball cap down as he walked up the stairs. Others followed, but I stayed. Chris Cooper did, too, and slid over to me. "Man, what the fuck does this all mean?" he whispered.

"Coop, it means this is going to be another long season," I said.

TV, radio and newspaper reporters got a hold of Curran and Bramburger, grilling them with many questions that all asked the same thing: "How could you let this happen?"

They contended they had a verbal agreement for space whenever they needed it, said it wouldn't have been good business to spend fourteen-thousand dollars — two month's rent — unless they were certain of using it, promised the team wouldn't be playing in the dingy, six-hundred-seat minor hockey rink, assured Lannie was breaching the contract, couldn't believe he was doing this, it would never work, they declared, no way, not in downtown Kildare of all places, the zoning laws alone, people wouldn't stand for it. Then Gary Curran, obviously flustered, went so far as to proclaim: "The Kougars will be in the playoffs and will be playing in Leroux Arena. I guarantee it."

Later, Curran approached our bus, already full with players, and apologized to Tyler Raycliffe, who was pacing outside. The lease agreement wasn't a reflection on Raycliffe or the players, Curran said. It was strictly a business decision, one he and his partners thought was the right thing to do, fiscally.

Raycliffe was nodding his head and nervously puffing on a cigarette. When Curran was done, they shook hands and Tyler stamped out the Marlboro. Wiping sweat from his face, our coach stared at the arena.

"Lannie-fucking-Land," he said and swatted the air. "This is insanity."

Curran, hands in pockets, walked back into Leroux Arena as the bus left for Deeringwood. For nearly the entire drive, Tyler walked up and down the aisle. He pulled at his hair, then scratched the back of his neck feverishly, brushed his hands over his face a few times, went back to pulling his hair. He would say things that belied his body language, such as, "Don't worry lads, things'll get sorted out. We just gotta go out there and do our jobs"; and, "This is just one of Lannie's jokes. A sick, sick joke. That's all."

Of course, we worried, and felt angry and insecure. Brendan, who sat stiff and picked anxiously at a pimple, was particularly peeved that the owners apparently had such little confidence in us, they didn't extend the lease to include the postseason. I told him we would just have to kick ass, and the town would get behind us and convince Lannie to let us have the rink for the playoffs, just like they got him to sell the team in the first place.

With few exceptions, the conversations to and from the game — a frustrating 4-3 loss that ended our five-game winning streak — surrounded Lannie Leroux. We were rapt in the events of the day. The ride was full of commotion and no one could concentrate on reading or doing homework. Amid it all, came the intermittent sneezing and sniffling of Gordie Joseph from the back of the bus. At the time, no one cared.

13

In November of 1995, the flu hit the Kildare Kougars with ferocity. It was three days before we were to travel to Coldbury for a rematch with the Chevaliers when Gordie Joseph, his sneezes echoing up the tunnel from the dressing room to the rink, showed up late to practice already sweating and with bloodshot eyes. His jersey, which never fit too-short-and-skinny Gordie properly anyway, was hanging out on the right side because he had been tugging it to wipe his nose. It ballooned at his waist like he was trying to hide a stolen loaf of bread.

Tyler, more alarmed by Gordie's appearance than his tardiness, let the whistle fall from his mouth as he leered at the rookie. Gordie's mom was in the stands and after seeing the distress on the coach's face, cupped her hands around her mouth and called out, "Don't worry, Mr. Raycliffe! The lad's just got a touch of the sniffles!"

Tyler, who couldn't stand the presence of parents at his practices, was livid that he apparently had such little respect a *mother* found nothing wrong with speaking during his drills. He took his frustration out on — who else? — his players, commanding, "Everybody, ten laps, now!" He blew his whistle. We groaned and began to skate.

Gordie Joseph lagged well behind the rest of us, even Dion Marcelle. In less than three turns around the rink, Brendan lapped Gordie, passing him so swiftly that the weakling nearly spun right around. As each of us sped by him, Gordie's balance eroded and he began to take quicker steps, shifting his weight from one side to the other as if he were traversing a rolling log. This caused a rapid change in his equilibrium and eventually forced Gordie to lunge both arms toward the boards, pulling himself to the wall like a drowning swimmer as he struggled not to fall. But the satisfaction he felt after rediscovering his balance was as brief as a simple breath and a "Whew!", because Gordie Joseph's legs were in fine form compared to his stomach. Gordie placed one hand on his aching belly, leaned over the bench and began puking while emanating a wretching sound that belonged to a body twice his size.

"Gordie!" shouted Mrs. Joseph, a robust, short-haired woman with a scratchy voice caused by too many cigarettes. She had come bounding down the arena stairs toward her son until the slab of protective glass behind the bench stopped her.

Tyler blew his whistle to stop the drill before most of us were even finished our sixth lap. He told Clyde Parker to run us through shooting exercises while he checked on the rookie. "You okay, son?" Tyler asked while setting a gloved hand on Gordie's back.

The kid shook his head slowly and managed a faint "Uh-uh" between dry heaves.

"Mr. Raycliffe, is it okay if I take him home?" Mrs. Joseph asked.

"Yes, ma'am," he said and showed he was eager to aid in the cause. Tyler took a few steps up the tunnel before shouting to the trainer: "Hey, Guy, come 'ere! We got a lad who's sick!"

Tyler walked back to Gordie, and helped him off the ice and into the hands of the trainer. "And, Guy, see if you can get a janitor to clean up that mess," Tyler said. He was crinkling his nose as the stench of the vomit began to rise.

"Mrs. Joseph," Tyler called as the mother of his problems began to walk away, "are you going to be taking him to a doctor?"

"I'm going to get him to Doctor Schellenberger as soon as he gets washed up."

"Good, please let me know what it is. If it's something contagious we may need to get the boys some shots."

"Of course. Sorry for the trouble."

Tyler waved a hand and amazingly managed a smile before blowing his whistle as he turned to us. "Okay, gimme seven more and we'll call it a day." We slumped our shoulders and groaned again.

The coach then frowned as he skated to the other side of the rink to speak with Gary Curran, who had come down from the press box to watch from the stands. "The kid got the flu?" Curran asked.

"I'd bet on it," Raycliffe answered.

"Oh, shit. Not now."

14

Paint was chipping off the porch of Clyde Parker's house and I picked at the wood splinters underneath while waiting for the door to open. There were no signs of flowers, just lots of weeds and bushes that were way overgrown. When I looked around the corner, all I saw was the usual stack of empties ready to be returned to The Beer Store. It wasn't a big house, an oversized cottage really, but with just Clyde and Johnny there was plenty of room, I figured.

The door creaked when Clyde opened it and he looked surprised to see me. "MacGregor," he said, "what's the word?"

"Hey, Clyde," I answered. "How ya doin'? Johnny around?"

"Yeah, come in," he said, then gestured to the car in the driveway. "That your girl?"

I looked back at Michelle, sitting behind the wheel, and said yeah.

He smacked his lips and grinned. "How the fuck'd you get her?"

I shrugged and said I didn't know, and followed him in.

He had a tumbler of scotch in his hand and already looked sauced. The house was dark and quiet, windows closed and blinds drawn. Really, the only noise I could make out was a Doors' tune coming from Johnny's room. If I was a stranger, it probably would've given me the creeps.

Clyde offered me a Molson's and I declined. He said that was good because I shouldn't be drinking the night before a game anyway. Then he reminded me about the midnight curfew and told me to wait there while he got Johnny.

Clyde was a hefty man with a ruddy face and large beer gut. Carefully, he would do things. He took his time getting to Johnny's bedroom door then paused in front of it before knocking and saying, "Hey, kid, your chauffeur's here."

The music stopped and I heard Johnny fumbling around. Clyde walked back to me and said, "Big dance tonight, eh?"

"Yeah," I said. "Should be a good time."

Johnny straggled out of his room, and Clyde and I turned to look at him.

"Hey," Johnny said when he saw me.

"Ready to roll?"

He said yes and put his boots on.

Clyde dropped a couple of ice cubes in his glass then walked over and patted Johnny on the back. "Try to get him laid tonight, would ya. Maybe that'll cheer him up," he said and chuckled. I chuckled, too, stupidly, but stopped as soon as I saw embarrassment on Johnny's face. "Christ, I'm just kidding," Clyde said. But Johnny wouldn't look at him and we moved out of the house without Johnny saying a word, either.

"See ya, Clyde," I said. Clyde shrugged and raised his glass.

When we got in the car, I asked, "Everything okay, man?"

"Yeah," Johnny answered and smirked, like it was a stupid question.

Michelle looked at him in the rear-view mirror and asked, "You're sure you won't need a ride home, Johnny?"

"Yeah, it's okay," he said. "I'll figure something out."

Michelle and I didn't want to seem too obvious, so we decided to mingle with our friends for a while, maybe dance a couple of times, then slip out. I gave her a kiss and, as she walked off, noticed her body, in a skirt and blouse that were red like her hair. When she got lost among her group of friends, I began to search for mine. Even before I knew where to turn, Jesse Sullivan pulled me into a corner of the Kildare High gym.

"Scotty Mac," he said over the music, "have a shot of this." He stuck a cup out at me. "Chaput's chick snuck in a whole mickey." I took a sip — vile stuff — and gave it back, my face scrunching from the bitterness.

"So where is everybody?" I asked.

"Coop's over there, trying to get into Dina's pants." Jesse pointed to our goalie on the dance floor. Coop was one of the few guys in the place with the nerve to go up to a girl. Like most school dances, the boys were on one side and the girls on the other, and very little was going on in between. Most anything that was, involved a Kougar. All the cliques were separated, making jokes about each other. It was funny, people paid a couple bucks to go to those things and just ended up doing what they did the rest of the time. What really got me were the kids with the spiked hair and all black clothes. They must have hated it, listening to music they didn't like, being around people they couldn't stand. But they always came. I guess it just shows how bad staying home and watching TV with the folks can be. At Kildare High, though, there were a couple of guys who had no boundaries.

"Hey, puckheads, want some a this?" asked Jungle Jim. He opened a bag full of dope in front of Jesse and me.

I said no thanks.

"That's cool. That's cool. Nothin' like livin' clean," he said, then laughed. "Not like I'd know." We called him Jungle Jim because he had a huge head of curly, brown hair that looked like an afro and had clumps sticking out like vines. (Plus, he was dense and stoned all the time.) He looked around and asked, "Where's Chaput? I can always count on him for a sale."

"He's outside," Jesse said. "I think he's got his own."

"Not like this," Jungle Jim said and began walking away. "Catch ya later, boys."

"Johnny with Chaput?" I asked and Jesse confirmed it. I shook my head in disgust. "What's with him?"

"Wha'doya mean?" he said. "The kid's set. He's got his scholarship, movin' south. You watch, he'll be livin' it up soon."

"Yeah, I know, but you couldn't tell by the way he acts."

"Man, that's just Johnny bein' a poser. I swear, he'd rather be Kurt Cobain than Ray Bourque."

"Now that's fucked up."

He laughed then I nudged him and threw a chin out to Chris Cooper, who was coming our way. When he saw us looking, he held up a piece of paper with both hands and snapped it a couple of times. "Got the number, boys," he said proudly and shook our hands. Coop then said it was a good thing Brigitte Chouinard and all the other Catholic school babes couldn't get in, too, because he was so hot he would have run out of paper. Then he swiped a hand under his nose and asked, "Where's the captain?"

Jesse gestured over to Brendan, who was with his girlfriend, Katie, and a couple of her friends. Coop coughed and said, "What do you say we go break up his little harem there."

We walked over and Brendan smiled when he saw us coming.

"Hey, B.," Jesse said, "keeping all the women for yourself, eh."

"No, just away from the likes of you," said Teri Williams, with a fake sneer.

We chatted a bit then a slow song came and Brendan led Katie to the floor; Jesse said, "You wanna dance, big mouth?" and took Teri by the hand; Coop paired off with Dina Harvey, the girl he was after; and I turned around to see Michelle beside me. I smiled and took her hand. We danced close. Her arms, thin and elegant looking, stayed wrapped around my neck. Her breath was warm on my collar and when she whispered, "Are you ready?" I didn't hesitate.

"Meet me outside," she said, and wiped her wet palms on her skirt, one at a time.

I kissed her cheek. The song ended and she slipped away from my fingers slowly, like ice melting.

Next, a heavy metal number blasted, drawing out Tim Chaput and his followers. They emerged drunk and high, and without Johnny Carruthers. He was supposed to find his own way home, anyway, I reminded myself. There was no need for me to be worried. But the two teachers who were chaperoning that night must have been. They stepped away from the wall looking concerned when Chaput's gang started moshing on the dance floor, taking turns flying into each other like they were throwing body checks. With that, I left.

I hurried into Michelle's car. The drive to Caledonia Hill was too long for both of us. She was nervous. Again, she talked about how much she missed Toronto, even if her parents didn't. It was good for them to be back, though, she conceded. Big-city life isn't for everyone and she was starting to see it was just too different for her folks, and it wasn't like she was on another world now; she could always go back when she started university. Besides, being back in Kildare was neat. She got to see how much people had changed, and to realize how much she had, too, after eight years. And, of course, it was nice to have met me.

The car stopped. We breathed and looked out the windshield as frost settled on it. I reached for her hand. She squeezed onto mine, and it was so quiet, or I was so keen to every sense, that I could hear distinctly the most delicate sounds: the throb as the skin around my fingers tightened, the wheeze of our breaths and the ruffle of her hair as her head began to turn. She looked at me and I at her, and when we saw each other, she opened her arms and I fell into them. We kissed long and deep, without stopping to say a word. She smelled like flowers and tasted like caramel. I drew her close to me and it didn't take long before she moved my hand down under her skirt, and to her crotch. I kept a finger pressed against her panties, and rubbed. Her teeth bit my lower lip a little. And I pressed a little harder, and rubbed a little more. Then her mouth broke from mine completely as she began to brush her hair against my face while swivelling her head so I could kiss her neck and her chin and her cheeks. She was losing herself in it and when I slipped my hand underneath, to feel her, flesh to flesh, she was gone. My hand was there, pressing and rubbing. She was moist and soft and free. Her arms gripped me now, clutching around my head, bringing me to her. "Oh, Scott," she said and rose a little from her seat. My fingers moved with her, and she with them, flesh against flesh. She rocked herself back and forth there, and moaned a little more. When her rocking got shorter, my hand rubbed faster. Her thighs began to stiffen and squeeze, and I rubbed faster. Then faster still, and

then not at all. My fingers were gripped to a halt, her legs clasping together to stop them. She was the only one moving now. I stayed still as she
vibrated against me, tense like something you pluck. Then it was over. She
relaxed and kissed my face and said my name. We made love while
parked there in the woods.

Then we drove back, holding hands and staying silent. The radio was on
loud, but I didn't notice what was playing. Nothing could get my attention,
I thought, and then I saw Johnny. We passed him on our way to the
Kowalczeks. He was walking alone and closing in on Clyde Parker's street.
I felt relief upon seeing him, knowing he was going to get home okay.

15

I t was around 3 p.m. the next day when Brendan knocked on Tyler Raycliffe's office door. The team had a rematch with Coldbury later that night and Tyler said he wanted to meet with Brendan and me beforehand. We didn't know what it was about and were very surprised when co-owner Arnold Bramburger, donut in hand, opened the door. "Come in, lads," he said, jovially. "We've been waitin' for ya."

General manager Gary Curran was pouring coffee and he looked up to nod a hello. Clyde Parker stood next to Tyler's desk with arms crossed and his usual surly expression. Equipment manager Peter Jones and Guy the trainer were taping sticks in a corner. Tyler was seated behind his desk, hands on top of his head, leaning back in his chair. The whole scene, with such a large cast, made me think something was up.

"What'd we get traded?" I asked.

They laughed, as if I had suggested an absurdity, and I was stunned that I felt relieved by their reaction.

"Oh, no, if they take you two away from me, they send me in the deal, too," Tyler said. He stretched an arm toward two chairs along the wall. "Sit down."

"So what's up?" Brendan asked.

"Well, we're thinkin' of makin' a couple of changes," Tyler replied. He paused to scratch his head, like a doctor giving a discouraging prognosis. Sitting up, he edged forward, clasped his hands together and fixed a steely stare on us. "We want to try Marcelle on your line."

I closed my eyes tightly, hoping to block out any thoughts of that pylon trying to catch one of my passes.

"But he's a lefthanded shot, like us," Brendan said. He was fumbling for anything that might change the coach's mind.

"Yeah, we know. I thought Scott could play the off-wing," Tyler said. "Look, fellas, we gotta get this lad goin'. He's got too much talent to be ridin' the pine two months into the season. If he can get hot with you guys, we'll drop him to the second line like we wanted all along."

Like a veteran salesman, Gary Curran stepped in to offer enticement. "Now, you guys know how much we trust ya, 'cause we shouldn't be mentioning any of this in front of you," he said, trying hard not to sound too excited, "but the other reason we want Marcelle to play with you is to see if he can handle it because we're looking at strengthening the team before too long. And if he can't fit in, we may get some people in here who can."

"Oh, yeah," Brendan said, perking up. "Who?"

"Hold on now," Curran said. He raised a stiff palm and took a sip of coffee. "We can't tell you everything just yet. Gotta make sure as few people know as possible to avoid leaks, you know. But we got things in the works. We know you boys want the Tremblay Trophy and I want to get it to ya."

"What about the whole Lannie thing?" Brendan asked.

"Yeah," I said, "what's going on with that?"

Curran was firm with his response. "Look, I don't want you boys worryin' about Lannie. He's just trying to get his name in the paper and his face on TV, that's all. Nothing more. This whole scheme of his has nothing to do with the arena."

Neither of us was convinced and Raycliffe knew it. "Look, lads, let's just concentrate on the game," he said with arms open. "There's nothing you or I can do about anything else, okay?"

We said alright. Tyler, satisfied, restated his position. "So, tonight, same lines as usual, but we're gonna try Marcelle with you boys in practice next week."

Brendan nodded, I said, "Yeah, sure," and, not expecting much of a reply, asked, "Is there anything else?"

Raycliffe started to say no, but then glanced up at Parker, who shook his head so swiftly it was almost unnoticeable. After taking a deep breath, Tyler said, "Yeah, there is." He looked us in the eye like he was about to impart a secret. "Johnny won't be making the trip. He's been suspended for this game."

"For what?" I said in shock. Inching up, I moved to the edge of my seat to hear Raycliffe's answer, but he wasn't the one who spoke.

"He missed curfew last night," Parker said.

"*What?* No way, I saw him walking home, at like eleven-thirty."

Parker tilted his head and shrugged. "What can I say? He didn't come through the door 'til quarter-to-one. And he was half-drunk."

I stared at him, shocked.

Clyde took a breath, shook his head and said, "I don't know what gets into that kid's head sometimes. I tell him he's fuckin' things up for himself, but he doesn't listen. Believe me, I didn't want it to come to this."

"We're keeping it quiet," Raycliffe said. "Sayin' he's got the flu. We told him to stop drinking and we're hoping you boys'll keep an eye on him. Johnny's a good kid. I think he'll get the message."

He handed over our forty-two-dollar paychecks and said he would see us on the bus.

16

The flu struck Dion Marcelle, two defencemen and our backup goaltender. They stayed in Kildare, along with Johnny Carruthers, as we made the trip to Coldbury, Quebec. Even before the game started, its outcome was not Tyler Raycliffe's main concern. Clearly, he understood that if his team's health continued to deteriorate winning would not even be a possibility. He had Guy write everyone's names in bold, black ink on our water bottles, making sure we didn't spread the virus through the sharing of fluids. Tyler convinced the owners to spring for a larger bus for the trip, and sat the players who showed obvious signs of being sick at the front while those who appeared healthy were spread throughout the back. We left for the three-hundred-kilometre ride an hour earlier than normal and Tyler made the driver stop twice so we could get fresh air while he opened all the windows and doors to air out the vehicle. He even made sure we got checked by a doctor for the flu and meningitis.

His actions were valiant and generous. Unfortunately, they were also useless.

Tyler's goal of keeping the team healthy and competitive at the same time faced its ultimate test when he had to decide whether to put Chris

Cooper in as the netminder or start the untested callup from the town's midget team. Declaring it unfair and potentially detrimental to the youngster to have him face Coldbury in his first game, Tyler opted to start Cooper and felt reassured because the goalie was practicing well, despite what appeared to be a minor case of the sniffles.

As it turned out, Cooper was marvellous, facing fifty-two shots and allowing only three goals — all to Alain Tallard, who was at his rat-like worst. He slashed and cross-checked me on almost every shift until finally I couldn't take it anymore. But when I dropped the gloves, he deviously backed off. I cursed at him all the way to the penalty box. He had goaded me into the stupid penalty in the third period, magnified because Tyler had to use inexperienced players on specials teams because more and more of our regulars were coughing, sneezing and feeling woozy, and needed extended rest between shifts. Needless to say, the Chevaliers stretched their winning streak against Kildare to a remarkable twenty-four games with a 3-1 victory. But our team's worst loss came after the game.

Cooper, who had been diving and sliding between his crease all night to make saves, did his most stunning movement of the season when he fell to his knees as the final whistle sounded. He should have already been to the bench, but we could never get the puck deep enough to get an extra man on. So, after being under pressure for three full periods, Cooper became easy prey for the virus already in his system. At game's end, he looked like he was beginning pregame stretches: on all fours, his goal stick flat on the ice but still clutched in his hand and his head bowed. I skated over and put a hand on his back. "Coop, you all right?" I asked.

He shook his head, keeping it stiff as if he was afraid to swivel it further than needed. His face wasn't visible to me, only the sweat dripping out from his mask, which wasn't unusual. The feverish shaking and groans of pain were.

Looking to the bench, I waved my stick. Tyler and Guy immediately started over. Brendan and Jesse Sullivan led a contingent of players coming to find out what was wrong. "Better tell the guys to give him room," I said to Brendan. He told our teammates to go to the locker room. Neither of us noticed the lurching foe still on the ice.

As Tyler and Guy were within a couple of strides of the goal, Alain Tallard skated over while I wasn't looking. He got our attention when he stopped abruptly in front of us, spraying snow on Cooper, who threw his head down further while letting out a loud, agonizing wail. "Hey, MacGregor, lost again, eh? Must suck to be you," Tallard said and started away before looking back over his shoulder. "Et goalie, merci beaucoup pour les buts."

At that moment, the absolute rage of playing against him and losing to him for more than three seasons climaxed. He also convinced me that he was truly demonic, that he didn't talk to get an edge or for competition's sake. He didn't like me, my team and all his insults in all those losses came from his heart. At that moment, when my stick went back in both hands, stretching behind my head, I hated Alain Tallard. The rest of his teammates were already on their way to the locker room. What purpose he served them by being on the ice eluded me. He was there to rub it in. To make it hurt more. And I screamed, my wits lost, as I plunged the stick down onto his right forearm. And through the bone. I heard the break, heard his scream. The brief sense of satisfaction fleeted with the realization of what I had taken.

Tallard immediately fell to a knee and threw off his left glove to grip his right wrist. He turned his neck to look at me, the tears were already streaming. "Batard! Voleur!" he cried. "You fucker!"

He got to his feet and pushed off, gliding toward his bench bent over at the waist, his shoulders drooping as he held his right hand with his left between his legs. Two of his teammates, neither of whom saw what happened, had puzzled looks as they helped him off the ice and to the dressing room.

"Jesus, Scott," Tyler said.

The fans began to shout obscenities at me. Tyler surmised the predicament and acted swiftly. He looked at me. "Get in the locker room, now!" He turned toward Brendan and Jesse. "You, too! Tell everyone: On the bus right away!"

Guy and Tyler helped Cooper to his feet and off the ice. "That's the last thing we need," Guy said. "And Cooper's burnin' up."

In the locker room, I stayed quiet, and Brendan and Jesse didn't say a word to me. They conveyed Raycliffe's instructions to the team to get dressed and out on the double. "But, why?" a few of the ill, young players whined. And got Brendan's curt answer: "Just do it!"

Cooper was dragged into the room by Guy and Tyler, and put in a corner. Guy helped him get his equipment off while Tyler went outside looking more frazzled than he had during our losing streak. He filled in Clyde Parker and Peter Jones then told Randy Delisle the players couldn't be interviewed and didn't comment on my hit against Tallard.

"What's wrong with Coop?" Tim Chaput asked after he exited the shower.

"What do you think? He's got the flu, you idiot!" Guy shouted. "Now shut up, get dressed and on the bus!"

"What's the big rush for?" asked Tony Lacroix, who was already in his street clothes, but was struggling to tie his shoelaces.

"The next guy who asks that, I'm draggin' naked through the parking lot," Brendan said. "Tyler said we gotta get outta here. So let's go!"

The tongues were silent, but the din of jerseys and equipment being tugged off, and feet scampering to and from the running showers filled the room. Too distressed and intent on leaving before the Chevaliers came after me, I didn't bother taking a shower. After toweling off the sweat, I shook nervously as I tried to button my dress shirt, even having to rebutton twice because I missed holes. My head was down and eyes away from everyone. I felt like shit and that's about all I felt. My heart was pounding like it wanted to yank itself free of me and that made it even harder to think. I just wanted to get away, find a minute to relax, to feel like it was time to turn off the lights and lay in the dark. I was reaching for my shoes when Jean Giguere's voice bellowed from outside the door and his large feet boomed down the corridor. "Hey, Raycliffe! Raycliffe! My player's got a fucking broken arm! You wanna tell me how!"

"Why don't you ask him what he was still doin' on the ice?" Tyler yelled.

"For that he gets a broken arm?" Giguere said. I pictured him glaring at Tyler as they stood toe-to-toe. "You're sick! Your whole team's sick! And that MacGregor's the worst of them."

"Look, let me get them outta here before this gets ugly."

"It already has!" Giguere said, so loud he sent an echo down the hall. His heavy feet began trudging again. "The league's going to hear about this. That kid's gonna be outta here."

The quarrel ended, and the only sounds we could here outside the room were Giguere's footsteps and Tyler's cigarette lighter flipping open. Inside the locker room, Tim Chaput, who was sitting across from me, raised his eyebrows and spoke in a hushed voice that was still audible throughout the room. "MacGregor, you messed up Tallard, man?"

"Shut up!" Brendan said. He walked over shirtless and raised an arm over Chaput's head. Chaput flinched away, Brendan returned to his stall to finish dressing and the first few changed players began to file out with Clyde Parker.

With a cigarette butt wiggling in his fingers, Tyler came in when he saw players heading for the bus. "Scott, you ready?" he mumbled.

"Almost," I said, without looking at him, and zipped up my bag.

Tyler whistled and waved a hand to Peter Jones down the hall. "Brendan, Jesse, go out with Scott and Peter," he instructed. "Don't say a word to anyone, even the Chronicle. Get on the bus and stay there. Everyone else hustle."

Like bailiffs, my two teammates and our equipment manager escorted me out. "Don't worry, it'll be all right," said Peter, who was also a grade school teacher.

As we walked out, Tyler asked Guy: "How's Cooper?"

I heard no response because my world quickly became one in which I was the devil. On my right were Coldbury players, who were being watched by two police officers and could not cross a designated line. To the left were parents and fans of the Chevaliers. All despised me.

"MacGregor, we're gonna kill you," one player shouted.

"Get outta here, losers," another called.

"You're a punk," a female voice said as I passed.

"That was my son you hit. Hope you go to hell," Tallard's father said as my entourage and I walked up the stairs that led to the parking lot. Cars were honking in front of our bus and passersby were slapping it while yelling profanities in English and French.

"Nobody do anything stupid," Peter said. Of course, he was directing the words at me, I thought. As we got within twenty feet of the vehicle, Jesse ran ahead to alert the driver to open the doors. When we got closer, a spectator shouted: "Vite, vite, allez-vous! There's the asshole!"

"Let's go," Peter said and we ran for the bus as snowballs came our way. We filed on safely and the sound of the closing doors amplified our collective sigh.

"How many left?" the driver asked.

"About ten, plus Tyler and Guy," Brendan answered.

"Let's hope they hurry before this thing gets overturned."

I walked to the back and cringed when Chaput said, "Way to go, man," and again after Lacroix slapped my back. Impressing them just affirmed what a stupid thing I had done. After finding the last seat in the farthest corner, I slumped down. A little later, the doors opened again and others rushed onboard. "Ah, man, I got nailed," one kid said. Then his team jacket ruffled with the sound of snow being wiped off.

"Okay, here comes Tyler and the others," Peter said. "We can get goin'."

"Anyone see Coop?" Jesse asked. He didn't get a reply, unless you count the ambulance siren.

The Greyhound's doors opened for a final time and the rest of the group climbed on. Tyler said, "Let's get the hell out of here."

The bus promptly shifted into gear and calls of "Whoa!" came from the players that were still standing.

"All right, everyone sit down," Tyler said. The seats around me started to fill up, but no one said a word to me and I wouldn't have responded if they had.

"What's up with Coop?" Brendan asked.

"Guy went with him to the hospital," Tyler said. "He lost about ten pounds out there tonight. We got some fluids into him. They're gonna check, make sure he doesn't have pneumonia."

"Is he going to be okay?" Manny Rivers asked.

"He'll be fine."

"Can he play Thursday?" Jesse asked.

"I don't know," Tyler said, curtly. "Where's MacGregor?"

No answers came, just the noise of several heads turning around synchronously. Then I looked up for the first time since leaving the ice to see Tyler making his way toward me. As the bus accelerated, he grabbed the backs of seats to pull himself forward. He arrived in front of me, waiting until he could feel we were on a steady course before plopping down. I edged closer to the window, wanting to be swept away.

"We gotta talk," he said sternly.

I was silent and didn't look at him.

"This has to end right here."

I glanced up. He had turned his torso to face me. His bushy brown eyebrows were raised causing his forehead to crinkle, and his mouth was open and I could tell his two front teeth were capped because they were much whiter than the others. "Scott, I haven't said anything to ya because I used to think you played better when you were angry. But that was a bonehead stunt tonight."

"But . . ."

Tyler raised a palm and turned his head slightly. "I know he was lookin' for trouble, but he didn't deserve that. Believe me, I know. There's nothing like having your career ruined by an injury. It's worse than anything Tallard or Giguere, or that entire team has done to us or you. I can tell you feel like crap, but believe me what that kid's going through tonight you wouldn't wish on anyone. Now, he'll probably be all right. And you probably shut him up, but that's not the point."

He paused, looked toward the front of the bus, sent his index finger back and forth on his upper lip, then turned back to face me. "Look, the reason Tallard gets on you and other guys on other teams, too, is because they know you'll do something. They'll get some kind of reaction, maybe a penalty. They don't talk like that to Brendan because he shrugs it off and goes about his business. You gotta do that."

"*I know*," I whined.

"I don't know what's going to happen with this, but if the league calls, I have to tell them the truth. We may be lookin' at a suspension."

I nodded and squeezed my eyes shut.

"That's why this has to stop. You're one of our leaders, our best goal scorer. I can't have you sitting out games. Especially after we've turned this thing around, okay?" He gripped my shoulder. "It ends here."

"Okay," I said, my jaw tense.

"You feelin' all right? Don't got the flu, do ya?"

"No. I'm fine," I answered and felt brief relief when Tyler got up to move to the front. As the drive to Kildare wore on, my stare fixated on the snow that flew by the window and I imagined slashing my stick through it aimlessly.

After we arrived, Brendan drove us home. He was quiet and seemed as awkward being around me as I was with myself. "The kid deserved it," he said finally.

"Nah, he didn't," I said. I paused before adding, "Think I'll get suspended?"

"Umm, maybe a game or two."

"You gonna make a star out of Marcelle?"

"No!" he answered. "But I'll make sure he sees stars if he doesn't finish."

We got to the Kowalczeks, and I went straight to my room, picked up the phone and dialed. "Hi, Dad," I said.

"Scotty. How ya doin'? You boys win tonight?"

"No," I said. "Dad, I messed up real bad."

17

The next day felt like a hangover, complete with a rude awakening. Brendan burst into my room, causing my head to ache, then flung a newspaper at my feet, making me stretch. "You made the cover, man. No way you can stay in bed today," he said. He threw me a towel and left. On the front page was my picture from the team program. It was below the banner headline:

Kougars' MacGregor Maims Coldbury Star

The story by Randy Delisle detailed the facts with cold objectivity. The "two-handed chop that snapped the forearm of the COHL's leading scorer" and "the near chaos that ensued." Jean Giguere's assertion "that his player 'was simply trying to congratulate Kildare on a good game,' even though Tallard's actions were obviously scurrilous." And Randy's summation that "the repercussions may be more harmful to the Kougars than any loss."

I closed my eyes. The words flooded me with shame and I sank back into bed. Maybe I could've skipped, but that would have just prolonged things; made them worse when I couldn't put off time any longer. It was no use, I concluded, there was just no getting around school.

At Kildare High, hockey players are not treated like other students. Most peers want to hang with the Kougars, because they are pretty much the closest things to celebrities in town. Plus the popular girls always gravitate toward members of the team, a sure sign of status. Even some teachers, the former Kougars usually, cannot help but display endearment toward one or two members who remind them of themselves. But there are the others in school. Slackers, nerds and artsies. Freaks, loners and wannabes. The ones that don't even know you, but look with contempt nonetheless. The ones waiting for you to fall. Hoping for something to assure them that you are nothing but the dumb jock they always suspected you to be. And when the moment comes, for a day or so at least, they react like the vanquished.

So, I was expecting to be a magnet for leers and smirks as I walked the halls the day after the Coldbury incident. And, believe me, my expectations were met. There were quick laughs, blatant chuckles and lots of squinting eyes.

"Don't worry about it," Michelle said, "they're just losers."

I bit my tongue at that.

On the way to gym class, one girl snickered, "Told you they were all goons," as I passed their clique.

"Let it slide," Brendan advised.

And I did. I let that slur slide. And the one in history class, when one kid wondered aloud if the Huns curved their blades. In drama, the joke was that Richard III would have made a good Kougar. "Please go easy on the frog," I was told in biology.

Just let it slide. Let it slide. Like a razor.

I grinned, made like I beared it and wished for the day to end. But when school was over, there was the rink.

"MacGregor, my girlfriend just broke up with me 'cause I stuck up for you," pointed Tony Lacroix, who was too mouthy for a rookie.

"Should I care?"

"Damn right," he said. "I was gonna bag her this weekend."

"Yeah, her groceries, virgin boy," Tim Chaput shouted from across the locker room.

"Shut up!" Lacroix said.

I raced to the ice, ridding my ears of them. It felt good to skate, to actually feel I was moving. But every time I wound up to take a shot, I remembered the grotesque sound of Alain Tallard's arm as it broke, like a room full of fingers cracking at once, the pained look on his crying face as he swore at me, his eyes wanting desperately to pierce me, to do anything to get even. But he couldn't, of course. Not on that night, anyway. His best consolation was likely that I had become a villain, one deserving of every chide remark, glare and dirty hit.

"Do you regret what you did?" Randy Delisle asked one of those stupid questions journalists have to.

"Of course I regret it. It was a horrible thing I did, but I can't change it. As much as I wish I could," I said, "I just can't."

Although Randy's story the next day reflected my remorse and referred to me as an "upstanding young man with good grades and amiable demeanour," it was dwarfed by the editorial that ran in the same edition.

"Violence in hockey is a serious issue in Canada," the article began, "any player who deliberately wounds another with the malice Mr.

MacGregor displayed in Coldbury should not be granted leniency, no matter his stature. It is not beyond the realm of reason to suggest it was a criminal act. With that in mind, we strongly encourage the team and the Central Ontario Hockey League to punish Mr. MacGregor with a lengthy suspension."

Even after reading it, I still had only a vague idea what the purpose of an editorial was, but I was certain I didn't want to see my name in one again.

"How can Randy let that get in the paper?" Brendan asked angrily as we ate supper.

"He has nothing to do with it," his dad said. "It's those stooges on the news side. The ones who never go to a game, or even care to mention the Kougars unless something like this happens. I tell ya, Scott, that kid had it coming to him. Don't worry about what these yahoos say, they don't know a darn thing about what goes on on the ice. You boys just put it out of your mind. It's over with now."

But really it wasn't and we all knew that. Coldbury would look for revenge; the league would be watching me; the schools in the States would be made aware. My future was at stake. Controlling myself on the ice had gone from a goal to a priority.

18

J ohnny Carruthers had been sober since his suspension. He had the shakes, at first, and was slow and sleepy during practices, but he actually had a little more stamina and that was important for him because Tony Lacroix and a couple of the other young defencemen were pushing for ice time. Johnny would still come out with us, but would have Coke or milk, and Brendan would make sure to drive him home. In school, he was improving, too.

We shared one period, Mrs. Nielsen's English class, and she was a pretty tough grade; didn't care about hockey at all. It was our own fault if we had to skip out early for a road game. If that's what we chose to do, then we had better make it up somewhere along the line. Johnny had a hard time getting that done at first and even when he turned things around, he still wasn't acing the class. But he did seem to get what she was talking about, and sometimes surprised us and her, and maybe even himself, by what he was thinking.

Mrs. Nielsen was one of those teachers that would put you on the spot. She would ask a question, then sometimes ignore the hands. Instead, she would go for the students who didn't have the confidence to volunteer an answer, or for those who were simply trying to hide. So, when she asked the class, "What is T.S. Eliot writing about?" she had plenty of options. First she called on the few familiar hands. One nerdy kid said the poem had something to do with the political climate in Europe back then, another said, "It's just so surreal, like a painting." Mrs. Nielsen said, "*Okay*," and then, "Anyone else?" She didn't see too many more hands, but did hear a bunch of bodies squirming in their seats. After surveying the room, she said, "What about you, Scott. What do you think the poem's about?"

I sat up, cleared my throat and said, "I don't know, I think it's just like a big soap opera."

There was some faint laughter and Mrs. Nielsen smiled at me, then nodded in a way that told me to continue.

"You know, there's the woman in the bar scared about her husband coming home from the war, then there's the fortune-teller who's predicting all kinds of doom and then there's that girl who isn't sure if she wants to be with the guy, but they end up doing it anyway." I got more laughs and a flirtatious look from Michelle. "It's like everything's way too dramatic. Even the title."

"Like a soap opera?" Mrs. Nielsen said, and I shrugged. "Or maybe like a Greek tragedy?"

"Yeah, maybe," I said.

"Okay, good. Interesting," she said and smiled at me in a way that said, *Nice try*. "Anyone else?" She looked around the room again and said encouragingly, "Remember there's really no wrong answer here," before calling on Johnny. He didn't say anything at first and kept scribbling in his notebook, so she said more firmly, "C'mon, Johnny, 'The Waste Land,' what's it about?"

Johnny looked up, a bit startled by her tone, then shifted his eyes down again before answering. "The fall of man," he said.

Mrs. Nielsen's eyes grew wide and she asked Johnny to explain.

"There's no religion or morals, that's what he's saying."

"And that's a wasteland?" the teacher said. "A world without God and values?"

Johnny nodded, then shrugged. "Yeah, people just do what they want and everyone else pays for it."

"Hmmm. Not bad. That's very good," she said, then moved on to lecturing more about the poem and Eliot.

Johnny wiped a hand over his forehead, trying to be discreet about it, then went back to taking notes and doodling. He was distant and becoming more so. Johnny missed home; he had told me that before. It was hard, because home for him was even farther from Kildare than it was for me. Johnny grew up in a little town outside of Kingston, where his parents gave what they could but were mostly able to just make do. There was Johnny and his younger brother, who he was close to but couldn't see a lot because his parents couldn't afford the time or money to make the trip up. The future would change that, Johnny thought, and his parents did, too, I'm sure. When I asked him how bad it was going to be living and studying in Minnesota for four years, where he might not be be able to get back at all, even for the holidays, he said, "If that's what it takes, then that's what it takes."

But it wasn't as if Johnny had big plans for himself. Back then, he knew as well as anyone how tough making it to the top was going to be, so he set his sights low. "There's this shit league in Texas where they pay forty-thousand a year," he said. "That's forty-thousand U.S." You had to be twenty-one to play, he told me, and it was real tough hockey, worse than Junior B, but that was good money, and he could help out his parents and kid brother. "And I read they'll give you an apartment, meal money, pay for all your equipment. Man, and that's the worst league. What if I made it to the East Coast league or even higher? Then they start paying seventy, eighty grand. That'd make this all worth it."

We were at a party when he said all this, so he was a little looser than usual. But after that last sentence he bowed his head and went back to being quiet, and I could tell it was something he had let slip out.

I understood missing home and family, but Kildare wasn't that bad. We had good guys on the team who would do anything to help Johnny if he just told us what was wrong. I can't tell you how many times I asked, "You alright?," and got back a quick nod and a "Yeah," that may as well have said, *Leave me alone*. Not to say he was ever rude, just not inviting. Tyler would talk one-on-one with all the guys at least once a month and, after Johnny responded well from his suspension, never appeared too worried about him. Maybe there was no reason to be. Some guys are just in their own world, Jesse said. And Johnny was definitely one of those guys.

"So what happened the other night, man?" I asked after Mrs. Nielsen's class. It had been last period for both of us and we were walking to the rink for practice.

He looked away and said, "Nothing."

"Come on, I saw you walking home," I said. "There's no way you were late."

He stared ahead, his stringy black hair covering his eyes, and said, "That's what Clyde says."

"So it's not true?"

He shrugged and say it didn't matter.

I said, "That's fucked up, man. Clyde can't be doing shit like that."

Johnny slumped his shoulders and looked guilty. "I guess I was pretty sauced. He said he was letting me off easy."

"Yeah, right," I snickered. "Wouldn't want to see him go hard on ya then."

We had reached the Leroux Arena main entrance by this time and I wasn't going to press further. "It's alright, man," I said and opened the door for him. "It'll blow over."

We went downstairs and found Chris Cooper, obviously fully recovered, hitting on one of the figure skating instructors. Coop was unbelievable; he would try any time, anywhere to get laid. Johnny and I waved to him, and after he struck out, he came over.

"Don't come close, boys," he said with a frown. "You might catch my bad karma." Coop had to spend a night in Coldbury General recovering from exhaustion brought on by the flu and it wasn't a pleasant experience, he told us. "They really hate you over there, man," he had said to me when he got back.

Now recuperated, he was to return to the lineup after missing one game — a 7-5 win over Otter Lake that maintained our winning record — but the sting from that latest loss to the Chevaliers was still being felt. Tyler Raycliffe heard our voices and popped out of his office. "Scott, come in here, please," he said.

I left Johnny and Coop, and closed Tyler's door behind me. He handed me a fax. "Got this today; it's what we didn't want to see."

The league had suspended me for three games. I sat and scratched my head as I read the fax, trying to figure away around it. But Tyler had already resolved there wasn't anything to be done.

"Well, I guess we'll see what Marcelle can do now," he said, then sighed.

19

I had never missed a game before and entered the Leroux Arena press box for the first time in a jacket and tie. The back wall of the room was wooden and painted white, but the rest of it was open so its occupants could overlook the rink. A scout for the Coldbury Chevaliers, there to watch Beavers Falls, their next foe, was sitting in the far corner. I felt his stare the moment I entered. Randy Delisle and the Beavers Falls reporter were sitting at a table in the middle. I took a seat next to Randy and as soon as I sat, the Coldbury scout came over, handed me a note and, with a sneer, said, "Watch your stick."

The note read: "Alain Tallard out six weeks with a broken forearm. Sends his regards."

Gary Curran, who was in and out of the press box, saw the exchange and immediately walked over to me. "Let me see that," he said.

He took the note out of my hand, read it and looked over at the scout. "Leave my players alone, or wait on the bus," our general manager ordered. The scout, an old curmudgeon, folded his arms and sat back in his chair, but not before flashing another evil eye at me.

My stomach turned and I tried to stay as still as possible, to be so still that I became like a structure, something you wouldn't notice after a while; something easily forgotten, maybe even invisible. This is what it must feel like to be on trial, I thought; to have everyone look on you with judgment, sizing you up because of an act, one single act, you did or didn't do. That's not me, I wanted to say. I'm not that type of player, that type of person. It was no use, of course. The best I could do was hope for it to go away and, in the mean time, try to be as inconspicuous as possible. That meant doing things carefully, even mundane things. When we stood for the national anthem, I made sure I wasn't the first one up or the last one down. I tried to blend in. Even during the first few minutes of the game, I was stoic, keeping still in my corner of the room, repressing every urge to shout out encouragement to my teammates. But you can't watch hockey like that. Eventually, the tension of it gets to you and you have to give in. For me, that time came when Dion Marcelle got his first touch.

We were pinned in our own end six minutes into the first period and the loose puck bounced to him. I remember biting my lower lip as I saw him reach out to settle it. He put his stick on it a couple of times to get it flat, then immediately shot it to the other end, icing it. It wasn't a bad play because we needed a whistle. So, I exhaled loudly, and even clapped, then looked around to see if anyone minded. (Randy Delisle smiled.) On Dion's second try, he made a nice move to get around a checker before sending a pass too long for Manny Rivers. I stewed my teeth, before realizing what Dion did was okay, so I clapped my hands again and said, "Good play!" Dion kept getting more chances and I kept applauding; he wasn't screwing up too bad and that earned him a regular shift.

Before I knew it, the second period was ending, tied 2-2, and I almost felt like myself again. I looked around, slowly, and saw the old man from

Coldbury had left the room. I stood to stretch my legs. During the intermission, my eyes settled on Randy, who was jotting stuff on a notepad,
scratching some of it out, then tapping on his laptop. It made me wonder
what he was writing about. "So what's the story?" I asked.

He looked at me smugly and said, "Well, my friend, unless I get something better real soon, the story is you."

"*Me?*"

"Yes. How your mates do without their leading goal scorer is the obvious
angle."

"An angle, huh?" I said and he nodded. "How can I get you a better
one?"

He laughed. "Go find out what Lannie Leroux is gonna do with this
place."

"Man, I wish I could." I took a glance around at the crowd, then turned
back to Randy. "So what do you think's gonna happen with that?"

"With Lannie?"

"Yep."

"Well, all I can say, Scott, is that with Lannie nothing is as it seems," he
said. "And I'm sure you figured that out a long time ago."

"Unfortunately."

Randy always was a good guy. He has lived in Kildare his whole life,
even though he's talented enough not to have to. He's an avid fisherman,
and every now and then he'll take extended leave to write a book on fly-
fishing or trout farming, or the like. Plus, he does freelance work on the
side. Together, the pay he gets supplements his income from the paper just
fine. The more I got to know him, the more I realized how dedicated he
was to covering the team. I don't know if he ever missed a game and there

were some nights he would be at the office until 3 a.m., doing research or working on upcoming stories. It was this dedication, I guess, that gave him the abilities of a sleuth.

At some point during that intermission, he turned around as if to scope the room, once confident he could speak, he looked at me and said, "Scott, there is one thing you might be able to help me with."

"Shoot," I said.

"You heard anyone talking about a guy named Bridgetower?"

"Bridgetower? The sports agent?"

He nodded like a hungry pup, but I made a face and shook my head, leaving him disappointed.

"Why?" I asked. "What's he got to do with the team?"

"Oh, I don't know yet," he said and got back to his story as the game resumed.

I remember thinking what a kick it was talking to him. Randy had a journalist's tendency of dropping these precious hints that made me realize I had no clue about what was really going on in my world. But I couldn't think of all the questions I had for him right then.

The game was still tied and it stayed that way until there was about two minutes to go. That's when Brendan got Dion Marcelle the puck at the Beavers Falls blueline. Instead of dumping it in, Marcelle tried to stick-handle through a defenceman. He lost the puck and the opponent seized it. A rapid rush the other way resulted in the winning goal and when it happened, I dropped my head until it banged on the table. Gary Curran said, "Fuck me," before walking out. Randy quickly typed the details into his laptop as his deadline approached. When he had a second, he said to me, "Tough break for the kid. He really doesn't need that."

Gary Curran came back into the room, handed Randy and the other reporter the final stats sheet, looked at me and slouched, then headed back out.

I stayed and watched Randy, deep in thought, continue to hack away. He would type something, shake his head, say, "No, no," and hit the backspace key. Once he finished, he would read the story from the top, urging his slow computer to "C'mon, c'mon," as he scrolled down. Once satisfied, he hit a large button on the top row of the keyboard and snapped out of his trance. Then his phone rang, he picked it up and said, "Delisle," and in between pauses, "Just sent it"; "Is that right?"; "What did he say?"; "Really?"; "Good, good, great."

He hung up, turned to me, pivoted his head slightly so he was certain the general manager wasn't in the room, then leaned over and whispered, "Do you speak any Russian?"

"No," I said, with a laugh.

In a hushed voice, Randy said, "You better learn." And he smiled slyly.

20

During the harshest days of winter, Kildare may resemble a mild Siberia, but certainly nothing from Russia, other than Lannie Leroux's caviar, ever made a home there. That is, until Vlastimil Skurilev and Dmitri Rushchenko arrived.

Thanks to Randy Delisle's reporting, the duo's entrance was anticipated with curiousity among the supporters of the Kougars. Both were ranked in the top forty in Rink Roundup, a quarterly publication whose main contribution to the information age is its "expert" analysis of young, undrafted hockey players. Yet asterisks appeared beside the names of Skurilev and Rushchenko, indicating neither had played an organized game in nearly a year. Their team, Rijstik '78, had become a casualty of the economic crisis in Russia. No money was left to fund the squad, forcing its closure without a chance to get the players onto other teams in the country. Nor was it a simple endeavour to put them on North American junior teams because of immigration procedures and because no team owned their rights.

The Kougars, though, found away around both obstacles. It turns out Skurilev and Rushchenko were represented by Frederick Bridgetower, the same sports agent as Matt Curran. The agent was about to begin negotiations with the Toronto Maple Leafs on Curran's behalf when he found out his most amiable client had been convinced by his older brother to go in on a Junior A team. Matt Curran heard of the two regarded Russians and knew they could help his new interest. Bridgetower balked at sending either Russian — especially the gifted Skurilev — to an inferior institution such as the COHL. Better off to send them a few Don Cherry videotapes, he must have thought. But Matt Curran, a ten-year NHL veteran fresh off a fifty-goal season and due to make a fortune in salary and endorsements, had learned the principles of hard bargaining, threatening to walk to another agent if the Russians did not sign with Kildare.

The immigration procedures began before our season even started, a beguiling move by the Currans and Bramburger. The only snag in their plan was Randy's reporting. Despite "No comments" by the Kougars' higher-ups, the planned gala reception to introduce the newest celebrities to Kildare was foiled. The story ran on the front page of the *Chronicle* two days after my conversation with the reporter in the press box. It was headlined:

Source: Russians Are Coming

Kougars may have highly touted duo in lineup soon

The story left Gary Curran and Tyler Raycliffe stunned, not to mention the gawfaw it put on the faces of every player in the room. (Except Tim Chaput, who never read the paper unless his girlfriend told him his name was in it.)

"I guess now we know what Randy meant," Brendan said as we ate lunch in the cafeteria.

"I don't believe it. What are they doin' in Kildare?" I asked.

"Let's see if they can play first. Sounds like Marcelle."

"No, man, Marcelle was never rated by Rink Roundup."

He shrugged — a gesture of reluctant agreement — then brought up a related, but much more compelling subject. "Who do you think's gonna lose a job?" he asked.

Yes, the majority of Kildareans who followed the team were excited about having Russians on the Kougars for the first time. But several citizens, mostly parents of players on the fringe, were critical of bringing in foreigners. The day the story ran, a half-dozen of them attended practice and did not sit quietly rooting for their sons. They stood on the first row of seats so Tyler Raycliffe could clearly hear their voices over the protective glass.

"Hey, Raycliffe, what's this about Russians?" demanded Fred Mackilwraith.

"Tyler, you're not cutting my Gordie, are you?" pleaded Mrs. Joseph.

"You cut my kid and I'm movin' to Beavers Falls, Raycliffe," threatened Terry Sinclair Sr.

"Why do ya need Russians, anyway? We're winning, you bums," said Joe Chaput. His son wasn't in danger of losing a position, but clearly he had already been dealt a worse fate; after all, it was obvious Tim Chaput had taken after his father.

"Hey, they're probably just as bad as Marcelle," called Sinclair Sr. as Dion skated past, making like he didn't notice.

Tyler raced us through our first two skating drills, his eyebrows furrowing like usual and the vein in the middle of his forehead popping further with each sentence spewed from a parent. Finally, he blew into his whistle so loud and for so long it sounded like an emergency alarm test. He turned his back on us and skated to centre ice where he shouted at his critics.

"Shut up! All of you shut up! Or I'll kick your kids off this team right now!" He spun in a tight circle before continuing. "This is my practice." He pushed an index finger to his chest. "If I hear another word, I'll throw you out of this building."

Mrs. Joseph, face red with worry, stepped down promptly and found a seat a few rows back, far enough to disassociate herself from the other parents.

Tyler blew his whistle to start our next drill and Joe Chaput said, "This sucks." Tyler swirled to glare at him, shaking his head as he saw the parents, having had their protest, clear out. Our practice continued tediously for the next forty-five minutes. We worked on nothing new and Tyler scratched his head often as he struggled to remember exact instructions. Without giving us our final exercise, which was always a random number of laps, he blew into his whistle and said, "Okay, that's it. We got Fairfield tomorrow night. I'll be in to talk about that and everything else before we go home." He began to skate off and we held our breath, hoping.

To no avail.

"You gonna give 'em laps?" Clyde Parker asked.

Raycliffe turned to look at him, then his whistle sounded for a final time. "Gimme five and hit the showers," he said.

"Ah, Clyde, what'd you do that for?" Tony Lacroix said, griping for all of us.

After we were all dressed, Tyler and Gary Curran entered the locker room with steam from the showers still creeping into the changing area like a curious spectator.

"Well, I suppose we got some things to explain," Gary said and held up a culprit copy of the *Kildare Chronicle*. "I'm sorry you boys had to read this. We wanted to tell you when everything became official . . ." He took a deep breath before exhaling like a confessor, "But it's true.

"These two players will make this a better hockey team and that's always been my goal and my brother's goal and Tyler's, and all of yours, I hope. It's exciting for us and for the town to have these kids coming here. We're not quite sure when they'll join us, but it should be around Christmas. Now it's going to mean things'll be shaking up. I'm not gonna bullshit you about that. Tyler and I couldn't be more pleased or proud of the effort everyone in this room has given, but changes are gonna be made in the next month or so. And we should all be prepared for that." He placed his hands in his pockets, puffed his lips and shrugged.

Anxiousness filled the room with a brief moment of silence. It ended when Tyler spoke with much more enthusiasm than Curran did. "Hey, we gotta look at it this way: These lads are gonna help us win more games. Now I haven't seen them, but from what we understand they both have a lot of skill. Like Gary said, this is exciting."

"Now, you boys know you can come talk to Tyler or me whenever you want," Curran said, "but if you have any questions about this, you can ask now."

We looked around the room, waiting for someone to orate. Tim Chaput eventually spoke in his father's surly tone. "Where're they gonna play?"

"We don't know yet. We don't even know when they're gonna play," Tyler answered. "They may need a few practices first, but we'll fit them in where they can help the most."

"Do they speak English?" Tahani "One-Axe" Kohono asked.

"Yes. Not well, but they understand, 'Shoot'," Curran said.

"What kind of vodka do they drink?" Manny Rivers asked, causing a relieving burst of laughter.

"I hope none of you find out," Curran replied.

"Where are they going to stay?" Gordie Joseph asked innocently enough.

"They'll be with the Chouinards," Curran said, matter-of-factly. But like a stranger in the company of good friends, he seemed perplexed by the response his answer got. Tim Chaput smirked and a couple of others giggled.

Brendan, wanting to end the moment without Curran or Raycliffe asking for the embarrassing explanation, made a query that was sure to snare attention. "Are pro scouts going to be watching us?" he said and the hush was quick. We awaited the response like a bingo player a square away.

"Yes," Curran said, emphatically. "I already got a call from scouts with the Senators and Maple Leafs. So you boys are gonna be in front of some powerful folks."

"All right," a few of us said, like dreamers.

"Okay, about tomorrow night," Tyler said, "bus leaves at five-thirty. Dion, you're back with Brendan and Manny. Scott, it's up to you. You can come on the ride, or stay home. Your call."

Shyly, I said, "I'm going."

"Atta boy," Tyler said. "Let's get that win back, eh."

Curran and Raycliffe left, probably still curious about the unexpected giggles, as Brendan delivered a damp towel into Chaput's face. Chaput brushed off the rag and said with an impish laugh: "Welcome to Canada, boys."

21

I watched as my teammates defeated Fairfield, 3-1. It should have been a shutout, but Dion Marcelle surrendered the puck near centre while we were changing lines. Jesse Sullivan said, "Oh, shit," and quickly hopped off the bench to give chase, but it was no use. Fairfield had a two-on-none rush late in the game that resulted in the only goal against Chris Cooper. The goaltender, who was playing his best game of the season, threw his arms in the air and screamed expletives at Marcelle. Dion sulked on the bench for the rest of the game. On the bus ride back, he sat alone and didn't seem to mind. "Changes were coming," Gary Curran had said, and more and more the words appeared to apply to Marcelle as much as anyone.

"Don't ever get suspended again," Brendan said after we reached his house.

"See! I've been carryin' you for three years," I said.

"You can't carry my jock strap," he said and passed me one of his mom's homemade cookies. "And that kid doesn't need one 'cause he's got no balls."

The next night, a knock came on the Kowalczeks' door about eight o'clock while we were watching a game on TV instead of studying for midterms. Mrs. Kowalczek answered and a man with a French accent said, "Allo, may I speak to Brendan and Scott, please?"

"May I say who's calling?" Brendan's mom asked.

"Ah, yes, of course. My name is Denis Marcelle. My son plays 'ockey with the boys."

Brendan and I looked at each other puzzled then went to greet our visitor. "Is everything okay with Dion, Mr. Marcelle?" Brendan asked.

"Oh, don't worry, there's no emergency. But I am here about my son," he said. Mrs. Kowalczek had shown him in and informed him it was senior league night, so he had just missed her husband. She then went to prepare coffee.

Mr. Marcelle blew his nose with a handkerchief then followed us to the living room. He seemed uncomfortable leaning back in the loveseat and settled for sitting at the edge of the cushion, rubbing his cold hands together in front of his mouth.

"This is odd for me, you know, but I'm here to ask you boys to help Dion," he said.

"*O-kay*," I said, dragging the word out skeptically. "How?"

"I know Dion is having trouble, but he's a good 'ockey player, and a good boy, believe me." He sighed and scrunched his face. "Ah, might as well get over with it." He took a deep breath, brought his hands in front of his chest — thumbs touching index fingers — and began to shake them gingerly. "The truth is," he said, "I'm very worried about my son."

Brendan flicked off the TV, and he and I sat up to listen.

"'Ockey to him used to be everything," Mr. Marcelle continued. "All the time he would play with the boys in town. He would score three, four goals and they would win, and he would come home grinning. We had a rink in our backyard over in Quebec, too. Dion would be on there so long, his mother would drag him off for supper. So much he loved the game." His hands fell to his knees. "But last summer everything changed."

Mrs. Kowalczek brought him coffee and sat in front of the fireplace to hear the story. Mr. Marcelle took a sip and although his lips came from the cup, his eyes did not. "You see," he said, pensively, "my daughter, Dion's younger sister, died in a car crash in May."

Mrs. K gasped, lifted her hands to her mouth and said, "My goodness, I'm so sorry, sir."

With his eyes still down, he nodded at her gesture. "Dion was driving the car."

Mr. Marcelle glanced up. Our eyes grew wide when they met his and suddenly a lot of things began to make sense.

After setting down the cup, he lifted his hands in front of his chest again and began to bounce them like before. "He'd just got his license, two months maybe, and wanted so much to impress Marie by driving her to gymnastics class. So what was I to do?" Shrugging, Mr. Marcelle this time broke off the index fingers from the thumbs, revealing open palms. "For sure, I let him do it. And I'll never forgive myself for it." After pausing to heave in air, he told the details. "It was a Saturday with no traffic and the school was ten kilometres away only. He had driven alone before, little errands about town, just like this. I thought nothing of it." Eyes closed, he shook his head. "But they never made it. A drunk ran a red light and slammed into them on Marie's side. The police said little Marie must have flew out of her seat and hit her head on the steering wheel." He slapped a hand through the air and brought it back, like it was her head. Or like it had propelled her head. "The ambulance came, but too much bleeding." He shook his head. "She never made it to emergency." After beginning to open his mouth again, he stopped and his lips pressed together. Enough had been said.

He took a sip of coffee.

"That's so horrible. Your family must be devastated," Mrs. Kowalczek said.

"Was Dion hurt?" I asked.

Mr. Marcelle just nodded at first, then he cleared his throat and said, "He had some cuts from the shattered glass and some back pains, but he's a strong boy. He was able to walk away from it. But it has not walked away from him. He couldn't go back to school. So depressed he was. His teachers and classmates tried to help, to get him to talk, but he didn't want that either. He was too embarrassed to face friends, or anyone, really." He stopped and his jaw clenched. "And the truth is, my wife and I were having a hard time with it, too."

"Of course you were. My gosh, I can't imagine it," Mrs. Kowalczek said. She shivered then put a hand on her forehead.

"I transferred here after the drunk's trial closed," Mr. Marcelle said. "Dion was drafted by Val d'Or of the Quebec League, but he didn't want to go and his mother and me did not want it, too. I called some teams. When I got to the Kougars, Mr. Curran said he had heard of Dion and would be happy to have him on the team. I told him and Mr. Raycliffe what happened, but asked them not to say anything to you boys." He turned to the two of us. "We thought it might help Dion fit in quicker."

His words made Brendan and me sink with guilt. Our judgment of Dion was shallow and base. He was supposed to be really good at hockey, instead he stunk and that's all that mattered to us about him. But now, so suddenly, Dion became someone to root for, someone to reach out to.

"How can we help?" I asked.

"If you boys can give him a chance. I mean, I see the way the others follow you two. If you were in his corner, it could really give him a boost. I don't know if it will help him, but if he feels more comfortable on the team . . ." Mr. Marcelle's eyebrows raised and his shoulders shrugged. He then looked at the Kowalczek family portrait, with Brendan, his sister in B.C., Claire, and their parents. He sighed. "You know, I only have one child left and I really must do everything I can for him."

"We'll give it a shot, sir. Don't worry," Brendan said and I concurred.

"Believe me, Mr. Marcelle, your son's in good hands," Mrs. Kowalczek said and patted Brendan's knee. She then sat up and spoke again, more carefully. "You know, we do have some very good counselors in town, if you think Dion should be speaking to someone . . ."

"Oh," he said. "Thank you. But we have him seeing someone in Ottawa. He goes once a week or so and it's helping, but I know he won't get through without hockey."

He stayed a little while longer before excusing himself. Mrs. K demanded he and his family join hers for dinner before Christmas. Mr. Marcelle thanked us then made us aware of the obvious, that Dion had not known he was there and he would appreciate if we did not tell anyone else about his family's tragedy. As Mrs. Kowalczek showed him out, I asked Brendan: "So, what are we going to do?"

"I don't know, but whatever it is, we better make sure he doesn't get kicked off the team, first."

22

One of the things you got to do as a graduating Kougar was give a hand to the kids in town. We would be asked to demonstrate a power skating drill or just come speak to the travelling teams, tell them how much work they would have to put in to get to where we were, and beyond. I have to admit, I got a kick out of it. Some of them, especially the really little guys in novice, treated us like gods. They'd call me mister and ask for my autograph. When their coach introduced me as "The Kougar who scores the most goals," they just went, *Wow!*

Sometimes, I wish I had a chance to go back and talk less about the hockey and more about the other stuff. The really important things, like how they should never take school for granted or forget the friendships they had made. But, then again, that's not what they were looking for from me. They wanted some escape and to dream a little. Or was it me who wanted that?

Anyway, we also volunteered with Big Brothers and that's the stuff that really got to me. They always had Kougars at their annual skating party, and Tyler asked Brendan, Coop, Jesse, Johnny and me if we would mind going. It was a good deal for us, we got free pizza and another half-day off school. But it was a real eye-opener, too.

We spent the first hour just skating with the kids, goofing around, nudging them into the boards and stuff. Jesse then started passing the puck back and forth with a couple of them, and Coop got the pads out and let them pepper him. Johnny looked happy. Being away from school and the pressures of the team was the main reason, but he was having as much fun as the rest of us. He was giving kids some tips on taking corners, and really getting into it, too, banging his stick when they made it around the bend. Perfect for him, I thought, considering how much coaching he got from Clyde. Brendan, meanwhile, got to show off how good of a skater he was. The kids couldn't believe someone could go the whole length of the ice backwards — without stumbling, no less — so a couple of them made Brendan do it over and over. They started chasing after him, too, like they were playing tag and he went along with it, letting them get close before swerving this way or that like a figure skater, causing them to squeal when they couldn't get their mittens on him.

I had my hands full, myself. I hit it off with these two brothers. They looked like twins, but one was definitely a better skater. He would get a good head of steam and go a little while, but his brother, who was trying to keep up, would always wipe out after just a few strides. So, the one who could skate would stop to come back for his sibling, get him on his feet and go again until the next time the poor-skating one dropped. After seeing them go through their routine a few times, I came over grinning, got the bad skater balanced then held his hands up from behind as we moved around the rink. I tried to go at his pace, but I couldn't help but speed up eventually. He was giddy because he had never gone that fast and his brother was cracking up because he couldn't believe they were actually right next to each other. The one I had was loving it, his hair was flying

back and he really howled when we passed his brother. He got a little
nervous around the turns, though, squeezing on my hands and losing his
feet a little. I steadied him through and at one point let him go when we
hit a straightaway, but he only got three or four strides in before losing his
balance, so I grabbed him again and kept moving. Cute little guys, those
two. After I had about three laps around the rink with them, it was time
for the food break. That's when one of the counselors filled us in on some
of the stories.

One kid was ten and hadn't heard from his deadbeat dad in seven years,
another was an eight-year-old foster child who had bounced around a lot
and had almost no hope of being adopted, and most of them were latch-
key kids who hardly ever saw their mothers.

Then there were the Ladouceur brothers. Joey, the better skater, was
seven and Mike was six. Four years earlier they had seen their drunken
father take a wrench to their mom, putting her in a wheelchair and him in
jail for a long time. I looked at them when I heard. They were several feet
away eating 'za and laughing with the other kids. They both had short-
cropped blond hair and big blue eyes. Dream children, I thought. Joey was
already having trouble in school, we were told, and Mike was a very timid
boy, scared to do anything without his brother. Their mom couldn't work,
so the only money they had coming in was from the government. I hadn't
noticed until then, but both had on drab snowsuits and the hood on Mike's
was sagging and looked like one good tug could rip it off. Too much of
Joey's clothes were from the Salvation Army and Mike's were Joey's
hand-me-downs, the counselor said. He was talking only to me now,
because the other guys had become distracted by the rest of the kids, and
I couldn't take my eyes off the boys. Both of them already knew they did-

n't have some of the things other kids did, he said, and pretty soon they were going to be treated differently because of it, too. That's just how kids are. And that's when it's really going to hurt.

All of these kids just need to feel special, some of them more than others.

Before the day was done, I gave Joey and Mike a couple of sticks, some pucks and had my picture taken with them. I promised I would see them at the rink and I did make an effort to say hi to them when they were at games. There was so much more I wanted to do for them, though, so much more I promised myself I would do when I was able to. But Joey and Mike Ladouceur never saw that much of me, really.

I remember feeling hurt when the counselor told me about their history and getting angry later when I thought about their future. It reminded me of all I had and all I had taken for granted. They didn't have someone like Grandpa Joe and I wanted them to, but I didn't think it could be me. And, yeah, maybe I was too selfish or too self-absorbed, at least, to tell myself otherwise. But, honestly, back then I never thought my time alone could mean much to two poor kids. Still, if I couldn't help them, maybe there were others whom I could.

23

Tyler Raycliffe waved Brendan and me into his office then continued to lace up his skates. A cigarette dangled from his lips and puffs of smoke would seep from the side of his mouth like steam from a boiling kettle.

"Tyler," I said, "we were wondering about the lines for when I get back."

That caused him to sit right up, shake his head vigorously and push the butt into the ashtray. "Okay, okay, you boys were right. I should've never put him up there. We'll be keeping Manny on the right side from now on."

"No," Brendan said, "that's not what we wanted."

"Yeah, I never got to play with Dion," I said. "We were talkin' about it and the line'll work."

Tyler rubbed his hands over his face then crinkled his forehead, looking like he had just woken up in a strange place. "Are you kidding me?"

We shook our heads. "We'll make it work," I said, knowing that if Manny Rivers returned to our line, Dion would again be in the press box, maybe before long he wouldn't be on the squad at all.

"Okay then. If I get a chance in practice to team you three up, I'll think about it," Tyler said. "But nothing's set." He scratched his head and sighed under his breath: "I don't believe this."

What Tyler did during that day's practice was give Dion a couple of turns on the power play with us. After he didn't mess up too bad, he got another shot the next day. He set up a goal and Tyler was encouraged. At the end of the week, he let Dion spend an entire scrimmage with us. Brendan and I were determined to make it work. To that end, we fed Dion the puck at every opportunity but he was slow to respond, fumbling passes, overskating pucks and rushing shots. He made one nice play, though — beating a defenceman, making a deft deke and tucking in a backhander —, and that's what we recalled. "Nice play rookie," I said and smacked his helmet. "Let's do it like that on game day."

He smiled as sweat poured off his face and for the first time I saw a little joy in his brown eyes.

Some of the guys remained surly toward him, jealous he was going to get more ice time. Slowly, it became obvious he deserved at least a chance. He began to show off his big shot with his fat, uncurved blade, even hitting the net a few times, and remembered his defence. On one play, Dion even showed a glimpse of brilliance.

"Get it to me behind the net," Brendan instructed before the drill. "Dion you set up at the halfboards here." He pointed to the left-wing face-off circle. "We'll try to cycle it around to Scotty Mac." Dion nodded.

Raycliffe's whistle blew and the three of us took off, streaking through the rink like jets in formation. I dumped the puck in and Brendan got it behind the endline. After we passed around a couple of times, Brendan found himself with some space and got the puck over to Dion. Immediately, a defenceman charged out to pressure him, but Dion slipped the puck between his pursuer's legs, shook off the check and moved forward to pick up the puck again. That play alone garnered a round of "Whoa!"s from our teammates, but Dion wasn't done. He closed in on Chris Cooper, looking right into the goalie's eyes with the puck in shooting position. Then Dion snapped it. The puck moved so quickly, Cooper didn't have time to budge; he was expecting a shot, after all. Instead, Dion had sent a pass across the crease and onto my tape for an easy tap-in. "Yeah," I said and pointed a glove at him. A couple of guys clapped, Brendan approvingly banged his stick on the ice, Clyde Parker scolded the beaten defenceman and Raycliffe quickly moved the drill along, trying to hide his delight.

For the next three games, Dion played intermittently on the top line, picking up a couple of cheap assists and earning himself more ice time. Tyler gave him a couple of turns on the power play and even trusted him enough to kill a penalty. But he had yet to start, or score. He was improving, but it wasn't enough; greatness had been promised and he still had not delivered.

It was late November and we had a Sunday home game, this one against last-place Deeringwood. Inside Leroux Arena, the town was celebrating the impending arrival of the two Russians by serving vodka for the first time. Maybe because of that we were playing before the largest crowd of the season.

Most fans cheered when our line took the ice for the opening draw, but there were the ususal critics who booed, calling for Dion's ouster and a labotomy for Raycliffe. By the end of the period, we had turned those sentiments around. Dion, a centre playing left wing, gained the blueline with five minutes to go, sent the puck to the middle of the ice where Brendan caught it, dropped a behind-the-back pass onto my tape and I whistled it home from my off-wing. Brendan and I each scored in the second period, but Dion, despite showing more confidence in two periods than he had in three months, still did not have his first goal as a Kougar. Then he whispered to me, "Let me play on the right," before we took the ice for the third.

I granted his wish, then he granted Kildare's. With a flourish, he picked up a loose puck in the neutral zone, beat one checker and went one-on-one with the lone defenceman between him and the goaltender. I trailed the play, watching as Dion faked a lefthanded shot, freezing the defenceman long enough to get a skate in front of him. Dion then dipped his left shoulder, staving off the same defender on his back, and closed in on goal with the puck on his backhand. The goalie dropped to his knees, expecting a low, weak backhander. But like a pickpocket, Dion changed the grip on his stick at the last moment, pulled the puck to his right and lifted a hard wrist shot over the shoulder of the stunned netminder.

Even the siren of the red light and the roar of the crowd, which reacted like a tilted slot machine, couldn't quell the sound of Tyler Raycliffe yelling, "Yeah! Yeah!" as he pumped his arms in the air. Brendan and I swarmed Dion, who was knocked down after he scored and merely raised his stick when he got up to celebrate his goal.

"Where've you been hidin' that?" Brendan said and rattled Dion's helmet.

"Shoot righty, too, eh?" I said laughing.

Dion wore a simple smile, like an exhausted runner who had just won a long race. Then he caught a look of his parents standing behind our bench.

His dad was applauding and giving him a thumbs up while his mom held her hands straight like a steeple under her nose. At the sight of them, Dion skated back to the linesman, asked for the puck, took it over to the bench and flipped it into his father's hands while grinning.

We won 7-0 and Tyler was so pleased he gave us all a day off from practice. Randy Delisle interviewed Dion after the game and went on to describe his goal, and all-around magnificence, in illustrious detail in the next day's game report. And Dion even came with us that night to Finnegan's, looking at last like he wore the same jersey as the rest of the team. "Thank you," Mr. Marcelle whispered to Brendan and me when we ensured Dion's safe return.

"Thank you," I said. "Your son sure can play when he wants."

Slowly, Dion continued to improve. He started throwing checks, playing defence, skating faster shift by shift, and working on his slickest move, faking a lefthanded slapshot before manoeuvreing to deliver a righthanded wrister. His improved play spanned five games in which we had a 4-1 record to move to 16-11-1 overall. It had become clear that Dion could do a lot for us, and that complicated matters for Tyler Raycliffe and Gary Curran. The Russians, it was announced, would be arriving four days after Christmas, and fitting them in wasn't going to be as easy as the team had thought.

24

Michelle broke from my kiss. She rubbed a hand on my chest and asked, "So how'd it go?"

"It was good," I said. "My dad's still having a hard time, but not as bad as before."

"That's good." She smiled a little, like she was shy. "Did you talk about me?"

I returned the smile and answered, "Yeah. They want to meet you."

"Oh, really! Cool!" Her eyes lit up. "I love Ottawa." I laughed and then she asked, "What else?"

I sat up straight, leaning back in the passenger seat. "Let's see," I said and sighed. "Oh, we talked about a lot of stuff. You know, they wanted to know about school and the team and how Brendan's folks are doing." I looked over when she didn't respond. "You know, the usual stuff."

But Michelle's eyes were narrow now and watching me like she knew I was leaving something out. Later on, it concerned me that she might know me that well, but at the moment I was just uneasy. My Christmas visit home wasn't something I was completely ready to talk about, I guess, but right then I felt I had to.

It had been my first time back with my parents since Grandpa Joe's funeral and it felt strange. The house seemed cold and the decorations were toned way down. Mom and Dad did their best, but they still looked stressed and I felt guilty for leaving them like that. At first, we talked a lot about the basics: grades and my wild dreams of turning pro. I asked about work and the weather, even though I knew the answers already. Such conversations are like the skin of a fruit, something we peel away at until we reach the heart.

During dinner, once we were all seated and done with the catching up, I turned to my father and asked, "What was Frank Masters like, Dad?"

The knife and fork in his hands paused, just for a second, and I knew he had also been thinking of the man who had saved my grandfather's life.

"Oh, Frank was a real nice man; the best," he answered. "Why do you ask, son?"

"Grandpa Joe told me in his letter that Frank saved him in the war and that's how they became such good friends."

Dad, still not used to talking about his father in the past tense, gave a nod. "Yeah, I guess if it weren't for ol' Frank Masters you and I wouldn't be here."

That's the thought that had been occupying my mind. If it wasn't for that man's actions, I wouldn't have been; and if anyone ever believed Frank Masters was never meant to be paralyzed then they also believed I was never meant to be here. It was all confusing and even more than that, it made me feel vulnerable. It was that part I didn't want anyone to know about; Michelle, too. But once she got me started, it became easier to say the rest.

Both my parents ended up telling me a lot about Frank over dinner.

"It's just amazing," Mom said, putting her elbows on the table and fold-ing her hands in front of her face, "how some people can just walk into your life out of nowhere and make such a difference. You know, I hardly knew Frank, but I remember his funeral and how shook up I was." She stopped to look at my father and then me. "I remember I was pregnant with you. When was it, John, November of Seventy-Five?"

"Yep," Dad answered. "Kitchener, just before Remembrance Day."

"What Frank meant to your father and grandparents," she said, "it was like he was part of the family. That's what friendship is supposed to be about."

I stopped to contemplate that then asked my father what he remembered most about Frank.

"Oh, there's so much. He used to ride me around in his wheelchair," Dad laughed. "Popping wheelies all over the place." He was keeping his head down and shaking it a little, like he was trying to jimmy free more memories. "Geez, I remember when your grandmother caught Frank teaching me how to play poker. Boy, that was about the only time I ever saw her scream at someone other than me! Let's see, what else . . . Oh, yeah, he'd even go fishing with us! I remember having to lift him into the boat. Then going back to chain the wheelchair to a tree. That was one heavy sucker, too."

"Him or the chair?" I asked.

"Both!"

He was flabbergasted and his cheeks took on colour as he laughed. It was good to see my dad enjoying himself again. When Grandpa Joe died he was so upset I wasn't sure how long it was going to take for him to get his spirit back. And when I saw him coming around, I couldn't help but think, *Man, that Frank Masters must've been some guy.*

"I bet!" Michelle said. "He sounds like a riot."

I didn't say anything else and maybe that was a signal.

"You miss him a lot, don't you?"

I bit my lip and looked out the window. I was telling myself, *No, no, no,* but it was useless, that pain that had become so familiar so quickly had a hold of me and I knew it wouldn't go away until I wept it out. I brought a hand up to cover my eyes, coughed out a cry and answered her with several quick nods.

Michelle touched my head and it fell into her shoulder. She brushed my hair and said, "Thanks for telling me, Scott."

"No problem," I said.

25

On the icy morning of December Twenty-Ninth, Tyler Raycliffe, general manager Gary Curran and co-owner Arnold Bramburger arrived in front of the Kowalczeks' house in a rented limousine. They were ready for the four-hour drive to Dorval Airport, where we were to greet Vlastimil Skurilev and Dmitri Rushchenko, return them to Kildare and present them to the Chouinard family, with whom they were to billet. The men wanted Brendan and me to join the welcoming party because they thought it would be good to introduce the Russians to a couple of teammates right away. As curious as we were, we were glad for the invite.

"Hey, Scott, perfect weather for Russia, eh?" jolly Bramburger said as I hopped in.

"That's for sure. Where's Clyde?" I asked.

"Couldn't make it," Tyler answered.

"Said he didn't wanna get stuck at the airport if they didn't clear customs," Bramburger said while fumbling for the handkerchief in his pocket, "or forgot where to meet."

"As long as they didn't forget their longjohns," I said.

"Hell, I hope they didn't forget how to backcheck," Tyler said.

"Hey, if they did, just stick 'em with these two," Bramburger replied, pointing at Brendan and me after wiping his nose. "You lads turned Marcelle around, imagine what you'll do with these kids."

"Is that what's going to happen?" Brendan asked, looking at Tyler. "You're taking Dion off our line?"

"We're thinking about it. I mean, we brought him in to play centre, may as well put him there now that he's got some confidence."

"You boys did what we wanted with Marcelle, may need you to do it with Skurilev," Gary Curran said. "We just have to see how ready these two are."

One thing was for sure, Skurilev and Rushchenko came off the plane well-prepared for and obviously accustomed to winter. Their bodies were hidden under thick parkas and scarves as they exited from the customs inspection. Their youthful, acne-plagued faces were ashen, eyes icy and tongues silent. That made the ride back as riveting as ice fishing without lures. At first, Bramburger, Curran and Raycliffe confused the pair's disgust at being humiliated to the Junior A level for youthful anxiety.

"Oh, you lads are gonna love Kildare," said Bramburger, a tall, fat, balding, near-sighted man, still elated with having a piece of his hometown team. "My God, wait 'til you see it in the summer."

The Russians closed their eyes. If they showed emotion, they would have been wincing. But any culture shock or apprehension they might have felt did not affect their appetites. After exchanging pleasantries, they commenced to each devour three Montreal smoked-meat sandwiches, four five-hundred millilitre bottles of orange juice, two Killaloe Sunrise beavertails and a big packet of almond M&M's Curran bought for them during a stop at a gas station, all before we had passed through Ottawa.

"Boy, they must not feed you much over there, eh?" Bramburger said.

They glared at him before continuing to feast. Indeed, their conversations with the five of us were limited to leers, nods, shakes, shrugs and one-word refrains. They weren't exactly surly about it — they had shaken our hands and said it was nice to meet us, and one of them did smile —, but our English was a bother to them, at least it seemed that way. Maybe clinging to what you know is a natural reaction when you've just arrived in a new place, surrounded by strangers who want to pull you into their world. Skurilev and Rushchenko spoke in Russian to each other and pointed out the window, perhaps commenting on the size of Montreal or simply noting the billboard advertising Alexei Yashin on "Hockey Night in Canada". Sometimes they would laugh, maybe at a joke, maybe at us; we didn't have a clue which. Brendan and I looked at each other knowing we were contemplating the same thing: How best to describe all of this to the rest of the guys.

Raycliffe, Curran and Bramburger each took attempts at getting the interest of their new trophies, but after presenting the food, none were successful. So Bramburger, being an astute businessman, went back to what worked. "How do you boys feel about getting more to eat?" he asked, with rush hour approaching.

In unison, they immediately said, "Goood, goood."

"Driver," Bramburger said, tapping his index finger on the glass partition, "pull over at the next truck stop."

After each having a bowl of beef barley, Brendan and I said we would wait in the limo until our new teammates finished their breakfast platters: four strips of bacon, three scrambled eggs, two slices of French toast, hash browns, orange juice and coffee.

"This really reeks," Brendan said after he popped a zit. We were back in the car, parked in a lot just off the Trans-Canada.

"Tell me about it."

"They know nothing about these guys and they bring them in like family." He stared out the window as he smeared pus and blood into his cheek. Trucks and cars were rushing past, throwing up slush when they whizzed by. The glass door leading into the restaurant opened and Brendan, pushing his chin up, said, "Look, even they're getting sick of it now."

I turned to see Curran and Raycliffe stepping outside to have a smoke. "Wonder how long Arnie will last," I said.

Bramburger was still sitting with the Russians, trying to coax responses, but, before long, he too gave up, heading to the washroom after settling the bill. He later exited the restaurant in a huff, tied the straps of his trenchcoat around his waist, and walked toward Curran and Raycliffe, standing in the swirling snow. Bramburger threw his arms up and his lips mouthed, "I give up."

At that moment, Skurilev and Rushchenko ran out of the restaurant, closely followed by a screaming waitress. "Hey, stop him. Stop that kid!" she said, pointing to Skurilev. "He stole my tip!"

Gary Curran yanked Skurilev by the crook of the arm and dragged him back to the restaurant. Bramburger, humiliated, coerced the kid to return the money, then doubled the amount and apologized repeatedly to the waitress. His face was red when he entered the limousine. He slammed the door then sat and stared at the two Russians. Curran, meanwhile, fixed his gaze on Skurilev and did not say a word while we resumed course to Kildare, still eighty kilometres away. For the first time, the Russian began to seem like a normal eighteen-year-old as he squirmed and avoided eye contact. His comrade, meanwhile, did the most frightening thing of all. Rushchenko revealed a set of knitting needles and went to work on a ball of wool that looked to be taking the shape of a toque.

Raycliffe ignored the whole situation and read *The Hockey News*, looking up only to Brendan and me to comment on the doings of Russian players in the NHL. He would whisper, "Says here Kozlov's got an attitude problem. Wonder where they could've got that?" or "Pushkin's new coaches are having trouble reading him. Wow, don't believe that for a second." Brendan and I tried to stifle our laughter.

For many minutes, the mood was colder than an icy snowball in the face. It began to change when we entered Kildare and saw the houses lit up and decorated, reminding us it was holiday season. We arrived at the Chouinards shortly after six, and bid farewell to the driver, who was poised to be the root of a grapevine.

"Hello, hello," said Mrs. Chouinard before we even got to the top of the driveway. "We've been waiting so long for you."

"Well, you know how time gets stolen away sometimes," Tyler said.

She began to laugh, but stopped when our looks told her she shouldn't be. Then she fetched her husband. "Joseph, the boys are here," she said. "And they're just in time for supper. You all must be starving."

Mr. Chouinard stepped immediately to the front door in a pair of untied boots, jeans and a Montreal Canadiens T-shirt. Beside him was his youngest daughter, nine-year-old Chantelle. Ignoring the frigid temperatures, Mr. Chouinard ventured out to greet his new housemates. "Let me help you lads with those bags," he said. He grabbed two suitcases, one belonging to each Russian, and brought them into the house.

"So, who is who here?" said a gleeful Mrs. Chouinard, an attractive blonde with a radiant smile.

"This is Dmitri," Arnold Bramburger said and held a palm up to

Rushchenko as if he was a museum piece. "Dmitri, this is Mr. and Mrs. Chouinard."

They shook hands, Mrs. Chouinard, who was to tutor the boys in English and social studies, said, "Privet, Dmitri," and Bramburger then pointed to Skurilev, and said with much less unction than he imagined he would: "And this is Vlastimil."

"Well, welcome home boys," Mr. Chouinard said and led us all inside.

The atmosphere surrounding the pair of newcomers had taken a turn for the better as the moment Brendan and I had most been anticipating was about to arrive.

"Darling," Mrs. Chouinard called up the stairs, "why don't you come meet the boys?"

And there, descending the staircase in white denim pants and a form-fitting red sweater was the one object in Kildare that had the potential to challenge the Russians' love for hockey, food and each other. Their eyes grew wider and wider, and did not blink at all when Mr. Chouinard said, "Lads, let me introduce you to my eldest daughter, Brigitte."

26

After thirty games, we weren't in first place but we were closer to it than last and Arnold Bramburger thought that was cause enough to celebrate. And no better time than New Year's Eve. He invited the Kougars, their parents, their billets, their girlfriends, their classmates, anyone it seemed, who was remotely associated with the team. I arrived with Michelle, Brendan and his girlfriend, Katie, around 9 p.m. Bramburger greeted us in his usual salesman-like way and gathered some drinks so we could have a cheer to "1996, the Year of the Kougars!"

"Thanks for the party, Arnie," Brendan said.

Bramburger slapped him on the shoulder and said, "Good to have you kids over. I wish I could do it all the time." He then bowed his head at the girls and pointed us in the direction of the basement, and the younger crowd.

The turnout wasn't huge. Some of the rookies couldn't come because their parents didn't want them out so late, others, like Johnny Carruthers, were still back home for the holidays, and then there were guys like Chaput and Lacroix who thought it too uncool to hang out with a bunch of thirty- and forty-year-olds who wouldn't let them do dope. All the better, I said. At least everyone who was there wanted to be there, and some more than others.

Nestled in a corner, beyond the strobe-lit dance floor, was a well-stacked buffet table being worked on by Vlastimil Skurilev and Dmitri Rushchenko.

"That's them, huh?" Michelle asked.

"Yep," I said. "The pride of Moscow."

The girls went to mingle with Brigitte Chouinard and their friends from the skating club, so Brendan and I found Coop and Jesse. They had heard briefly about the disaster trip from Montreal and were howling as we recounted it in detail.

"I can't believe he stole the tip!" Coop said.

"Which one's which?" Jesse asked.

I pointed out Rushchenko, but had to look around the room to find his countryman. Brendan gave me an elbow and pointed over to our girl-friends. Their whole group was giggling because Vlastimil Skurilev, his belly presumably satiated, had come over to them, reached out an arm to Brigitte Chouinard and in a thick accent asked, "Dance?"

Brigitte smiled and shrugged her shoulders. "Sure," she said.

"Oh, man, he's got balls," Coop said. "I guess you didn't tell 'em."

"Nope," Brendan said. "They'll find out."

What was to be found out was the reason Brigitte didn't have a boyfriend: she couldn't. Her father, rumour went, prevented her from dating until her eighteenth birthday. That frustrated many boys in town and even made the last player the Chouinards billeted ask the team for a trade after he became lovesick over Brigitte. From the looks of it, one or both Russians were heading there, too. Brendan went over to get the scoop from Katie. Jesse and Coop said Tyler wanted me to say hi, then went to find their dates. I told Michelle I was going upstairs, and on my way I turned back and laughed when I saw Dmitri Rushchenko walk over to his comrade and Brigitte. He promptly cut in.

Upstairs, Tyler came over to me after I picked up a beer. He clanged my bottle with his glass of club soda. "Better make that your last one," he said, straight-faced. "Eight a.m. practice tomorrow, eh."

"No way," I groaned.

"Two hours of doin' laps. To get the New Year off right," he said, then waited for the stunned look on my face before breaking out in a laugh. He bounced a hand off my chest. "Just shittin' ya."

"The guys said you wanted to see me."

"Yeah, yeah. Just wanted to see how the holidays went."

"Good, good."

"Folks doin' okay?"

"Yeah, you know, Dad's still getting over it."

"Oh, yeah. I bet. It's a tough thing to deal with."

I nodded and looked around the room. "Big turn out, eh?"

"Yep, Arnie knows how to throw a bash."

I saw all the faces I expected, except for one. Clyde Parker wasn't around, again, and when I asked, Tyler looked away and told me he left early.

"Clyde?" I said, shocked.

Raycliffe raised his eyebrows and looked down to find the bowl of peanuts on the table next to us.

"No way. He must be sick or somethin'."

"Yeah, maybe that's it."

But I knew it wasn't. "C'mon, Tyler," I said, "what's going on?"

"It's nothing, really." But I looked disappointed and he said, "It's better you boys didn't know."

I must have seemed scared or hurt, or both, because Tyler sighed before looking me in the eye like we were near the end of a close game and he was about to reveal a play.

"Keep it quiet, okay, Scott," he said, and I nodded. "Clyde's not real happy about all the changes with the team." My gut knotted with worry. "Now, we'll work things out, I promise," Tyler continued, "but right now, me and him," and he shook his head before finishing with, "well, let's just say we're not seeing eye-to-eye on some things."

"But we're doing great. What's the problem?"

He squinched his face like he was trying to hold himself back, but couldn't. "Well, with the two new guys, we're gonna play a little more uptempo, take a few more chances. Clyde doesn't agree; strongly disagrees is more like it."

"He's still with the team, right?"

"Yeah, yeah," he said with a snort. "Nothing big, I'm tellin' ya. We need Clyde; he's too good a coach. He's got the defence down."

I didn't say anything else right away and he took the opportunity to change the subject.

"We did get some good news today."

"Oh, yeah."

"Gary and Bramburger think they might sort out this whole mess with Lannie."

"Really!"

"Uh-huh. They're supposed to meet with the lawyer in a couple weeks, but sounds like things may be worked out."

"That's awesome."

"Yeah, yeah, it is."

We talked a bit more about the team and about the games we had coming up. Pretty soon, Michelle came running into the room and took me by the arm. "C'mon, it's almost time," she said. "The big ball's movin'!"

All of us gathered in the living room to watch the scene from Times Square. Bramburger led the countdown: "Three, two, one . . .," and the chorus of cheers and whistles that followed. Glasses of champagne were passed out as the stereo began to blast "Auld Lang Syne." I kissed Michelle, and Kildare seemed as normal and happy as any place on Earth.

27

S kurilev and Rushchenko became official members of the team on
January Second and immediately delighted, kicking up ice chips as
they whizzed around the rink like uncaged horses. After practice, the team
announced it had traded our third-line right winger to Beavers Falls for a
draft pick and returned another player to the midget team to make room
for the Russians.

General manager Gary Curran and the rest of the Kougars' braintrust
truly believed both players, especially Skurilev, were going to catapult us
to the top of the COHL. They thought they had the equivalent of a
windup toy. "Just put him on the ice and watch him go," Arnold
Bramburger said with a laugh. The Russian's mischief on the trip from the
airport had only deterred their faith in him for a short time, but after
Skurilev's performance against Otter Lake in the first game of 1996, sweat
poured down the faces of Bramburger, Curran and Raycliffe as if they had
just lost an expensive wager.

Skurilev played more than twenty minutes, not the fifteen Raycliffe
intended him to, because he refused to change with his linemates, staying
on for thirty seconds, sometimes even a minute longer than Tahani "One-
Axe" Kohono and Dion Marcelle. That caused confusion for all and

induced us into a pair of too-many-men-on-the-ice penalties. When Skurilev got the puck, he tried to carry it from end to end, never passing, never dumping in, just skating hardheadedly through the neutral zone before being checked by a defenceman, who often started a rush the other way while Skurilev loped back shaking his head in disbelief. His actions caused little Tahani to shout, "What's Russian for 'Pass the puck?'," and Clyde Parker to take on a look of conceit as we lost 4-2.

Skurilev confounded all of us, even Brendan, who prided himself in being able to get his charges to listen and be motivated, but he didn't know how to get through to the Russian. Unfortunately, neither did anyone else. "We just have to hope he comes around," Brendan and I heard Curran whisper while we passed Tyler's office a day after the loss.

Conversely, Rushchenko was turning out to be surprisingly effective. He didn't have nearly as much ability as his countryman, but he was coachable and made few mistakes with the puck. His size helped clear the front of our net and his speed allowed him to jump in on rushes. He had trouble skating backwards and didn't take to bodychecking, but because he had a good attitude he was excused. His knitting habit — he completed his toque and immediately began working on another accessory — got him teased, but he reacted by creating a mitten with the middle finger missing and presenting it to Tim Chaput, a move that won many of us over. And after we beat Fairfield 3-2 in overtime, Rushchenko and Skurilev were invited to Finnegan's. Skurilev, probably sensing animosity toward him, declined. Rushchenko accepted and tried his best to avoid Skurilev's glare as he did.

"How you likin' Canada, Dimy?" asked Jesse Sullivan after we had all unbundled from the cold.

"Gooood," Dmitri answered. "Eet's warm."

28

Johnny Carruthers didn't barf, but his dryheaves were so bad he had to keep his head over the Lacroixes' toilet bowl just in case. He seemed to have no control of himself. His body would twist like it was possessed and he would make that grotesque cackle people make when vomiting, but nothing would come out and his body would try again. When it let up, his chest would heave rapidly and quiver like it was in a spasm. Eventually, Johnny would be able to lift his head from the bowl, take a few breaths and relax for a second.

"You okay, man?" I asked.

He nodded without looking at me.

"I thought you'd stopped," I said.

"I did," he said, his voice hoarse.

"Then what the fuck happened?"

He couldn't answer; his body was going through the sick motions again. That's what someone looks like when they've been poisoned, I thought, and then I realized what had happened. I told Johnny I'd be back in a minute, then ran downstairs.

It was exam week, but I was all done; wrote my last one that day. Michelle was still cramming and that gave me a night out with the boys, but I should've known better when Brendan said he had to study, and Jesse and Coop said they were broke until the next team payday. They convinced me to go to Tony Lacroix's place with them. Lacroix wanted to make friends with the rest of us, not just Chaput, and with his dad out of town a lot, he figured he knew how. He gave the guys on the team, and a lot of others, a standing invite whenever we wanted to shoot pool or raid the liquor cabinet.

"He okay?" Jesse asked when I reached the basement.

"No!" I shouted and headed for Tim Chaput. "You spiked his drink didn't you?"

Chaput got up from the couch and said no, but when I raised a fist at him, he confessed.

"Okay, okay," he said, backing away. "I put a couple shots in his pop, but it's not my fault he drank it."

"You're a fuckin' idiot!" I yelled.

Coop and Jesse had left the pool table to come between us or else I would have smacked him one.

"Is he still pukin'?" Lacroix asked, without turning from the porno he had on. Jungle Jim and two other guys I didn't really know were watching, too. None of the girls Coop and Jess were expecting had shown up.

I said Johnny was in bad shape and Jesse went to see how he was doing.

"This could get him kicked off the team, you know," I said to Chaput.

"No way," he replied, in his usual arrogant way.

Chaput followed Jesse upstairs, and Coop and I trailed them. Jungle Jim got up, too, but Lacroix said something about being there "right after this fuck scene," and stayed on the couch. When we saw Johnny, he was struggling to stand, but at least Jesse had gotten him on his feet.

"How much did you put in?" Jesse asked Chaput, angrily.

"Just a shot or two," he answered. "I swear." Chaput touched Johnny on the shoulder and said, "Sorry, guy, didn't think you'd mind."

Johnny shrugged him off and kept his head bent over the sink while he continued to get washed up. He started to dryheave again, and Jesse patted his back and told him it'd be okay.

It was sad, especially because Johnny had been having such a good time. Lacroix had a bunch of video games and Johnny got lost in them. He grabbed a joystick as soon as he arrived and took care of all challengers in NHL '96. His back and shoulders were straight, and head up. When he scored or delivered a big check that caused the other guy's player to bleed, he would laugh and high-five one of us. There was a look of escape on his face that was rare for him, one Chaput stole with a stupid prank.

Jesse ducked his head out of the bathroom and looked upset. "He ain't sobering up any time soon," he said to Coop and me.

"Give him mints," Jungle Jim said. "It'll take the smell away." We didn't pay attention to him. "It works for me."

Johnny went back to the toilet bowl now, and Jesse came out to talk to us.

"Let's just take him home," he said. "Clyde'll understand."

"*What?*" I said. "No way! He'll freak, just like last time."

"Yeah, but even Johnny says that was legit. We gotta get him home some time tonight; earlier the better, right?"

Coop agreed. "Clyde's all right," he said. "If we're all there and we explain what happened . . ."

I shook my head and Coop asked, "Did you and Clyde duke it out or something?"

"No," I said, defensively. "I dunno. Whatever. Let's just go if that's what we're gonna do."

Jungle Jim said it was cool hanging out with us and he'd catch us later. Lacroix came up when he heard we were leaving and handed Cooper a videotape. "Hey, man, give this back to Clyde for me, eh."

On the ride there, Johnny was still the whole way until Coop stopped the car abruptly and said, "Okay, J.C., we're home." Then Johnny opened the door, stuck his head out and puked. He wiped snow on his face then kicked some on the vomit before we escorted him to the front door.

"What'd someone call a team meeting?" Clyde said when he saw the four of us standing out in the cold. But after he recognized Johnny's state, he got pissed. "He's fuckin' wrecked!"

"Clyde we can explain," Jesse said.

Parker watched us skeptically as we entered his house. Johnny went straight to the washroom and Clyde didn't take his eyes off him until he disappeared around the corner.

"So what is it?" he asked.

"We were hangin' out at Lacroix's, just us," Coop said, "and Johnny must've just picked up the wrong glass or something."

"Bullshit!"

"C'mon, Clyde," Jesse said, "really he didn't know there was booze in it."

"He must've known when he started getting buzzed, eh?"

I was still standing in the foyer, cringing at Clyde's words. When I opened my eyes, he was staring at me. "MacGregor?" he bellowed. "What's the word?"

"Clyde, can you just give him a break, please?" I said. "He's been sober for two months before tonight, and tonight wasn't his fault."

He stood leering at me, a condescending look on his face. And I leered back, hoping I could see what was going on in his head, and just when I thought I might have been close, he looked down. Then he exhaled and said, "Okay, no promises."

That's when Johnny came out of the washroom. He went directly to his room and shut the door. Clyde had taken a glance at him then turned back to us. "I'll talk to him when he sobers up and if he says it was a mistake, then it stays here."

"Alright, Clyde," Jesse said. "You the man."

"But if I get the feelin' he's lying, then I'm going to the superiors. Got it," he said and started pointing a finger around at us. "And don't you go fucking blaming me if he gets his ass suspended again, or booted off this team for good."

Jesse and Coop bowed their heads; I looked right at Clyde. He walked toward me, but ignored my stare. Instead, he went for the door, opened it and kept his head down as we filed out.

"You see," Jesse said to me after we left, "things worked out."

"Yeah, right. No promises, remember."

"Ah, shit," Coop said after he started up the car. "I forgot to give him the fuck tape."

He asked me to bring it in and when I knocked on the door, Clyde took his time answering. "What now?" he asked.

"Lacroix said to give you this," I said.

He looked down at the label. I peeked behind him and the only thing I saw was light coming from Johnny's room.

"Fantasy Island," he said. "Great, now I got something to do tonight."

He went to take it from my hand, but I pulled it back. Clyde looked me in the eye, angry, yes, but a bit spooked, too.

"What would Tyler say about this?" I asked.

He snatched the tape from my hand, sneered and closed the door.

I don't know, maybe I was being hard on Clyde. He did supply Johnny with room and board, took time to give him a little extra coaching, said he was doing what was best for the kid. Maybe he never had a billet as difficult as Johnny and that was probably irritating to live with, too. So, I suppose, it was none of my business. Clyde, by the looks of it, was giving Johnny everything he was obligated to.

In all that time, though, it never occurred to me what Johnny might give Clyde. Indeed, what Clyde might take.

29

In the winter of 1996, scouts flocked to Kildare as if it were a century-and-a-half earlier and the centre of a gold rush. Besides the usual representatives from American collegiate teams, NHL clubs eager to sign Skurilev, and possibly Rushchenko, to six-figure salaries were sending evaluators to eye the Kougars. Quite a coup for a team whose entire alumni during the Lannie Leroux era made more from their summer drive-thru shifts at McDonald's than they ever did from hockey.

"How many we got tonight?" asked Tim Chaput, a good defensive forward, which meant he had a better shot at gaining tact than playing professionally. Of course, that didn't stop him from strutting into the dressing room, gleeful about all the hoop-la.

"About a good dozen," Gary Curran said. "From all over; even Los Angeles."

Without missing a beat, Chaput sang, "Hoo-ray for Hollywood, Holly, Holly, Holly-wood," causing Curran to chuckle as he left. "Woo-Hoo! Here I come!" Chaput continued.

"Yeah, you're gonna be on 'America's Funniest Dweebs'," Tony Lacroix said.

"Shut up, asshole, or I won't make you one of my entourage."

"Oooh, there's a big loss," Lacroix retorted just when Tyler Raycliffe walked into the dressing room.

"Okay, let's get serious," the coach said, even more firmly than usual. "I just found out Timberton lost today, so we're playing for first place in the division. And we have no excuses."

We had won three straight to improve to 19-12-1 before hosting Crowne Place that night. Increasingly, the attention was being drawn from the team and toward Skurilev, who, despite his maddening antics, was a wonder on skates. He drew penalties and along with keeping the puck from his teammates, kept it from the opposition, as well. Maybe because he sensed the spotlight on him, Skurilev was at his mesmerizing best — and worst — during the first period against the Royals. The Russian's dexterity was too much for their checkers, who flailed their arms and sticks when he sped by. Two hooking penalties gave us power plays that resulted in Brendan setting me up twice as we led 2-0 after the first. But Skurilev, whose aloofness had quickly devolved to bitterness toward his teammates, especially the more popular Rushchenko, would seethe at his stall during the intermission.

As a talent, Skurilev was above us, as a personality, he was below us. Either way he wasn't one of us. No one congratulated him on his play. No one walked out to the ice with him. No one extended themselves for him. In the second period, his icy facade began to crack. On his first shift, he grabbed the puck behind Chris Cooper in our end, rushed up ice, weaving around between the bluelines like he was in the Ice Capades before slamming the puck into the corner and skating off. He made sure not to look at anyone, especially Raycliffe, who denied him another turn until near the end of the frame. When Skurilev finally took the ice again, he began to enact the same stunt, showing off his puckhandling, probably believing he was making fools of everyone on the ice. Then he did the unthinkable. Before coming off, Skurilev carried the puck slowly up the right wing and to the front of our bench. He looked over as Rushchenko prepared to hop on, then lured two Crowne Place defenders closer. The Royals stormed toward Skurilev, looking like they couldn't wait to finally get their shot at him, but the slick forward slipped the puck behind him to Rushchenko, who had barely gotten onto the ice and wasn't expecting the rubber. Skurilev lithely ducked away from the checks like a trickster. He found his way onto the bench, then watched his scheme unfold.

An opponent crashed into Rushchenko, hurling the big Russian to the ice. He landed on his right side and immediately curled up in pain. I jostled with the player that hit him causing a brief melee as gloves, sticks and equipment went flying off bodies. After order was restored, Rushchenko was carried off, his separated right shoulder hanging like a slashed branch. I didn't catch the look on Skurilev's face when his roommate was injured, but I did notice his shock when he heard Brigitte Chouinard call out, "Dimy, are you okay?"

Skurilev didn't take the ice again and between periods was told by Gary Curran, who had seen right through the ploy, to change into street clothes and watch from the press box. Without either Russian, we were more comfortable and had our strongest period since the Christmas break, scoring three goals and winning, 6-1. Personally, it was my best game of the season: five goals and an assist. Afterwards, I did my usual routine: showering, changing, packing my gear. But as I began to head out, Tyler called me into his office. "Scott, there's someone here who would like to talk to you," he said, his eyes bright.

I walked in to see a familiar, bespectacled man in an oversized parka holding a clipboard. He was a scout.

"Hi, Scott, Rich Eisener from Rochester State," he said, offering his hand. "We met last year, maybe you remember."

"Oh yeah," I said. I shook his hand. "Good to see you again."

"We'd like to talk to you some more about our school, if you've got time."

"For sure," I said.

We went to Finnegan's, where Rich told me that Rochester State had been looking at me for a couple of years. They were serious enough to talk to Tyler and some others around the league; they all said good things. Some people at State were concerned by my suspension, Rich said, but not so much to stop them from offering me a full four-year scholarship. "State's a terrific school," he said. "I know we've been through this already, but we really like you, Scott. Our top two scorers are graduating and you'd be able to step right in and get a lot of ice time. And we love your toughness. I knew you could score, but what really impressed me tonight was the way you stuck up for your teammate, that Russian, there when he got banged around."

"Thanks, that's just part of the game, I guess," I said, sheepishly.

"Yeah, well, we're hoping you could bring that to our game. I'll be honest with you, Scott, some of our guys don't have the heart you do. That intensity you've got could mean a lot to us." It was ironic because ever since I axed Alain Tallard's arm I was trying to become *less* intense. "Last time we spoke, you said you would be interested in studying English, is that still what you want?"

"Yeah, it is. And I know you guys have a good program."

"We sure do, but so do a lot of schools." He stopped to sip his beer. "So, tell me, you and Brendan Kowalczek seem real close, you boys wanna stick together after Kildare?"

"Oh, that'd be great," I said, "but it's probably not going to happen. Brendan's pretty much decided on B.U. They only have one scholarship to give a freshman, and he's the one."

"Well, we'd love to have him, too. But believe me if that makes it easier for us to sign you, we're happy to make the trade." He slid some papers in front of me along with a brochure about Rochester State, and a bulletin on its courses and campus life. "Why don't you look these over and let us know."

"Sure. I'll have to talk to my folks first . . ."

"Oh, of course," he said. "Don't rush. You have until April Fifteenth to make a decision. But if you're really interested in us, please we'll fly you and your family down, show you around town. You'll love it."

For four years in Kildare, I gave up time with my parents and Grandpa Joe, pushed back my education so I could get in another season and never gave thought to another career. My life was hockey. And, back then, that didn't seem at all unusual or foolish. Until that moment I wasn't sure if my efforts were going to pay off. But I felt a rush when it seemed all I needed to secure my future was my signature on an officious sheet of paper. Although I was still a few months from graduating the Kougars and high school, I truly believed I had already moved beyond on that night.

30

The Leroux mansion was a bit too close for me. The "No Trespassing" sign at the property line had me worried and the "Absolutely No Trespassing, violators will be prosecuted" sign in front of us got me anxious. "Michelle, maybe we should go back," I said.

"Scott, don't worry about it. I used to do this all the time."

Used to?, I thought.

"C'mon, we're almost there."

She continued trudging through the woods that led to the rear grounds of the mansion. I followed, of course, aware that even if I had the where-withal to turn back, I wouldn't know how to get to her car. We had parked at the edge of the river and began walking through Caledonia Hill's back woods full of spruce trees and ice because "it'll be fun," she said. "You won't believe the view when you see it."

That she was right about. Once we finally came clear of the woods, we stood on a precipice and could see Leroux mansion in full view, lit up like Christmas. It was a calm winter night, typical of Central Ontario. The stars seemed close enough to be street lamps and the cold air was so still I got to thinking 20-below wasn't so bad. It was an awesome sight and I wanted to stay a while, to take it all in, to see Kildare as a postcard for once.

Instead, I heard, "C'mon," as Michelle tugged my hand, "we can get closer."

Before I knew it, we were heading downhill — fast. We both nearly fell, but that didn't stop her from dragging me up to another plateau. "Are you nuts?" I said when she stopped to plop down.

She didn't answer. Then she yanked my hand and I dropped beside her. Before stretching herself out on her belly, she smiled and kissed my cheek. That relaxed me, made me feel warm and, as I watched her rest her delicate chin on her mittens, realized how good it felt to be with her then, and how necessary. Because I only had one class that final semester and she had a full course load, we hadn't been seeing as much of each other as before. I wasn't there to talk with before class, or for our spontaneous drives to the hill at lunch. That was frustrating, and sometimes we took it out on each other. I was spending too much time at the rink and gym, she was trying to fit too much in with school and visits to universities and the skating club — and me.

During that last year of school, both of us had a lot of pressure. We were dwelling on our futures all the time and it was a confounding pastime. (Where would I be? Where would she be? Would we be able to keep in touch? If it seemed at all hard now, how about then?)

Thing was, neither of us knew the answers, so we often chose to recall the past, instead.

"We used to toboggan here after school a lot," she said as we overlooked the grounds. "That was when Lucinda Leroux was still alive and she'd let kids on the property."

"And Lannie doesn't, so what do you think he'd do if he found a couple of big kids trespassing?"

She smiled like a mischief and squeezed my arm. Then she was up and gone. "I'll show you the gazebo," she said. "I bet it's still heated."

After rolling my eyes and slumping in defeat, I got up and followed.

"He's asleep by now, anyway," she said.

"But all the lights are on!"

"They're always on." She wrapped herself around my arm, and rubbed a hand up and down it. "No one'll know we were even here." She looked up at me as we approached the steps to the gazebo and grinned. "Besides, what's the worst that could happen?"

This time, I had to look at her like she was crazy.

"Probably a slap on the wrist, maybe a fine." She let go of me and placed her hands close to an outdoor heater meant to keep the benches warm. "Maybe Lannie would have us for breakfast. And he likes boys, so he'd probably keep you for lunch and dinner, too."

"Get outta here," I said, keeping a wary eye on the mansion.

Michelle hugged me, then we kissed and held each other for a while, and I asked if she was happy to be there again. "It's not the same." She sniffled and wiped a mitten under her nose. "It seems too lonely." It was Lannie's own fault, she said, and I asked what she meant.

"He just uses people, you know. His mom was so cool to everyone in town and he's so cruel sometimes." She sighed and got up, and I knew it was finally time to leave. "I mean, I don't think it's right the way people make fun of him and all, but he's not been a nice man, when it comes down to it." I agreed and she noted he's been hurt by it, too. "No one really hangs around Lannie or this place anymore," she said, "unless they really have to."

We began to walk back up the old toboggan hill, but my mind was still on Lannie, wondering what he might do if . . ., and that wasn't a good thing. Had I been concentrating, had my head not been down, had I been more focused, I wouldn't have been so flustered when Michelle slipped. She had turned around to say something and lost her footing on her next step. I saw her about to fall and hurried to catch her, but couldn't. And didn't have to.

Michelle was fine. She got her balance back on her own. On the other hand, I was in deep shit. My feet came from under me when I reached up for her and I plunged down the icy hill. Michelle let out a scream and I must have, too, because huge, brilliant flood lights came on in response. When I saw them, I started to panic. I tried my best to slow down, pressing my hands and feet against the hill, but it was too slick, and I kept going down. The lights were now turning toward me and I still hadn't reached the bottom. "Scott! Scott!" Michelle screamed.

When I finally skidded to a stop, I didn't even have time to take a breath. The mansion's backdoors were swinging open.

"Scott!" Michelle called.

"Run, Michelle!" I shouted. "Run! Get outta here!" Desperately, I tried to get up the hill. If it had been more vertical, I would've looked like a rock climber. But I didn't appear to be anything that cool. I was clumsily trying to traverse the ice, keeping my toes and hands on the hill and my knees bent as I trudged forward, desperate to maintain my feet.

"C'mon, Scott! Hurry!" Michelle shouted.

"Run!" I yelled. "Go!"

She was bouncing nervously on her feet, her mittens against her cheeks. I don't know how long she waited before she decided to leave, but it was probably until she saw the Dobermanns. "Oh, God, Scott," she said. "I'm sorry." And I heard her boots pounding in the snow as she ran away.

I was pushing hard to get up. The insteps of my feet pressed against the ice as I inched forward, but I hadn't even gotten halfway to the top when I lost my ground again. I went tumbling back down on my belly, the only sounds being my knees scraping the ice and the barking that kept getting closer. When I came to a stop this time, I turned over to see two huge black dogs with stubs for tails, and white teeth bright like snow and how sharp I didn't want to know. I started to pant fearfully, holding a hand to my face as I backed away on my butt. At the moment they were about to jump on me, my mind went completely numb. By instinct, I turned to my side and balled myself up, bandaging my skull with my arms. But my head wasn't so covered that I couldn't hear the whistle that stopped the dogs. I stayed curled up until I could feel them backing off. Even after I knew it was safe to turn around, I did so slowly, scared of what I might be in for. When I looked up, I saw a brawny, bald-headed man in blue jeans and a silk shortsleeve standing in the freezing cold petting one of the dogs.

"Well, look here, boys," he said. "I think we got ourselves a trespasser."

31

"What happened?"

"They kept me there for a while," I told Michelle over the phone the next morning. "Wanted to know why I was trespassing."

"Oh, Scott. I'm so sorry!" she said. "Do you hate me?"

"No."

"I'm so happy you're okay. I couldn't sleep all night."

"Me either."

"They didn't do anything to you did they?"

"No."

"Are you sure?"

"Yes."

"What happened then?" she asked. "Did you have to talk to Lannie?"

"Yeah," I said. "I had to talk to Lannie."

First, though, I had to deal with his manservant, Brad. After he hoisted me up off my back, he led me into the mansion and the Dobermanns started barking again.

"So, what the hell were you doin', man?" Brad asked after he closed the doors.

"Nothing," I said. "Really." I was shivering from the cold and backed into a corner by the dogs. One of them started clawing at my leg and I must have yelped because Brad quickly shouted, "Down!" He then whistled them quiet before, mercifully, sending them into another room.

"So what's the story?" He didn't sound mean, but he sure looked it. Tattoos of sharks decorated his arms, several studs pierced both ears and steam was rising off his bald head.

"My, my, ah, my girlfriend just dragged me up here."

"Girlfriend!" he said, then laughed. "Christ, in this weather! You coulda gotten stuck together for good, you know."

I looked at him blankly.

"This is private property, you know."

"Yeah, I know. I told her," I said. "I'm really sorry."

He raised his eyebrows and said, " 'Sorry,' doesn't cut it much around here." Then he picked up a phone and dialed.

"Are you calling the police?" I asked, with alarm.

"No," he said. "Not yet, anyway. That's not up to me." He then switched his attention to the voice on the other line. "Hello, sir. Brad, here." He must not have received a pleasant reply because his next words were, "Yes, I know it's late, sir, but we got us a young trespasser, wanted to see what you wanted to do with him." He paused before saying, "The police it is."

I closed my eyes and tried to figure out what I would say to Raycliffe and Curran, then I heard a whirring sound coming from above my head. I glanced up to see a camera shifting its gaze straight at me. Then Brad looked me over once before fixing his eyes on my Kougars jacket. He threw his chin out and asked, "Are you on the team?"

"Ah, yes," I said, into the camera.

"He is," Brad said into the phone. "Okay, then, I'll hold off on the cops."

I looked at him startled and more worried than before. "Come with me," he said.

"Where are we going?"

He looked me in the eye, compassion on his face, and said, "Lannie wants you."

My heart raced and my feet refused to move until Brad shouted, "Come on!"

I followed him through double doors and up a spiral staircase that led into a sitting room with a fireplace and view of the frozen river.

I was told to "Wait here. He'll be right in." Brad exited from where we came and as soon as he was out of sight, I began looking around for a way out. My first try was the French doors that led outside, but they were locked. There were two open doors leading into adjoining rooms, but the one I went through took me to a dead end of solid walls with bookshelves and family pictures. I hurried out of it and began heading for the other doorway, as Lannie Leroux was coming through it, pulling the door closed behind him.

"Uh, uh, uh," he said, with a lilt. "Not before you have a drink first."

I started to back up and he kept coming forward, smiling and holding a glass of brandy out to me. My leg hit a chair and I finally stopped to take the glass, but did not drink.

"Good," he said. "Now have a seat."

When I sat, Lannie's grin grew and he threw back his glass of liquor then walked to a barcart to pour more. After taking a seat himself, he crossed his legs and began to lean back, but his spine didn't even press against the back of the chair when he vaulted forward and yelled, "Ha, I can't do this without a snack!"

Do what exactly?, I thought.

He threw his arms up, walked back to the barcart and retrieved a bowl of peanuts. Then, with his happy gait, he came over and asked, "Want some?" I shook my head, he shrugged and retook his seat. "What's your name?" he asked and began popping nuts into his mouth.

I managed, "Sc-Scott MacGregor."

Lannie's face was full of makeup and his cheeks were puffier than usual because of the peanuts. He had on pyjamas under a green robe with an ornate "LL" stitched over the breast. Pretty normal looking attire for him, I thought. After placing the bowl of nuts in his lap, he pushed a hand to his chin and set an elbow on the armrest. Then he stared at me.

I looked down.

"You're not scared, are you?" he said. "Not a big boy like you?"

"No."

"What are you thinking right now?"

I got brave and looked right at him, trying to zap him with my eyes, then said, "I'd like to know what's going on?"

"Come on, Scott," he replied, in an even higher octave, then leaned back in his chair. He got snug and let his right hand with the brandy fall limply over the armrest before saying, "We both know all I want is to get you stinking drunk and jump your bones."

I can only imagine how grim I looked. My fists clenched, and I made sure to keep my chin down and eyes steely, all while racking my brain for an escape plan.

Then Lannie slapped his knee and let out a bellowing laugh that could have come from a bear with stomach cramps. And he kept laughing, grabbing his gut and doubling over, a prankster enjoying his own work. "You should see the look on your face," he was able to say between hysterics. Tears began to form in his eyes while he struggled to gain composure by letting out loud heaves instead of coughs of laughter. Eventually, he began to calm, slowly sitting back again and wiping his eyes. "That is priceless. Simply priceless," he said, still chuckling. "That is what you feared I would do, isn't it?"

In those few moments, I truly believed I would remain mute for the remainder of my life.

"It's what everyone thinks," he said. "I know it. I'm just some queer, sex-starved lunatic, right? Let's see, what is it . . ." He raised his eyes to the ceiling. "Loonie Leroux, they call me? No, no, that was a few years ago. Come on, help me, what is it? Lassie? Lucy? Come on, you can tell me."

I sighed heavily and, under my breath, said, "Loopy."

"Ah, yes, Loopy!" he shouted, elatiously. "Loopy Leroux! The crazy old fart — or fag, depending on your ignorance — who owns this despicable town. That's me, isn't it?"

I nodded twice, quickly.

"I la-uh-ove Kildare! And all the people in it," he said, clasping his palms. "They're my playmates and don't even know it!"

This is Lannie Leroux, I said to myself. *I have nothing to be afraid of.*

He was not going to use me for any inane fun, I decided, and began to walk to the door. Lannie didn't get up, he just followed me with his scheming eyes. I turned the knob, but had no luck. "Uh, uh, uh," he said. "Can't do it without this." He was holding up a key in mockery.

Leaning against the door, fizzling like I was beaten, I finally asked, "Lannie, what am I doing here?"

"Well, come on, you're having a drink with good ol' Loopy Leroux," he said. He looked hurt that I wasn't having fun, or drinking.

"Lannie, seriously," I said, raising my voice slightly. "What do you want?"

"Okay, fine," he said and caused a boom when he slammed a hand on a wooden armrest. He gulped down his liquor and angrily went to pour himself another. "I need you to help me with something."

"Why me?"

"Well, because you're the only one here, silly."

I exhaled and he begged me to sit again.

"Oh, Scott," he said, acting glum. "I really miss being part of the team, especially now that you boys are doing so well. I just can't help but think I had a part in it."

I had to wince.

"I just want a little, teensy bit of recognition, something that says, 'And let's not forget about good, ol' Lannie,' you know?"

Although I knew better, I had to ask what he had in mind.

"Well," he said and nearly leapt out of his chair, "how about a parade?" His arms flew open as if he was about to take flight, his smile growing again. "We'll have floats and balloons and cars all decorated. You and the boys can stand next to me, we'll ride down Main waving at the minions. It'll be splendid, don't you think?" He looked at me wide-eyed like an expectant kid in a toy store.

"Lannie, I don't think the guys would buy that."

The words deadened him and he sank back in his chair, slouching like a beanbag. "Oh, I don't like it when that happens," he said with spite. He huffed and puffed then sat up to smack a hand across his knee. "I've got it," he cried. "We'll have a Lannie Leroux Day. They'll roll me out on a red carpet, I'll do that drop the ball thing, they'll cheer when I leave."

They would do that, I wanted to say, but chose to just shake my head.

"Oh, pooh," he said and got up to pace, keeping a hand on the side of his face. "Scott, you're going to find this hard to believe," he said and hurried over to me, "but I don't know that much about hockey!" His arms were spread now and eyes bulged like he was pleading for relief.

I looked at him, trying to stay expressionless, then he raised my concern even more.

"I'm supposed to sign this deal with Curran and Bramburger in two days, and I'm getting nothing out of it," he said and crinkled his nose. "That would be giving them the win in all this. You can't do that in business, mother always told me." He sat again, massaging the seat with his ass until comfortable. "I just can't give them free run of the arena without getting something." He paused to look at me then moved forward. "I won't give it to them unless I get something from them. I just don't know what. What do hockey teams have? *What? What? What!*"

He looked at me so desperately, I couldn't help myself. "How about a trophy?" I said and regretted it as soon as I spoke the words.

"A trophy?" He inched closer to the edge of his seat, eyes alive with interest.

"Yeah, you know, the Lannie Leroux award or something."

"That's it!" He suddenly had a faraway look on his face. "The Lannie Leroux Award, given annually, forever and ever. And ever." He flashed his gaze at me — "My goodness, Scott, you're brilliant!" — then stood. "A bronze statue of me, presented to . . . to . . . To whom?" Again, he wanted an answer.

"I don't know," I said. "We've already got awards for rookie of the year, best goal scorer, MVP."

"What does that leave?"

After mulling it over, I had to snicker when I came up with it.

"What is it? What is it?" he asked.

"How about best defensive forward?"

"*Best defensive forward?*"

"Yes," I said. "Every team needs players like that to win and they never get recognized."

"The Lannie Leroux Award, presented to the Best Defensive Forward," he said like he was rehearsing a scene. "I like it!" He took a breath and circled the room before asking the obvious. "By the way, who's the best defensive forward on the team?"

"A guy named Chaput."

"Chaput, eh?" he said. "That's a good hometown name. Good. It should go to a Kildare boy." He relaxed and sipped his drink. "Thank you, Scott. You don't know what a cure that is for me."

I thought I would be free to leave, but Lannie didn't move. He checked the wall clock and stayed recoiling in his chair, readying for another crazy conversation it seemed. "You're not from Kildare, are you?" he asked.

"No, Ottawa."

"Ah, Bytown. It's a fine town."

I nodded.

"So, you trespass here often?"

"No," I said and felt my heart racing again. "Never."

"How can I believe you?"

"I'm telling the truth."

"I don't know if I believe you."

"Why not?"

"I could have Brad interrogate you more, ummm, forcefully."

"*What?*"

"Or I could call the police."

"No! What for?"

He got up to pace again. This time, he kept his index finger on his lips. "Let's see," he said. "Who else knows you were here?"

"Just my girlfriend."

"That's it!" He didn't seem happy about that.

After pacing a bit more, he said, "You know, you're the first trespasser here in three years. Why do you think that is?"

"I don't know. What'd you do with the others?"

"Oh, nothing. Nothing," he said. He faked a shy look and squeezed his robe. "Oh, I might've had Brad's predecessor rough them up a little."

I raised my eyebrows.

"And I might've had them prosecuted, too."

I nodded at him and told him word probably got around. He then waved a hand to me and said it was time to leave. Quickly, I popped up and followed him through the door.

"This is what I'm going to do for you," he said. "I'm not telling on you, so you tell on me."

"Huh?"

"Tell them you were outside in the cold and I invited you in," he said, looking off to the side. "I gave you something to warm you up, had a nice chat. You had a grand time with Lannie." He turned and leaned toward me. "Didn't you?"

"Yeah, yeah," I said. "I did. Thanks, Lannie."

"Do you need a ride home?" he asked. "I'm sure Brad would be happy to provide one."

"No, no. I can walk it."

"Okay, then," he said and opened the door. "Don't be afraid to drop by again. Bring your girl, if you like."

And I walked away, thinking that was the most stupefying evening I had ever had, and that Lannie Leroux had been a horrible owner, yes, but maybe wasn't all that bad a guy, after all.

32

Gary Curran enjoyed game days as much as anyone, mostly because the other days were grating. Running a hockey team was business and in Kildare that business was often infuriating. The day he was supposed to sign the arena deal began badly, ended miserably and had many aches in between. First, before he even began thinking of Lannie, he found himself in his office pacing, and checking his watch over and over. He was about to give up and move on with other business when the cause of his irritation came through the door. Vlastimil Skurilev was late for an overdue meeting with our G.M., and had no apology for it.

Curran knew it was imperative he had a sit-down with the young Russian, but Skurilev obviously did not see things the same way, Gary would tell me. Skurilev simply sat — slouched, really — in his designated chair, chewing gum and staring blankly at the wall. Trying his best to keep calm, Curran chose a diplomatic approach by explaining that the latest scouting reports had moved Skurilev into the middle of the first round. NHL teams had been impressed by the Russian and were ready to pay him thousands and thousands, but it was all in jeopardy; Skurilev was perilously close to being benched. That didn't seem to faze the star prospect, who kept his mouth quiet and eyes peeled to the wall. His behaviour so irked Curran that he finally addressed the juvenile as a teenaged boy with ill discipline.

"Vlastimil, listen to me: I don't care where you're going to play next year, but right now you're on my team that means you do as I say. Got it!" the G.M. shouted while leaning over his desk, knuckles pushing down. Skurilev looked up stunned. "If you can't get with it, believe me, and a lot of people will tell you the same thing, the NHL will be looking. Now what are you going to do?"

Skurilev did not answer.

"I said, what are you going to do?" Curran yelled. His face turned red and veins popped.

At last that startled Skurilev into compliance. The millionaire-to-be bowed his head and shook his legs nervously. "I play," he mumbled. "I play."

Curran sighed and stood straight. "Good. Now, apologize to your team-mates," he said.

Several minutes later, after we had arrived for morning practice, Curran and Tyler Raycliffe accompanied Skurilev into the dressing room.

"Vlastimil has something to say," Curran said.

We all looked at Skurilev, who fidgeted with his sleeves, bit his chapped lips, and resembled a scolded child rather than the cool athlete he had proven to be. He stuttered as he spoke in his thick Russian accent. "I am sor-sorry for how I play. I will be bet-better. I will d-do what coach says. I am sorry," he said. He sat in his stall and lowered his head.

A pause fell over the room as the rest of us looked at each other. Some shrugged, some smirked, most didn't know how to respond. I decided enough was enough, and went over to shake his hand. "It's okay, Vladie,"

I said.

Skurilev beamed a smile and before long the other guys came over to punch his shoulder or slap his back or rub the top of his head, any gesture that showed we had accepted his apology. But the one player who did not mete out forgiveness that day was the one who could not. Dmitri Rushchenko was probably still asleep after spending another night in the hospital, Brigitte Chouinard at his side, as his separated shoulder was tended to.

Yes, the Russians' quarrels would have to be dealt with, but that was for another day, Curran thought. Right then, he was anxious to get done with his next priority, shaking hands with Lannie, and putting that whole arena mess behind him. But when he showed up with Arnold Bramburger to sign the deal later that day, Lannie postured. He trifled on meaningless points and quibbled about phrasing, and when his counterparts were sufficiently worked up, Lannie said, "Also, I would like to donate my name to an award."

Curran closed his eyes and drooped his shoulders as if to say, *You've got to be kidding*. By this point, though, he and Bramburger were weak and submissive. "Oh, all right," Bramburger said after mulling it over briefly with his partner. "What kind of award?"

"I believe it would be fitting, and long overdue, might I add, to honour the best defensive forward. The Lannie Leroux Award, you see, for a player in the background, quite essential, but often overlooked," Lannie said. "Apropos, is it not?"

Curran rubbed his eyes in disbelief. "Is that all?" he asked, through clenched teeth.

Lannie said yes and the team's owners let out a mighty breath in relief.

The two sides signed papers, without delay, securing a contract that freed Leroux Arena to the Kougars — for a large sum — whenever they wanted it. As for LannieLand, it was being moved to the outskirts of town, where it would be bigger and more splendid, a beacon for weary travellers on the Trans-Canada, Lannie told reporters. "But let's talk about my award!" he said. "You know, I do believe a fine lad named Chaput from our town here could be the first recipient. Wouldn't that be grand?"

As Lannie vamped for the press, Curran retired to his office, collapsed in his chair and dozed. Unfortunately, there wasn't much rest. Gary couldn't even get into dreamstate before the phone rang. Randy Delisle was calling and Gary shook his head, wondering what more the paper could possibly want to know about the contract with Lannie. But Randy had other questions. He began by asking about the Russians and their apparent fallout. Curran got around those easily enough, blaming growing pains and new-country blues. Then the reporter got to the heart of the matter.

"I've been told, by my sources," Randy said, "that things are a little shaky with Parker and Raycliffe, maybe a lot shaky. Just want to know how you feel about that?"

Curran bent his head and rubbed a hand over his aching forehead, then answered decisively. "Believe me, there's no battle of wills between the coaches on this team," he said.

"Gary, you should know we're running a story tomorrow saying it looks like there's tension between the head coach and his assistant, and I'm giving you the chance to address it."

"I just did." Curran hung up, wiped his hands over his face then picked up the phone again.

"Tyler," he said. "It's Gary. We gotta talk about Parker."

33

C lyde Parker was not his usual self, and that was a pleasant sight. The assistant coach came to practice with such a light step, Tim Chaput wondered if he had finally gotten himself laid. (Assuming he had, Chaput went on to describe the act in stark detail, grossing out all of us.) But in Clyde's gait and easy laugh that day, there was method.

"Let me tell you lads, we're going to settle a lot of bets today," Tyler Raycliffe said after we were all on the ice. His statement got a smirk out of Clyde, who stood with arms crossed, looking smug as he surveyed us.

Tyler, grinning like a kid about to hop on a new bike, blew his whistle and pointed his stick at Brendan then waggled it. Our captain didn't get it; none of us did. We kind of looked at each other with confusion until Clyde said, "Cooper, over here," and waved a hand at our goalie. That's when we knew we were being drafted. Raycliffe called Jesse's name next, causing Clyde to shout, "Bastard!" as his opponent nabbed the most reliable defenceman. "Alright, J.C., you're with us," Clyde said, settling for Johnny Carruthers. Johnny bowed his head and skated away from the pack to stand behind Cooper and Clyde. Tyler, meanwhile, picked me as the players continued to be divvied up for a scrimmage that offered peculiarity, and little else.

Clyde, too slow and out of shape to get up and down the ice, tried to stay within his own blueline while Tyler — for the first couple of shifts anyway — scooted about the rink as if his body possessed a revved-up engine. Still, Clyde had to skate to and from the bench, and Tyler, who insisted on being our right winger, just couldn't keep up with Brendan and me after a while. By the time they got what both wanted — a one-on-one against the other — it was a test of guts, and in no figurative sense. As Tyler took the puck against Parker, he actually began laughing in that ticklish way men do when they know they're not acting their age. Then his rival stunned him back to reality. Clyde got his hands — and belly — on Tyler and gave him a shove to push him wide. Barely able to keep his balance, Tyler, struggling for air, stumbled, and Clyde pushed him again, this time right into the boards. Tyler bounced back, though. He had a step and enough leverage to shrug off Clyde, throwing a forearm into his chest and gradually breaking free of the check. Then Tyler took a few choppy strides before gliding behind the net. Clyde tried to pursue, desperately reaching out his stick at, then lunging after Raycliffe. He fell to his knees and from the ice watched Tyler straining to come around the goal. Tyler's eyes were hard with concentration and his heart was definitely in it, but his legs were tired and lungs empty. That state induced a lazy pass out front and as soon as he made it, our coach threw his head back in defeat. The puck went right to Johnny Carruthers, who quickly slapped it away.

"That's it, J.C.!" Clyde managed and banged his stick on the ice. "I'll get the next one."

He used his stick as a cane and got himself to one knee, then leaned over and didn't move for a few moments. Tyler was no better off. He was collapsed against the glass, trying to catch his breath.

We played on, but a few of us kept glancing back with worried looks. Of course, with Tyler winded at the other end, our squad was always offside. Brendan urged him to get out of the zone, and he was able to push off and make it to the top of the faceoff circle before we decided to put an end to it. When we stopped play, Clyde and Tyler turned to each other, and Tyler shook his head. Tyler got to the bench okay, but Clyde was still on one knee, huffing. "Man, does everyone suck this bad when they get old?" Cooper asked after he helped him up.

"Fuck you, kid," Clyde said. Once he was on his feet, he yanked his arm away from Coop and skated, in a crooked line, to the bench. To punctuate the episode, Coop mimicked our fat coach behind his back by stretching his hands out wide to mark an invisible belly and puffing his cheeks. He got a few of us on the ice to giggle and we weren't the only ones. Whistles and applause were coming from the few onlookers in the stands and press box as the coaches successfully made it to the boards. Parker waved the finger back at them then sat.

Tyler guzzled down water and spat some of it back out, too, when someone suggested, "Next goal wins?" He then leaned over to Clyde and said, "We're never doin' this again."

"Damn, right, we're not."

Above, Randy Delisle was straight-faced. The reporter had been intently looking at Clyde, observing him to see what else lay beneath all this.

34

Fifteen games remanied. And Vlastimil Skurilev was becoming a force. Through that February, he had eighteen goals and six assists in twenty games as we improved to 25-14-2 and were one point behind the Coldbury Chevaliers for the league lead. But he and Rushchenko still were not speaking. Dmitri, who had missed four weeks with a separated shoulder, was not about to forgive Skurilev for his injury. Their fallout concerned Tyler Raycliffe as the playoffs approached. The Russians had solidified the team talentwise, but it was important for his players to be focused, and together.

"Okay lads," Raycliffe said on the bus trip east to Salterton, "be ready, this isn't gonna be easy tonight. Nobody gives you first place."

If Raycliffe was anything, it was prepared for this. He would pour over scouting reports and videotape, check stats sheets, talk to reporters to find out which opposing players were hot or playing hurt. All of this to get even the slightest edge, to remove as much doubt as he could. When reviewing Salterton, an up-and-coming team, he must have noticed they were playing their less experienced players more because of injuries and had become prone to taking penalties. So he gave Skurilev a lot of ice early, and the strategy worked.

A few minutes in, Dion Marcelle won a draw by tying up his opposing centre's stick and kicking the puck up to Skurilev. The Russian went like a streak through the middle of the rink as the Thespians lunged desperately at him. Eventually a defenceman tackled him illegally before Skurilev could unleash a shot. Right away, Raycliffe's plan had earned us a man-advantage, then he pushed his luck.

Our power-play unit consisted of myself, Brendan and Dion with Skurilev and Rushchenko as the point tandem. By forcing them to work together on the ice, Raycliffe was attempting to seam the gap between them. Unfortunately, stitches mend matter, not pride.

After winning the faceoff, Brendan sent the puck behind the net where Dion picked it up and spied the ice before him. He passed out front when I moved into the slot, but my shot was stopped and the rebound was sent up the middle toward the blueline, where the Russians were. Both started to go for the puck, then backed off thinking the other was going to take control. Neither did, forcing Rushchenko to stretch to keep it inside the blueline before sending a weak backhand to the boards while glowering at Skurilev. Salterton gained control and sent the puck down the ice, causing Rushchenko and Skurilev to give chase. Rushchenko picked it up and began to move out of our end before dropping a pass to Skurilev despite not being forechecked. Skurilev, not expecting the puck, overskated it. While slowly retrieving the rubber, he yelled something in Russian to Dmitri. The defenceman stopped skating and turned to shout back. Skurilev then ignored the puck and began spouting harsh-sounding words in his native tongue as he moved toward Rushchenko like a boxer coming out of his corner.

"The puck! The puck!" Chris Cooper screamed in desperation from the goal-crease, poking his stick in the air like a pointer. But his pleas were lost.

The Russians met at the blueline where Skurilev, displaying his swiftness, shook off a glove, unhooked Rushchenko's facemask, removed the helmet and delivered a right cross to the chin. Rushchenko, legs like roots, barely flinched as he threw off Skurilev's faceguard to retaliate. The pair exchanged blows while a Thespian moved in to grab the puck, looking behind him with awe when he passed the duelling Russians.

The Salterton crowd roared as the combatants flung punch after punch at each other while the perplexed officials were idle, probably aiming to remember what the rulebook said to do in such a case.

Too intent on stopping the Thespians from scoring, Dion, Brendan and I skated by our scuffling teammates to chase down the puck, which was still in our end after Cooper stopped the breakaway but couldn't corral the rebound. After some pushing and shoving, I got control in the corner and slapped the puck down the rink, conceding the icing to restore order.

Brendan skated over to the Russians. They had lost their balance and were now wrestling on the ice. "Break it up! Break it up!" he screamed while jerking Rushchenko, who was on top. Dmitri had a good hold of Skurilev's throat and his thumbs appeared to be inching up the face in hopes of gouging at the right winger's eyes. Skurilev, meanwhile, kicked his skates in the air as one of his hands pushed against Rushchenko's chin, sending it off to the side.

Dion and I began to pull Skurilev away. He spat blood as we skated with him to the bench. In the mean time, Brendan and Cooper took Rushchenko by his arms to the other end of the bench. When we were through, we looked at each other in disbelief.

"That was fucking pathetic," Coop whispered before going back to his crease.

None of us disagreed, of course, but we didn't have anything more to say, either. Seeing our teammates brawl was so strange, it was difficult to comprehend. Maybe that's why it was so easy to go about our business like it never happened. It helped, too, that our coach didn't say a word.

Raycliffe's only reaction was to stare down and rub his forehead, but underneath his sportscoat he must have been seething. His fists were clenched and elbows bent slightly, like he was being held back from a fight. Guy the trainer attended to the Russians' cuts and Raycliffe kept them on separate sides of the bench for the rest of the game. Between periods he had Guy watch them on the bench as the rest of us spent the intermission strategizing in the dressing room. Raycliffe made no mention of the incident during the game.

"Okay, lads, you're doin' a great job out there," he said, clapping his hands, during the second intermission. "Just keep muckin', keep grindin'. The goals'll come. We *are* gonna win this game."

It was then I realized Tyler Raycliffe believed in serendipity. He had laid himself bare that night, entrusting whatever forces were in command to guide us to victory, and he was preparing us, and himself, to recognize the opportunity when it was presented. Doubt was not going to enter him. That's why he ignored the Russians' fight, even their mere presence, that night.

"Scott, when I think about the night I ripped up my knee," he would tell me, staring at the lit cigarette in his hand, months later when I needed to hear it, "it isn't the accident that haunts me, it's the doubt. It was a frigid night, eh. The wind was swooshin' all around, you know how it can get. It was over the holidays and I was supposed to meet up with some lads from the team over here. Now, you know Muskegee's about ten minutes from Kildare by car, twenty when the road's icy, and it sure was that night. So, I decided to be a show-off. I'd just got my snowmobile license and knew a shortcut — illegal one, of course — to get me to the ski lodge in seven minutes, five-and-a-half if I really floored it. And I remember tellin' myself when I stepped outside and felt the whip of the wind, 'Don't go, you'll never make it.' And that's when I was doomed. The whole ride, I just kept waitin' for the accident to happen. Of course that didn't slow me down any, dumb ass. Anyway, I was crossing through the Murphys' farm with snow flyin' in my face and I wasn't used to wearin' a visor, so before ya know it, up comes this huge bump. I think it might've been part of a snowman the Murphys' kids'd made. I tried to turn away, that's when she began to flip on me, as we went over ol' Frosty there, eh. My leg got caught and I couldn't throw myself free, and most of her landed on my knee. Jesus, pain you couldn't imagine. My screams must've wokin' up the farmers 'cause the police got there real fast. Wrote me a ticket after they called the ambulance, too! Bastards." He snickered, shook his head and took a sip of club soda, collecting himself to deliver the ending. "But that was it. Blew out the whole knee. Never played again. Tried, but didn't.

"After I quit, I went a long while before I even put on skates. Then my girlfriend's kid needed a coach for his team three, four years ago. Figured, what the hell, may as well start livin' again, eh?"

My empathy for Tyler never stopped growing during the time I played for him. Often, he would start to skate full out with us on warmup laps in practice, beating all but our best skaters the first couple of times around the rink before his smoker's lungs or tired body forced him to pull up. Sometimes when I sat with him in his office, he would tug his track pants up almost to the knees to remove his socks and the scar would be revealed like a loved one's ashes. He would come to the three schools in Kildare and Muskegee to lecture on snowmobile safety, telling his world not to be like him when so many of us felt there were much worse people to be than Tyler Raycliffe. "He was the best," Randy Delisle had told me. "Skated through teams, he did. Not just one or two guys, the entire team. Unbelievable. God, what a tragedy that accident was."

But Tyler recovered emotionally and physically enough to be a remarkable coach. He had taught us to have faith in ourselves and did all he could to give us a chance to win. That night in Salterton, we gave him a big, just reward.

Despite a short bench and weary legs, we managed to eke out victory when we caught Salterton on a bad line change and Johnny Carruthers smartly got Brendan the puck for a breakaway goal, the only one we would need. With the win, we unseated Coldbury for first place in the COHL. At the end of the game, Tyler looked up at the scoreboard and nodded with a contented smile.

35

The confidence we got from being in first place springboarded us to a remarkable finish. We had a 12 win-2 loss run that clinched first-place overall and made the final game of the season meaningless. Tyler told us he would rest most of the top players for the last game. It was a convenient break, because the season closed on the Sunday after Brigitte Chouinard's eighteenth birthday party, a day she graciously allowed to share with the Kougars' victory celebration. While Tyler and his staff declined the invite, insisting we hadn't won anything yet, all the players showed. Some came with presents in hand, others with wary girlfriends clinging to them. After all, Brigitte would now be free to date any boy in town.

Michelle and I, fresh off a spat about me not inviting her on my recruiting trip to Rochester State, were the first to arrive, and Brigitte bounced to the door to greet us.

"Oh, my God, Brigitte," Michelle said and hugged her, "I love your hair."

Brigitte had a lush doo that resembled a honeycomb. When she got the compliment, she patted her head with both hands and batted her eyes. She then pulled Michelle to the basement steps and continued their girltalk. I followed, like an afterthought, and things seemed stranger because the only others present were Vlastimil Skurilev and Dmitri Rushchenko. After their spat in Salterton, Tyler scratched both for a game and they got the hint, being as amiable to each other as they had to be to get back playing. Off the ice, though, nothing had changed.

"MacGregah," said Dmitri, alone at the pool table, "want to shoot a game?"

"Sure, Dimy," I answered.

"We play for food, none of thees silly papers with Queen's face." He smiled, then racked.

"Vladie, you wanna play?" I asked Skurilev. His mouth was too stuffed with potato chips to answer, so he shook his head and turned back to the food tray.

The room filled quickly. Brigitte's parents politely came and went from the basement, disguising expedient trips to investigate the scene by bringing more food or taking away empty dishes. The party was less than two hours old when Mr. and Mrs. Chouinard each brought in a cake lit with candles.

"Scott, Brendan, you boys do the honours with this one," Mr. Chouinard said. He plopped down a dark chocolate cake made to resemble a hockey puck. Written on the treat was: "Kildare Kougars 1995-96 COHL Champs." It had one large candle in the middle that had an ornament shaped like the Stanley Cup sitting below the wick. Next to it was a white sponge cake decorated with eighteen candles for Brigitte.

I stood between Brendan and Brigitte behind the table with Mr. and Mrs. Chouinard. In the back of the room, Dmitri presided over the pool table while Tim Chaput and Tony Lacroix stood next to the bar, each with a hand behind his back. Skurilev, dressed immaculately in a suede jacket and bow tie, reached the front of the table first, apparently anxious to get a piece of both cakes.

"Hey, kids, let's gather 'round here," Mr. Chouinard said. "Now I've been a Kildare Kougar and I've been a Kildare Kougar fan, and I gotta tell ya I've never seen a team in all these years work so hard as you lads. You boys deserve your title. And I know that Tremblay Trophy's coming soon enough. So here's to the Kougars!" He held up a glass of beer as the room filled with whistles and applause. Brendan looked at me, laughed and blew out the candle.

After the roar quelled, Mrs. Chouinard pressed a kiss against her daughter's cheeks and said, "Well, sweetheart, happy birthday. My baby's an adult now."

Mr. Chouinard gave Brigitte a kiss on the top of the head and said, "Happy birthday, kiddo."

She thanked them and blew out the candles, spurring more applause and a rendition of "Happy Birthday to You," as Skurilev grinned with anticipation.

"Now, the best part," Mrs. Chouinard said while carrying wrapped boxes. "The gifts."

"Oh, good," Brigitte said. "Let's see, I'll start with Mom and Dad's."

From her folks, she received a new pair of skis and keys to the family's second car. She hugged and kissed her parents again before moving on.

"Okay, let's go in order, then. Vlastimil and Dmitri's are next." She picked up an ordinary-sized box with an extraordinary gift from Skurilev. Brigitte read the card first and seemed puzzled, if not stricken, by it. She opened the gift deliberately as if she was trying to give herself time to prepare. But when she lifted the lid, she was still overwhelmed. "Oh, my God," she said and held up a silver-plated tiara with a diamond in the center. "Vladie, it's, it's . . . I don't know what to say. "

Unknown to us at the time, Skurilev, his NHL Draft day fast approaching, had signed an endorsement contract with a trading-card company and promptly spent most of the upfront payment on Brigitte, who he sought to be his "queen," as the birthday card read.

Brigitte, stunned by the gift and discomforted by its meaning, fumbled as she put it back in the box. Looking flushed, she said, "Thank you" to Skurilev like a girl reluctantly being initiated into womanhood. While Brendan and I wondered where Skurilev stole the tiara from, the others were still "oohing" and "aahing" at the sight. "Put it on, Brigitte," someone called, stirring a grin from Skurilev.

But Brigitte did not respond. She was careful not to look at Skurilev as she moved on, reaching for Dmitri's present. It was perfectly wrapped, and topped elaborately with ribbons and a bow. Brigitte, her hands shaking slightly, opened the package and pulled out a beautifully woven white wool sweater with a tiny Russian flag patched on the left shoulder and a large, script-lettered "B" over the left breast. "Oh, my gosh," she said. "Dmitri. It's beautiful."

Finally realizing what he was doing with his latest patch of wool, I said to him: "You did that yourself?"

He nodded and Brigitte bulged her eyes. "*You made this?*" she asked and stretched out her arms to view the sweater in its entirety. Rushchenko, sipping a glass of tomato juice, nodded again. "Dimy, I can't believe it!" She leaned over to kiss him on the cheek. "Thank you."

Skurilev stood straight and crossed his arms, his forehead crinkling as he watched Brigitte neatly fold the sweater before placing it right beside her, close enough so she could touch every now and then. She then continued opening gift after gift, reading the cards and graciously thanking each giver for their sweetness. When it was all done, we clapped our hands and got set to party again. Brigitte started handing her little sister some of the presents to take upstairs and one of the first to go was Skurilev's tiara. That depleted him. And when Brigitte swooned over the sweater again, freeing it from its fold with a quick thrust in the air, propelling it near Skurilev's face, it riled him. She held it in front of her again for all to admire, causing Skurilev to turn and push beyond the crowd. Immediately, he bumped into Rushchenko's shoulder and Rushchenko jabbed back, throwing an elbow out at Skurilev. That exchange caused the tomato juice in Dmitri's glass to swirl uneasily and when Skurilev flung an arm to smack him on the back, things got ugly. The glass sailed out of Dmitri's hand and toward the celebration site. He lunged for it, but missed grabbing it. Instead, his fingertips hit the bottom of the glass and pushed it further along its course, directly toward Brigitte and the sweater. The tomato juice leapt out of the container like a thrown gauntlet and spilled on the gift, bloodying the white wool.

Brigitte shrieked as the rest of the room gasped. Jumping back, Brigitte tried to avoid getting hit by the juice. After the initial shock, Rushchenko raised a fist as he turned after Skurilev, who even looked guilty. A look that quickly turned to fear as Dmitri was about to deliver a blow to the face.

Before he could, Brigitte shouted "Stop it! Stop it!" Rushchenko complied, stepping back as a couple of spectators came between him and Skurilev. Brigitte was still holding the sweater outstretched, but was now staring at it with disgust not amazement. She threw it down in front of Skurilev and walked around the table to face him. "Why are you like this?" she said moving closer to his face. "You want to ruin everything. I don't understand it!"

Skurilev put his hands in his pockets, hunched his shoulders and lowered his head.

"Look at what you did," Brigitte said, pointing to the sweater on the hardwood floor. "Dmitri made that and you wrecked it." She clasped her hands and held them to her chest. "I appreciate your gift. It's beautiful. But you can't expect to buy me or anyone else. Okay, Vladie?"

He gave a slight nod, because that was all he could do with his chin touching his chest.

"You think you're one of them," Brigitte said and gestured to a framed picture of the '93 Canadiens over the bar, "but you're not. Not yet, anyway. You're still one of us."

Skurilev raised his head to look at Brigitte. He let out a sigh and sincerely said, "I'm sorry."

Brigitte, still shaken, patted him on the arm. "It's okay. Just be part of the team from now on."

She then turned to head upstairs. Her mother, claiming she could get the stain out, picked up the sweater and went after Brigitte. Amid the clamour, Chaput and Lacroix had rushed forward with joints and beers in hand to get a glimpse of the distraction, and when the crowd separated, they were stuck in the middle of the room surrounded only by the smoke and smell of marijuana.

Mr. Chouinard, who had doggedly contained his anger while Skurilev marred his daughter's day, finally lost it. "That's it!" he screamed. He flung his arms like a scorned king. "Get out! Everyone!"

He promised Chaput and Lacroix he would inform their parents of their actions while muttering under his breath about the magnitude of their impudence to bring marijuana into his venerable home. He leered at Skurilev as the cause of the party's demise found his way up the stairs. Michelle volunteered us to help clean up, but was instructed to go home. Outside, the crowd scattered, some decided to go home, others chose to start another party elsewhere and some went to Finnegan's. Skurilev sat on an ice-covered chair on the front porch looking like a disappointed kid at Christmas. Dmitri, meanwhile, was at the bottom of the driveway hanging out with some of the guys. Michelle was talking to another friend when Brendan came over and asked what we were doing. I shrugged.

"Man, we've gotta get this thing settled," he said in a low voice so no one else could hear. "The playoffs start in three days and these two are still fighting."

I asked what he wanted to do, and Brendan looked down and shook his head like a man out of options. Then he turned his gaze to pouting Skurilev, and sighed before saying, "Let's take 'em across the border."

36

In the Valley, not even the Ottawa River's treacherous white-water rapids can separate the peoples of Ontario and Quebec. To go about their daily business, workers and students zip across bridges that bind the two provinces, skiers and sportsmen adopt the land on either side as favourite spots, and drinkers gather in the flexible bars of Quebec.

With later business hours and a legal drinking age a year younger than in Ontario, watering holes over the river are often full of anglophone teenagers seeking a buzz and the sensation of beating the system. In Bordeleau, some of the more frequent patrons have traditionally been members of the Kildare Kougars. After the unfortunate end to Brigitte Chouinard's birthday bash, Brendan was as intent on getting the team to act like one as he was on scoring any goal. That meant some team bonding and a trip to Quebec.

"Come on, Vlastimil," Brendan said. He grabbed the well-dressed and disheartened Russian from the cold chair on the Chouinards' porch. "We're gonna cheer you up."

Brendan escorted him to his green Tempo, where his girlfriend had vacated the passenger side. He then walked to the bottom of the driveway to take Dmitri by the arm. Before pulling him away from his conversation with Johnny, Jesse and Coop, he informed all four of the plan. He put Dmitri in the backseat, finished an apology to his understanding girlfriend, kissed her, then slapped my arm and said, "Let's roll."

I couldn't go so quickly, though. Michelle saw what was going on and rushed over. "Scott, what're you doing?" she asked, in an accusatory tone.

"Just goin' out with the guys," I said, defensively.

"Were you going to tell me?"

I looked off to the side and didn't answer.

"I told Mary we'd meet her and Joe at Finnegan's."

"Were you going to tell me?" I said it coldly, in a whisper, through gritted teeth.

She looked hurt and sober of affection for me. It was painful to stare at, so I didn't, opting instead to turn and walk away. I didn't hear or feel Michelle move after me.

"What happened?" Brendan asked.

"She's pissed," I said from the backseat.

"What for?"

"Ah, bullshit. You know."

"It'll blow over."

"I don't know," I said. "We'll see."

He said he was sorry and I told him not to worry about it, then stayed quiet the rest of the drive. Our carmates were silent, too. Skurilev was in front sulking and Dmitri was beside me looking out the window. Brendan kept his eyes on the road except when he glanced in the rear-view to make sure Coop's Audi was behind us. We crossed over the icy Nation Bridge and into La Belle Province. Both cars pulled into the first parking lot on the right as we entered Bordeleau's city limits and La Maison du

Bon Temps.

"Ah right, we're going to see if these Ruskies can hold their liquor, eh?" Jesse said.

Six of us began to walk up to the bar's doors in the middle of a light snowfall when I finally asked, "Where's Johnny?"

"He passed out in the backseat," Coop said. "Just hope he doesn't barf."

"I thought he wasn't drinkin'?"

Jesse and Coop shrugged and shook their heads. Brendan said, "We're gonna have to straighten that kid out."

Coop, Jesse and I nodded, but didn't know what to say. We wanted to help Johnny, but, like always, it didn't take much to convince ourselves we could put it off.

"Well, what are we havin', boys?" Coop said over a U2 song. "First round's on me."

"Vodka and orange juice all around," Jesse said.

"Just orange juice," Brendan said.

After we all had a glass, we cheered, "To mother Russia." We clanged our tumblers, which even coerced a smile from Skurilev.

After we all had a sip, Rushchenko said, "To Can-ah-dian friends."

The glasses clanged again and I remember being amazed at Dmitri. He already seemed to have gotten over the disappointment from the party and was even smiling. It was hard not to like the guy. Inside, he must have been writhing, but he didn't let it drag us down. In fact, he was actually trying to make the rest of us feel more at ease.

Brendan and I moved to the pool table with the Russians while Jesse and Coop approached two women at the bar. I began to shoot a game with Dmitri while Brendan and Skurilev chatted. As far as hockey went, the two of them probably had more in common than the rest of us. They had a mutual appreciation for what the other could do on the ice and Brendan was probably the only one of us Skurilev respected for his ability. Like two physicists discussing the atom, they spoke of staring down goaltenders before making a deke, the difficulty of avoiding getting a shot blocked, and the advantages and perils of working behind the net. That obsession with hockey is what set them apart from other Junior A players, including myself, who also loved to play and had dreams of becoming pros but lacked the confidence and focus the best always seem to have. While I was claiming a rare victory against Dmitri on the pool table, I couldn't help envisioning Brendan and Skurilev facing off against each other in NHL uniforms, with all the glory and wealth that accompanies those colours. I lined up to hit the eight-ball — "Corner," I called — and rifled it in with such force it banged into the back of the pocket like a puck against a post, causing a couple of bar patrons to turn their heads.

"Nice shot," Dmitri said, with his eyebrows raised.

Skurilev came to the table next, nodding politely to Rushchenko as he passed. Brendan and Dmitri went to the bar to fetch more drinks. I broke while Skurilev searched for a stick.

"Scott," he said, "I am sorry for ruining pah-ty."

"It's over," I said. "Don't worry about it." I passed him my stick, the only one in sight, after missing a shot.

"No, I have done wrong. I promeese to stop," he said and sank a stripe. "I will be paht of team from now on."

"You always were," I said.

"Thank you. You a good man," he replied. "But I want to help win. I promeese to help win thee Tremblay Cup."

"Trophy," I corrected. "Tremblay Trophy."

"Yes, trophy. I promeese we will win eet," he said. He handed me the cue stick after a miss.

"Well, we got a long way to go yet."

"We will win eet," he said again. He watched Brendan and Dmitri return with drinks, and added, "I promeese."

Brendan came over to me as I aimed at a ball. "Shank this game, would ya," he whispered. I did as he asked, missing a couple of shots on purpose, allowing Skurilev to win.

"Brendan, your turn," Vlastimil said afterwards.

"Nah, I hate that game," Brendan lied. "Dimy, you go ahead." He patted Dmitri on the back so hard it was like a shove toward the table. Dmitri began to rack the balls while Skurilev waited, shuffling his feet and taking frequent sips from his glass.

Brendan told me to go to the bar with him and we left the Russians alone.

"You think it's safe, or should we tell the bartender to put away all sharp objects?" Coop said, after he and Jesse struck out with the two babes at the bar.

Because they had to share the cue stick, Rushchenko and Skurilev began to talk, but with the jukebox blaring, none of us could hear the conversation. "C'mon, I gotta know what they're sayin'," Brendan said.

He led the four of us to an adjacent pool table and picked up three pool sticks he had placed behind the jukebox without anyone seeing. I began to rack and Jesse got ready to break. Coop, meanwhile, got the Russians speaking English when he asked them what they thought of our imported vodka. The Russians exchanged knowing looks and even snickered.

"That bad, eh?" Coop said, looking curiously at his glass. "At least the O.J. helps, right?"

Dmitri started to chuckle and Vlastimil joined him before long. They looked at each other and Dmitri said, "Remember what Coach used to say?"

Vlastimil nodded.

" 'When you get to Canada, never drink their bad vodka.' "

Coop, shocked, looked at Jesse and me, then stretched a hand out toward Dmitri. *Do you believe this?*, is what he wanted to say.

Dmitri kept laughing and glanced at Skurilev, who came through with an assist. " 'And don't poot orange juice in eet,' " he said. " 'If you have to drink eet, drink eet straight.' " He then slapped a hand on top of the pool table as if it were a knee.

Coop, Jesse and I looked at our glasses with disgust; a few feet away, Brendan smiled.

"Well, I bet Russian beer tastes like shit," Coop said.

Dmitri laughed, nodded vigorously and blurted, "It does!"

The laughter must have gotten us noticed, because a customer called, "Hey, it's the Kougars. Don't you boys got a game tomorrow?" Then someone looked at the bar clock and shouted, "Later tonight, you mean," and laughed.

Jesse looked at his watch right away. "Past midnight," he said and turned to us, looking concerned.

"There wasn't curfew tonight, was there?" Coop asked.

I shrugged and said, "Tomorrow's still a game day, I guess."

"Yeah, but it's not like it's a real game, right?" Jesse said.

The three of us faced Brendan.

"What do you think, cap'n?" Coop asked.

"I don't know. I didn't think about it," Brendan answered. "But maybe we should go. Just to be safe."

The six of us headed out of the bar and to the snow-covered parking lot, where Johnny Carruthers had managed to open the door enough to slink his head from the backseat, sparing Cooper's Audi the contents of his stomach.

"Oh, Christ, he puked," Coop said. He ran to the car, almost slipping on an ice patch. "Come on, Johnny, get up. Let's move." Cooper was tugging Johnny up by the collar, being careful not to touch any of the vomit. Finally, he got him awake enough so Johnny could pull himself into the backseat again. "Alright, just wipe your face, man," Coop said. "Don't get it on the seat or my dad'll freak."

Jesse hopped into the passenger side of Cooper's car as Skurilev, Rushchenko and I filed into Brendan's Tempo, this time with the Russians together in the back, tension still between them. Brendan and Cooper got their engines started, and began wiping snow from their windshields.

"Think we'll have trouble?" I asked Brendan when he sat.

"Not really." He paused to strap in. "Besides, my folks won't say nothin', neither will Jesse's or Coop's," he said. "The Chouinards'll be glad not to see these two tonight. That just leaves Clyde."

"That's it. We're dead. No way he's gonna give us another break with Johnny wasted."

"Who knows? He's probably out getting tanked himself."

"Man, I hope so. If nothing happens, this'd be bigger than beatin' Coldbury," I said. We rolled out of the parking lot, following Cooper's car onto the road with single-lane traffic.

The thick snow flew into the windshield like a repellant while we shivered, waiting for the car to heat up. Brendan gripped the steering wheel like he did the top of the boards just before he jumped over. He didn't turn on the radio, concentrating instead on the Audi's taillights. Although he was only going about fifty, he had to pump his brake constantly because of Cooper's driving. "Fuck," Brendan said, slamming his hand on the wheel, "he's all over the road."

Coop, who was getting much more snow in his face than we were, would inexplicably swerve, although we hadn't hit any black ice. "Were you watchin' him, tonight?" Brendan asked.

"No," I said. "Why?"

"How much you think he had?" He put one hand to his forehand while exhaling a heavy sigh.

"Oh, no. He can't be." Then I realized how buzzed I was from the two vodka drinks.

"I'm going to get around him after we cross the bridge."

We never made it that far.

37

As we went over the Nation Bridge that night, Cooper hit an ice patch. His black Audi veered chaotically from side to side. He frantically pulled the wheel from left to right like he was trying to grab a puck with sticks waving in his face. The brake lights flickered as he pumped the pedal repeatedly, desperately trying to regain control. But Coop failed.

After spinning out, the car skidded sideways, front facing Bordeleau, and toward the wooden barrier. I didn't see what happened next, because Brendan hit the same ice patch while braking and we lost control, too. However, the Tempo was not going nearly as fast as the Audi, so when Brendan pulled up the handbrake, we slowly flung around to face Quebec again. During the spin, we heard the loud crash of Cooper's car into the frail barrier of wire and oak stumps. When we came to a halt, we saw the backend of the Audi hanging over the edge with its bright headlights slightly tilted up, the beams cutting through the swirling snow. It looked like a tank having trouble getting on shore as it inched forward when Cooper pressed on the accelerator, only to fall back when he let up. It appeared as though there was a magnet pulling it toward the frozen river.

"We gotta hurry," I said and exited Brendan's car as soon as we came to a stop. I heard Brendan and the Russians behind me, but only saw the panicked face of our normally cool goaltender, sweating so heavily from under his woollen toque it looked like he was shedding his youth. "Come on! Come on!" he yelled, shaking the steering wheel with both hands as the car continued to slide away from the direction he wanted it to go. Jesse was sitting limp with his head thrown back and there was no sign of Johnny as I approached the passenger side.

"Hang in there, Coop," I said when I opened the door. Blood was coming down Jesse's forehead. "You okay, Jess?"

"Fuck no!" he yelled. Brendan and the Russians were standing behind me as I reached over, hands quivering, to unbuckle Jesse's seatbelt.

"C'mon, let's get 'em out," Brendan said.

Jesse put his right arm around my neck and I could feel his weight on my spine as I stumbled backward out of the two-door. Brendan grabbed him by the waist to get him further out before ducking his head under Jesse's other arm so we could haul him out like a cross. But when the car lost the two-hundred pounds it took a significant slip backward, causing Cooper to scream.

"Push it up, boys! Push it up!" I commanded the Russians, who were watching Brendan move Jesse away. Rushchenko came into the area between the passenger-side door and the seat and began to push against the edge of the windshield. Facing him was Skurilev, who was pulling on the inside frame exposed by the open doorway.

"Poool, Vladie," Dmitri said. Skurilev nodded and put more weight into his effort.

They managed to keep the car steady long enough for me to push up the front seat and see Johnny, still unconscious and with his ankles hanging out the passenger door. "Oh, Christ," I said. "He's still out."

"Get him out! Get him out!" Coop yelled. "I think it's gonna slide."

Grabbing Johnny by the ankles, I yanked him like a wet cloth and was surprised how light he was. After I got half of him out on the first pull, I slipped and Brendan had to help me. I strained to ask, "How's Jesse?" and groaned as we began to pull Johnny by his waist, manoeuvreing around Dmitri. "I dunno," Brendan said. We got Johnny out, but shook the car when we did, causing Dmitri to stumble.

"Oh, shit!" Cooper screamed.

Rushchenko was about to fall to a knee and the passenger door about to close into his body when Skurilev reached out a hand. He grabbed his comrade and pulled him back up. They looked at each other and smiled a little. At some point soon after that, Skurilev started to whimper.

"Dmitri, I am sor-sorry," he said.

Rushchenko gripped Skurilev's hand like an arm wrestler and shook it. "It's okay, Vladie," he said. "I forgeeve you."

Skurilev started to bawl. He put a glove to his face to wipe away tears and Rushchenko had taken both hands off the car to console his friend. As badly as we wanted the Russians to reconcile, their timing was brutal. Without their muscle, the Audi took a significant slip.

"Fuck!" I shouted. "Keep pushing boys!"

The rear tire on the passenger side was almost over the edge by now and Coop was in a complete panic. "Oh, shit! I'm goin' down!" he screamed. "I'm goin' down!"

"I'm comin'!" I said and circled over to his side. Brendan was taking Johnny to safety while the Russians got back to trying to steady the car. When I got around to Coop, tears were streaming from his eyes and snot was around his nose.

"Where're my pads when I need 'em, eh?" he said.

"Come on, we're gettin' you outta here." I reached over to undo his seatbelt.

"No," he said. "I can't leave the car."

"*What?*" I thought one of us was beginning to hallucinate.

"I can't go," he said. "My dad'll kill me."

"So you're gonna do it for him!"

"What's goin' on?" Brendan asked. He was breathing hard when he arrived beside me.

"He doesn't want to get out."

"*What?*"

"I can't go 'til the last second," Coop said, shaking his head.

"Fucking goalies!" Brendan screamed and pulled his hair. "Wear a god damn mask and they think they're fuckin' Spider-Man."

"I'm not goin'," Coop said again. He kept his foot flat on the accelerator, causing the spinning wheels to begin emitting the smell of burning rubber, that raunchy odour that made me envision hell.

"Alright, alright," I said, turning to Brendan. "Grab the back, I'll go to the front."

As I moved, gravity pulled the door in until it closed on Coop. I went to the hood and started to push down when I saw the first set of approaching lights since the accident. The vehicle was coming over the bridge from Kildare and when I began to wave at it, its sirens went on.

Officer James Gregoire squealed his tires to a halt in front of me. "What the hell happened?" he asked. He then called in his location to the OPP dispatcher.

"We spun out," I said. I was pushing down on the hood when I realized that if we were successful in boosting the car, I would end up under it.

When he got out of the cruiser, officer Gregoire pointed toward Jesse and Johnny. "Are they okay?" he asked.

"I dunno. I think so," I said.

He must have recognized our jackets right away, because he asked, "You lads all with the Kougars?"

"Yeah," I said.

He stood close to me and whiffed. "Drinkin' in Bordeleau, eh?" He moved past me toward Cooper. "Okay, let's get this driver out."

"I'm not goin'," Coop said.

"*What?*" the cop asked, looking back at me.

"He's our goalie," I said, then shrugged.

"Of course." Gregoire looked at Brendan and the Russians. "Well, you lads are holdin' her up all right. The tow truck'll be here in a minute." He turned to Cooper. "But if she slips any more, I'm orderin' you outta there, got it?"

Coop didn't reply, and Gregoire rushed over to check on Johnny and Jesse as the ambulance sirens became audible.

"The four of you in the other car?" the cop asked when he passed me.

"Yeah. We're not hurt." I was bent over, tugging the car from under the front bumper.

The officer ignored Johnny once he caught sight of him, but kneeled over Jesse, who was laying on his back on the frozen roadside. Gregoire reached inside his uniform jacket to grab a handkerchief then instructed Jesse to hold it on his bleeding forehead.

"This boy may have a concussion, maybe worse," Gregoire said to the

EMTs when they emerged from the ambulance.

"Can he walk?" one of them asked.

Jesse gave a nod, and the two EMTs helped him up and into the ambulance. Then they came back for Johnny, who Gregoire diagnosed as "just needing his stomach pumped."

"What about the other ones?" the ambulance driver asked.

"They're fine, for now," the cop said. "Driver needs a labotomy, though."

"Lemme guess, he's the goalie?"

Gregoire laughed as he confirmed the suspicion and waved on the just-arrived tow truck. "Let's get 'em outta there," he said, and we let up to cheer, causing Cooper's car to slide back.

"Keep pushing!" Coop screamed again while another vehicle — this one unexpected — slowed to a stop.

The tow-truck driver hurried to clasp the hook of the lift underneath when Charles Goring of the *Chronicle* arrived, no doubt after hearing of the incident over the police scanner. He hurried to the scene. His hands were on the top of his flash-equipped camera and he soon began snapping shots, sending light bursting over the scene as Cooper's car was slowly lifted onto level ground. "Okay, no more pictures," officer Gregoire told Goring once the car was safe. Goring obeyed, but then began seeking answers. He asked when and why the accident happened, who was involved, where we were coming from, how hurt we were, what we thought the team would say, and if we were drinking.

"No comment," Brendan said, for all of us. "We're not sayin' a thing."

It didn't matter much, though, the paper already had a front-page photograph that pretty much told the story.

Officer Gregoire was restrained enough to wait until Goring left before performing the task that more than anything set us trembling.

"Blow into this," he told Cooper, now in the back of the cruiser. The cop had stretched a plastic tube attached to a breathalyzer toward our goaltender. Coop took the tube, and looked over in fear at Brendan and me leaning against his recovered Audi.

"Oh, shit. I can't look," Brendan said. He closed his eyes, breathed out frosty air and walked to the overhang, staring down at the Ottawa River to contemplate a postseason without our only qualified goaltender.

Coop began to blow. A red light meant a suspended driver's license and possible permanent expulsion from the Kougars. "Green," I said under my breath. I bundled my arms into my body and held my hands to my mouth. "C'mon, green."

"Blow, blow, blow!" Gregoire urged Coop, whose cheeks puffed. Brendan, his head still down, had his arms stretched apart, each hand gripping a stump of the guardrail. The Russians had patted each other on the back and were now sitting in Brendan's car with the heater on. Coop withdrew his mouth then had to wait for the result. "Green," I said.

Coop must've felt like he was facing a penalty shooter charging down the middle of the ice, readying to make his move; a whole existence living and dying within those few seconds.

The breathalyzer buzzed. I stood straight. Cooper peered at Gregoire, who read the result: "Yellow."

Yellow?

"You blew point oh-seven-eight," the cop said.

"What's that mean?" Coop asked.

"It means it's your lucky day," Gregoire said, probably quite aware of the irony. "The legal limit is point oh-eight. You blew under that. Barely."

Brendan and I sank to the ground, in relief.

"You're not going to be charged," the cop continued, "but you can't operate a vehicle tonight."

It wasn't like Coop had made the save, but more like the puck stopped on the goal-line for him.

38

Kildare woke to the news of our hazardous night because the *Sunday Chronicle* posted two pictures from the scene on its front page. One was an inset of Jesse Sullivan sitting head down in the ambulance and the other of Cooper's car being wrenched from a fall by the tow truck and our arms.

Before Tyler Raycliffe called to fume, Brendan's mother shook her head as she dished out our breakfasts while querying about how we ended up in Quebec when we were supposed to be at the Chouinards and what in the world made us drive in that storm. "Just thank God you're okay," she said.

Mr. Kowalczek, meanwhile, was shaking his head, too, except he made it feel like he was in the presence of lesser creatures. He looked at the pictures, and said nothing, while standing bespectacled in a robe near the kitchen table. When he was done, he dropped the paper in front of us and walked away.

Raycliffe called during breakfast and Mrs. Kowalczek took a message that strongly requested us to be at the rink by noon, well before anyone was to arrive. It was supposed to be the last game of the season. A meaningless one that allowed the team and its coach a little relaxation before the playoffs. Tyler was very disappointed that that was stolen from him.

"What the hell were you thinkin'?" he screamed when we walked through his office door. He pushed his head in the direction of the locker room. "And why did they stay here?" Fearing the wrath of Mr. Chouinard, Skurilev and Rushchenko decided to sleep in the dressing room.

"It's a long story," Brendan said and took a seat just before the door swung open again.

"Ah, Mr. Villeneuve himself," Raycliffe said when Cooper entered.

"I'm sorry, Coach," Coop said.

"Tell it to Jesse. He's got a concussion; could miss two weeks," Tyler said. "I just got back from the hospital."

"How's Johnny?" I asked.

"I was hoping you could tell me," Tyler said and lit a cigarette.

"He was supposed to be at the hospital."

"I know!" Tyler said, emphatically. "He left before being admitted. Called Clyde, doesn't know where he is. Called the cops, they haven't seen him. I don't know where he is."

"This just keeps getting worse," I said, causing Raycliffe to snicker.

"Just wait until Gary shows up." He lifted his eyebrows and pointed his cigarette at us. "You lads pulled one hell of a stunt last night."

"Tyler, it wasn't like that," Brendan said. He sat up in his chair and pulled down his baseball cap. "There was trouble at the Chouinards and I just wanted to stop these two from fighting." He threw his head back in the direction of the Russians in the adjacent room. "We got it straightened out, but then Coop hit ice and . . ." He shook his head and sighed.

"And, and. And you're lucky to all be alive!" Tyler shouted. "And you," Tyler pointed his two fingers, cigarette in between like a dart, at Cooper. "You . . .," he paused to take a breath and scratch his head before looking up again. "Geez, look Chris, you're a good kid, but I know you were drinkin'. Be grateful the cop didn't let it get out."

That was when Gary Curran walked in, holding Johnny Carruthers by the arm. "Found him passed out in the press box," Curran said. He shoved Johnny toward a chair in the corner before turning to face us all. He started to speak, but then stopped and opened the locker-room door. "You two get in here!" he called to Rushchenko and Skurilev. The Russians moved to the doorway at the edge of the crowded room, then Curran began a harsh monologue.

"This is a disgrace," he said standing tall, hands in pockets, jaw stiff like stone. "An absolute disgrace. I thought this team meant something to you. You," he looked at me, "you wanted to win so bad this year you carry around your grandfather's cap like it's a safety blanket. And you," his gaze shifted to Brendan, "you're the captain for Christ's sake, where was your sense last night? I nearly flipped when I heard you were behind this! And you," he glared at Johnny, "if you even so much as sniff a beer again, you're off this team!" Johnny looked up shocked and ashamed. "I mean it," Curran said, "and I'll talk to you later about it." Then, shaking his head, he turned to Cooper. "And I don't even want to be in the same room as you," he said, looking at the goalie with a mean stare. "Just remember, you would've been off this team if you were arrested." He paused for a moment, the shame seeping in on us like some invisible, odourless gas. Up until that point, I think we all felt a little contentedness — and a lot of relief — in just being alive that day. Physically, we were numb, the kind of numbness you feel when the mind hasn't had time to decipher and deal with trauma, but Curran stung us when he accused: "Did this year mean nothing to you?"

It was a vicious thing to say, but how could we answer without sounding trite. So we were silent, pulses beginning to race. Frustration came, too, because we knew we deserved it all.

"Your teammate's in the hospital, the Chronicle keeps calling, God knows what you've done to your parents, and there's a game tonight!" he said. "Do you realize the fucking mess you've caused?"

We shifted our eyes between each other.

Curran shook his head like a judge then pronounced the sentence. "You all know the rules: Anyone who misses curfew is suspended for a game, at least. But since this was more than just missing curfew and because tonight's game means shit and everyone knows it, you're all suspended for three." We groaned, our heads sank, and he twisted in the wound. "And that's going easy."

Brendan slouched in his chair and pulled down his cap even more so it covered his eyes.

"If anyone asks me," Curran continued, "I'll tell 'em we still have talent and we can win these games without you seven. It's bullshit. You're going to watch your teammates work for nothing. They're gonna lose these next three. We all know it. But if we go out in the first round, if someone gets hurt on the ice, who's fault do you think it's gonna be?"

Another question unanswered and Curran finished by holding up two patches in front of Brendan and me. "You're going to have to earn these back." He left the room as Brendan eyed his captain's 'C' and I watched my 'A' sitting on the table in front of us. Untouchables both.

Raycliffe dismissed us, saying we left him with much work to do. Johnny stayed to talk to Curran and the rest of us went to visit Jesse Sullivan, who was being released from Kildare General. He told us not to worry, he would be back banging heads again in time for the second round. His parents, who exchanged no words with us, took him home as soon as the paperwork was finished.

We moved on to the Chouinards, where the Russians would gather their belongings. Over night, Skurilev decided that he would use the remainder of his new fortune from the trading-card company to pay for a hotel room for Rushchenko and himself until the season was complete. Even though Mr. Chouinard sounded welcoming over the phone, the guys were scared he might not have calmed down yet, so it was decided Brendan and I should be the ones to approach the house.

"Scott, Brendan," Mr. Chouinard said, a copy of the *Chronicle* in his hand, when he opened the door. "Thank God you're all right." He peered over our shoulders to the carload. "Are they coming in?"

"I think they still feel bad," I said.

"Well, they should," he said before waving an arm to the car, "but you boys have been through enough."

Brigitte came slowly from the kitchen, said hi and moved to Dmitri's side. "Are you guys okay?" she asked.

Skurilev and Rushchenko explained their plan to the Chouinards and the parents agreed it would be for the best if the two billets moved out. They hurried to pack their bags, and Brigitte told me I should call Michelle. "She's really worried," she said, in a knowing tone. I asked if I could use the phone and when I called, Michelle said we should talk and she would be right over. Brendan and Coop took the Russians to check in at Kildare Inn and I left the Chouinards with my girlfriend. We drove to our spot on Caledonia Hill.

"I was scared when I heard," Michelle said.

"I know," I said. "I'm sorry."

"Me, too." She reached out a hand and I cupped it between mine. "I love you, Scott."

I turned to face her, but didn't say anything.

"I mean it," she said through glassy eyes.

"Michelle . . ."

I paused for a long time. The longer the silence and the longer I stared into her eyes, the more grim her face grew. I looked down, then out the windshield and, after a little while, back at her. I wiped a tear from her face. By then, we both knew I couldn't return the words; and though we talked a lot and said we could try, some things about relationships remain universal, no matter how young or old you are. If it's there, it's there, and it's beautiful. If not, then no matter how much you wish it to be, no matter how much you try for it, no matter how much you pretend it is, love won't come when forced.

Michelle Lessard and I ran in the same circles, so we still saw each other after that day. We said hi and how are you and that's good, but we never talked again. Sometimes, politeness is all you can give, and the most you should expect.

When I watched her drive away, I felt loss and a hollowness like grief, and I felt tremendous guilt, for not being the one with the broken heart.

Not since minor hockey had I or most of my teammates reached a postseason. We all imagined it would happen, however, each of us dreaming of the moment we scored the goal or made the save that ensured a title. But none of our fantasies began like this.

Gary Curran's prediction was correct. Except for Dion Marcelle, the Kougars were uncompetitive. Dion scored four impressive goals in the first two playoff games we were suspended for, but that was not nearly enough as the Kougars were embarrassed in front of our fans. The prospect of the team's magic season melting away before the spring thaw had not seemed possible just a few days earlier. But now the *Chronicle* was predicting we would not overcome the deficit against Otter Lake because we no longer had home-ice advantage and were faced with having to win four of the final five games. Even more insulting was word that our opponent's general manager had already begun selling tickets for the second round!

As I marched back on the ice, I remember thinking that after all my teammates and I had gone through, after everything we had shown, we still had much to prove. Our coach let us know it, too, by not being there. Tyler took a scouting trip to watch Coldbury, a more dangerous and much-improved team according to reports, the night of our return from suspension. That meant, for one day, Clyde Parker got his wish. Raycliffe left him to run practice, and, from above, Curran spied him as much as us.

"Okay, green and whites, let's go!" Parker yelled. "Right now! Get in line!"

Two boxes full of sports vests were in his hands and he slid them to centre ice before moving toward Tony Lacroix, the first player in line. Clyde pointed at Lacroix's chest and said, "Green." He went through our line, slowly, designating each of us either green or white. As soon as he did, we skated to the boxes and picked out a vest of our colour. When the sides were complete, Clyde approached centre ice with a puck and blew into his whistle.

"Okay, twenty minutes; I want you to go all out," he said. "Change lines yourself, winners watch losers do up-and-backs. Let's go!"

Clyde had purposely not balanced the sides. The green team was bent toward defence, with Johnny and Jesse, Chaput's line and Cooper in goal. The white team had Brendan and me, the Russians and the Gords.

Parker dropped the puck and continued to play the role of referee. He coached, too. Whenever there was a stoppage, he would yell instructions before restarting the game. Lacroix was told not to be afraid to rag the puck behind his net and Tahani "One-Axe" Kohono got scolded for not skating hard to chip the puck out of his end. All of us, though, were found guilty of one thing: not being intense enough.

"This isn't fuckin' ringette!" he shouted after Brendan only gave Manny Rivers a lovetap in the corner. "Now let's see some checks!"

He blew his whistle and dropped the puck again. "That's it! That's it!" he shouted to Dion when he pinned one of the Gords against the boards. He clapped his hands and carefully enunciated, "Good," when Dmitri

Rushchenko took the man, not the puck. But there was still no score and we were starting to get tired, and Clyde knew it. "Did I mention those up-and-backs, boys, are going to be backwards," he said.

That was enough motivation for me. I came off the bench with purpose and forced Chaput against the boards, freeing the puck for Brendan. He drew a couple of guys to him, then dumped the puck off to Vlastimil Skurilev, who quickly tipped it over to me. I was one-on-one versus Johnny Carruthers, who was shadowing me perfectly with his stick stretched out and head up watching mine. But that's not what Clyde Parker wanted.

"Hit him!" Parker yelled. "C'mon, take him out!"

Johnny made a move toward me and I put the puck between his legs, then got around him to pick it up again as we crossed the blueline. He regained position quickly, getting his shoulder up against mine and reaching after the puck with one hand on his stick. "Hit him!" Parker shouted. But Johnny kept holding me off with his shoulder while trying to make the play with his stick. He had tied me up so well, I couldn't take a shot — and it still wasn't enough. "C'mon, put a lick on him!" Parker screamed. By now, I had lost control of the puck and Cooper was coming out of his goal to cover it up. I could feel Johnny easing up on me, too, but when Parker shrieked, "Hit him!" so loud it sounded like a thundercrack and Johnny just reacted. He put both gloves on my shoulder and shoved me to the ice. It was a clean play, but I was still pissed and got up ready to nail him. But Johnny looked more hurt than I was, so I dropped my fist. He skated to the bench and put a towel over his face.

He was under a lot of pressure, a lot more than any of us knew. Curran had told Johnny that he would have to tell his parents about the drinking, maybe get him into a program, or something. And if Minnesota State ever found out about that . . .

But Johnny had enough time to fix things himself and Curran was going to help. After the season, arrangements were going to be made for him to see a guidance counselor regularly and Johnny was going to follow through once he left Kildare. Johnny was supposed to talk to Gary, or us, if anything was wrong or needed. (He never did, though. When we asked, he would shrug it off and say he was okay.) Gary said the most important thing was for Johnny to focus on hockey, concentrate on that. It was the best thing he had going.

I liked Johnny a lot. I really did. But there was something about him that just made you uncomfortable. It was an odd discomfort. When I thought of the Ladouceur brothers, I felt a helpless kind of unsettledness and when I broke up with Michelle, it was more of a shameful guilt. With Johnny, it was sort of a mix of the two. Maybe that was because I didn't really know what was wrong, and was bashful about prying too much. But Johnny's demeanour heightened everyone's discomfort, and maybe that's how it should be. His quietness, his solitude, the drinking, the way he hung his head and frowned so much, looking back, I see now it was all a cry for help. One none of us really answered. We tried and Gary Curran came closest to doing something about it, but Johnny was adrift, and I just knew being around someone as grating as Clyde Parker so much wasn't good for him.

"We gotta start sending messages," Clyde said. He was continuing practice after Johnny's hit on me. "If they wanna come near our goal, they're gonna pay for it."

Our side had a line change and I glanced up to Curran on my way to the bench. He had his eyes fixed on the scene, and seemed concerned. Randy Delisle was there, too, and looked intrigued. On the next shift, Dion Marcelle scored for the greens and Clyde called the game. And it was a welcome end, even for those of us who lost. "All right, gimme ten," Clyde said and paused before adding with emphasis: "*Backwards.*"

The guys on our side dropped our shoulders and some moaned as we began the wearying exercise. Clyde was happy as he skated to the bench to greet the winners. He patted Johnny on the shoulders and started talking to him while jabbing his stick through the air, pointing to the spot where Johnny had hit me. But Johnny, who was usually attentive to instructions, just looked off and nodded like he had to.

"Okay," Clyde said after we completed our ten trips up and down the ice, "we got breakouts next. Now, I want the forwards to stay . . ." But Clyde couldn't finish his thought, because Curran, with two fingers in his mouth, whistled down.

All of us, Clyde and Randy Delisle included, looked up and our general manager called, "Power play."

Everyone turned to Clyde. He was leering at Curran, who tapped his wristwatch three times. Clyde got the point.

"Alright, sorry, boys," he said. "My mistake. We're running outta time here, so let's work on P.P."

Randy Delisle, pen and notebook ready, immediately went up to speak to Curran. It was weeks before I found out what was said, all I knew then was Clyde Parker probably wasn't going to be running any more practices for us.

"This is some scrimmage," Randy said.

"Well, Clyde knows how he wants things to be done," Curran said.

"Does his way mesh with your way?"

"Ha-ha, no comment."

"Clyde's a tough coach."

"Tough-minded, I'd say, but fair."

"You know anything about his past?" Randy spoke with a knowing hint, causing our G.M. to stand up straight and look the reporter in the eye. Gary then shook his head. "He had a run-in with the minor hockey folks out west just before he moved here."

"What kind of run-in?" Curran asked and braced himself.

"There was a complaint about the way he was treating players. Or mistreating, whatever you like."

"What?" Curran was shocked. "What kind of mistreatment?"

"I'm still searching on that, but probably some parent got sick of seeing his kid getting chewed out every practice."

"That's not much of a reach."

"No, it's not," Randy said and paused for a second. "What do you think of it?"

"I don't know what to think." Gary sat and put a hand to his chin. "So what happened to him after that?"

"Looks like Clyde made a clean break," Randy said. "Got out before the shit hit the fan, but the complaint was still filed."

"When did this all happen?"

"The year he moved here; almost six years ago now."

"And you're saying he came right here and began working with the team just like that?"

Randy nodded.

"No one did a background check!"

Randy chuckled and began to make a wisecrack, but Curran beat him to the punchline. "Yeah, yeah, I know: Lannie Leroux."

"So, still nothing to say?"

"No, not until I talk to Clyde myself."

"When will that be?"

Curran rubbed his hands over his face. "You going with a story on this?"

"No, not yet."

"You waiting for a comment from us?"

Randy grinned and did nothing else.

Curran sighed and said, "Off the record?"

"Sure."

"I was planning on making a change anyway. What I saw today just convinced me more and if what you say is true, that seals it," Curran said. "But not now. We're in the playoffs and the team's just getting over that nonsense on the bridge. I just want them to be able to focus on hockey." Randy nodded. "But if you find out anything else, let me know."

"Otherwise . . .," Randy said, stretching out the word.

Curran huffed then looked at the reporter and spoke with sincerity. "When the season ends," he said, "you'll have a story."

40

Is on da house," said Nehru Ramsingh, the West Indian manager of Finnegan's, who, on more than one occasion, has tried to introduce Jamaican beef patties and ox-tail soup to the menu only to be foiled by the franchise's head office. "You boys bringin' me beeg business, ya know."

"Oh, yeah. How so?" Tim Chaput asked. He was hoping to keep him talking so he could get more material for his impression of Nehru.

"Yeah, mon," Nehru said while serving us our usual bland cheeseburgers and chicken nachos. "You boys been kickin' some serious ass and they been comin' in ta celebrate. Before game, is full. After game, is full. Got me workin' round da clock."

Yes, we were winning again. Kildare watched with pride as we triumphed over Otter Lake, taking four straight games. Then, with all players healthy and ready to show what we could do, we quickly dispatched the Moosehead Wheat Kings and marched into the semifinals, a round away from a likely showdown with the Coldbury Chevaliers for the league championship.

With hope alive, our group of young men, twenty-one strong, had become revered citizens. Everyone, it seemed, wanted to be around us, to wish us luck, offer advice, recount a favourite game or play, even present us with a charm.

"Here, Scott, try dis, mon," Nehru said. He put a tiny bottle of tabasco sauce next to me. "Made juss fa you, help ya score, ya know."

I thanked him and he punched my biceps before walking back to the kitchen with a delightful smile. Before Nehru was out of sight, and before we could eat, Casey Milgrew, a career councilman, approached our table with his politician's grin and forwardness.

"Let me shake your hands, lads," he said and rudely took my arm away from my meal. "By gosh, you're doin' wonders for this town. We've all forgotten that crazy incident on the bridge, not to mention old Lannie, too." He winked as he finished his handshakes.

"Yeah, I just hope no one catches Lacroix's mono," Tim Chaput said. "That would really suck."

Milgrew was startled and when Tony Lacroix lifted his plate up to offer a fry, the councilman looked grim. Lacroix played it up, too, with an impish smile and hacking cough. "No, no, thanks," Milgrew stuttered and, trying his best not to appear disgusted, put a palm up to keep back the fries. Then he pulled out some folded bills from his pocket and put down three twenties. "This one's on me, lads," he said. "Keep muckin' out there."

He rushed from the table, wiping a hand on his pants, causing Chaput and Lacroix to crack up. I was about to go tell Milgrew his money wasn't needed when Chaput elbowed me and said, "Forget it, this'll get us two cases."

I looked at him disapprovingly. "Don't worry about it, man," Lacroix said. "The old guy just wanted to make himself feel good."

After Milgrew, came Fat Willie Savard, one of the loudmouth fans who used to boo us, but now wanted something from us. "Can I get your autograph, kid?" he asked, and passed a napkin and pen to Skurilev, who signed it quickly and calmly, like he had been practicing. Other autograph seekers followed, then more politicians to shake our hands and former Kougars to tell us about the good ol' days, all as we tried to dine, causing Skurilev to deduce, "Thees must be what eet's like in NHL."

While the townsfolks' adoration took our egos to new heights, Tyler Raycliffe was determined to pull them back down. "Get those grins off your faces," he said to Chaput and Lacroix specifically during our final practice before the third round. "You haven't won a thing yet!"

A coach can't be a coach without observing, and what Raycliffe saw in us was as unsettling as the sight and smell of rotting equipment idling in afternoon heat. Some of us horsed around during drills, trying to outstick-handle the Russians when we should have been helping them with break-out schemes. Others practiced new ways of celebrating a goal, including Tahani "One-Axe" Kohono doing a few steps of a tribal dance. And there were the less talented players who became lackadaisical because their already limited ice time was cut further, to one or two shifts a game, once the playoffs began. They loped around the rink with the sullen looks of the underemployed.

None of this sat well with Raycliffe. He instructed us to huddle in front of him, then delivered a harsh assessment.

"I just don't understand this. You're eight wins away from being god damn champions. You've got every bloody scout you could possibly want watchin' ya. Some of you are leavin' this town once we're through here. I figured, 'Yeah, they'll wanna work their tails off. They'll work for this town and for themselves and for each other. Hell, maybe even for me.' But what do I get?" He paused with his mouth and eyes open like a shark. "This!" He held his hands out as he skated backwards, moving away from us like he had just been ostracized. "A bunch of superstars you are, eh? The whole town thinks you're hot shit. Now so do you. Well, I don't. Neither does Timberton. Neither does Coldbury, who haven't lost a game in the playoffs, by the way. But, hey, who am I? You boys just show up for the game tomorrow. But remember no team's ever won anything without everyone workin' for it. I hope you lads can find a way to be the first."

He reached the boards and turned his back as he began to head up the ramp, and away from the ice. Then he got the desired response.

"Coach, wait," Brendan said and skated away from the pack. "We wanna skate."

41

Before the first game against Timberton, Brendan was reinstalled as captain and I got my 'A' back. We led the team onto the ice as more than twenty-two hundred fans, all on their feet, cheered and sang to The Tragically Hip's "50 Mission Cap."

The energy in the building made Kildare feel like a bustling place and the fact that it was awards night only punctuated the mood. After a short warmup, our players stood on the bench as a red carpet was rolled to centre ice and a table full of awards followed. Tyler Raycliffe and Gary Curran walked out to applause while a dolled up Lannie Leroux struggled to stay seated in the very first row.

As Tyler presented small trophies to every player to honour our participation on the team, he said something funny or kind about each of us. He then gave way to Gary, who would present all but the final two individual awards. The general manager, eager to get the game started and fearful of Lannie going on and on, made it quick, saying a few generous words before presenting Brendan with the MVP award, the goal-scoring trophy to me, Skurilev as rookie of the year and Jesse Sullivan, the best defenceman.

He then began to introduce Lannie and we harrassed Tim Chaput.

"Here she comes, Chaput," Jesse laughed; "Make sure you pucker up, big boy," Tony Lacroix said and hung an arm around his friend's neck; "Just don't bend over to take a bow," Chris Cooper warned. To each joke, Chaput responded with a "Fuck you," "Fuck you, too," or "Very funny, mother fucker." Intermittently, he would cause me to grin when he threw in something such as, "MacGregor, if I ever find out you were behind this, I'll kill you, you fuck!"

Luckily, Gary Curran, not Chaput, was holding the mic.

"Ladies and gentlemen," Curran began, "we have a special guest here tonight, someone familiar to all of us. He wanted badly to be a part of this night and we've done our best to accommodate him. I'm sure you'll do the same. So here, to present, for the first time, the Lannie Leroux award, Lannie himself." Curran looked behind him and pointed an arm. Strutting out, white teeth shining for all and eyebrows newly waxed, Lannie waved a hand like a scrutinized politician as boos and whistles were hurled his way. He was wearing an elegant, not-too-tight fitting, black evening gown that, believe it or not, he almost pulled off. The shawl covering his bulky shoulders and chest was a big help in this. About his neck, though, was a gem-studded choker that was a bit much. As was his speech.

"Friends, Kildareans, fellow fans," Lannie started, sending several spectators to the washroom and concession stand, "many great accomplishments, in history and in our everyday lives, no matter how pitiful and meaningless, go unrecognized, even, I fear, unappreciated. One of these is the work of young hockey players that some of us have come to call defensive forwards." He paused for effect and looked up. "Tonight, we are here to honour such a player. But first, some history . . ." Catcalls joined the boos as Lannie was urged to "Get on with it." Of course, he did not, rambling on about the past glories of his family and of his own, much of which was news to us, saying how happy he was that his name will forever be linked to the Kougars, and begging for recognition himself. These pleas, however, fell on deaf ears as the crowd spat jeers and insults and curses so cruel and loud that eventually even Lannie couldn't put up with it. "Oh, alright!" he finally shouted then took a second to gather himself. "The Lannie Leroux Award and all the responsibility it carries, goes to . . ." He actually had an envelope, and took his time opening it. "Tim Chaput! Tim Chaput, ladies and gents!" Clapping his hands, Lannie tried to look stunned while Jesse and Cooper all but hoisted Chaput onto the ice then gave him a shove toward the lectern. The fans, relieved, cheered as Chaput skated slowly to receive his award, which had a bronze statue of Lannie holding a hockey stick in a shooting position, the blade curved the wrong way. When Chaput got close enough, Lannie, quick as a trap, reached out and grabbed him by the shoulders, kissing him on both cheeks and applying a hug before our dumbfounded teammate could react. We all started to howl and some of us urged Lannie to give him the tongue. With that, Chaput had had it. He turned and raced back to the bench without taking the award.

"Tim, Tim," Curran called, but with no luck.

Chaput had already escaped up the ramp to the locker room, swearing under his breath. He left Lannie standing with the award, looking like a groom with a ring and no bride. (Or the other way around.) Angrily, he stepped to the microphone again and spat, "Well, how rude!"

Curran acted fast. He took the award out of Lannie's hands, told him he would make sure Chaput got it and asked the audience to please give Lannie a big round. Enough of them obliged that Lannie felt compelled to take a bow. Then he walked off, slowly, spinning like a model.

"Well, we look forward to seeing Lannie doing this again next year, don't we?" Curran said and got no response from the crowd. But Lannie apparently appreciated the gesture as he waved to the G.M. and retook his seat. Relieved, Curran continued. "Now, I know we all want to get on with the game, but we do have one more award to go, folks, and this one is very special. And, if you all bear with us, I think you'll agree." He stopped for a moment until the chatter died down. "Okay, this last award is a brand new one, too, and what makes it so great is that it comes from the players. Our fine boys here have gotten together and chosen a teammate they feel deserves to be honoured, not just for skill, but for heart and dedication and hard work. All the things maybe we don't always see and maybe the people in the media who vote on the other awards don't always see, but they're what a teammate really notices. So, I'm gonna get a couple of the fellas up here — captain Brendan Kowalczek and assistant captain Scott MacGregor, come on up here guys — to present the first Kougars Team Spirit Award."

Brendan and I skated toward Curran as the fans applauded. After thanking everyone for the cheers, Brendan said into the microphone: "This award came about when Scott and me were talking one day and we both agreed that this one guy on our team had worked his butt off to get better, and it would be really great if he got recognized for it."

With a look, he gave me my cue.

"Yeah," I said and surveyed our bench until I found the face I wanted then smiled, "when I came to training camp this year, there was this skinny kid who spoke with a French accent and looked too goofy on skates to be a hockey player. And he didn't play real great in the beginning, either,

but Dion, you've really turned things around for yourself, and we appreciate all the effort you've put in and you've made us a better team, bud."

This time, I looked at Brendan, who was smiling for the same reason I
was: From Dion's tender brown eyes, we could tell we were doing the right
thing. Brendan picked up the award and said, "That's right. So from all
the guys, we want to present this to you; you deserve it, man."

With his hand around the award, Brendan gave a punch in the air
toward Dion. In tears, he came off the bench to loud cheers to collect it.
We gave him a hug like he had scored a goal and Gary Curran said, "Dion
Marcelle, everybody!"

Even though he was wiping his eyes, Dion, smiling, was still able to find
his parents in the stands. His dad held up two triumphant fists and Dion
lowered his head to hide the rush of new tears. When he did, Mr.
Marcelle mouthed, "Thank you," to Brendan and me.

42

When I saw my dad next, he was acting like my grandfather. He wanted to know why I wasn't getting more ice time — "You should be on PK, Scotty. You gotta have your best players killing penalties. Any coach knows that" —, what strategy changes we were going to make, and who was injured and how badly. It was easy to understand his interest and anxiety; after all, we were only one victory away from advancing to the COHL Finals.

"How about these boys, eh, John?" Mr. Kowalczek said after my parents arrived the day of Game Five.

"You bet, Murray. You bet," Dad said, looking at me. "All that hard work and wishful thinking sure paid off."

Mom and Dad, taking up the Kowalczeks on their invitation, were there for an early supper. The Marcelles came, as well. After the accident on the bridge, Mr. Marcelle was less friendly with the guys on the team. He still said hi and asked how we were, but it was obvious he was upset and disappointed — for good reason — that we had been involved in a crash after leaving a bar. That changed after the awards ceremony. He and his wife were quite grateful to Brendan and me, and to the Kowalczeks, too, for their generosity.

"One day, Pam," Mrs. Marcelle said, "I will have you and Murray over for dinner."

"Oh, don't fuss," Mrs. K said. "You folks are still settling in."

"How is Kildare, Josee?" my mom asked.

"It's splendid," Mrs. Marcelle answered. "We miss Quebec, yes, but it's nice and quiet. Dion likes it. Likes the boys and the team, the school. That's the important thing."

"Well, that son of yours is turning out to be quite the little player," Mrs. K said. "He's just a zippy thing the way he skates around like that."

Dion's mom laughed and said he couldn't have done it without our help. She said Dion was really going to miss having Brendan and me around the next season. Mrs. K said she would, too, and Mom said she's missed me since the time I was fifteen. "What can you do?" she said. "They have to follow their dreams."

Supper went pretty quick because Brendan, Dion and I had to be at the rink early, but I still had enough time to perform a very important function, one I had promised my parents I would do with them there.

"Wait, Scott," Mom said. "We brought you something for that."

She handed me a gold pen with my name inscribed on it. I took it, turned it in the middle to reveal the tip and signed my name on my next step in life.

"Alright, Scotty," Dad said as he shook my shoulders.

"We're so proud of you, dear," Mom said. She kissed my cheek while the Kowalczeks and Marcelles clapped and Brendan offered his hand, congratulating me on choosing Rochester State.

With my decision made, there was relief. I had realized a goal, and felt proud and confident because of it. In the game, I had the extra focus ath-

letes chase, the concentration that allows every task to be precise. I
passed crisply, delivered strong checks and wended my way around the
rink with ease. But it wasn't enough. I wanted to do something special
that night, to give it a memory. And Tyler Raycliffe would help me. With
about five minutes to go and the game tied 1-1, he put our line on. We
controlled the play, keeping it in Timberton's zone, pushing the puck
around the boards, trying hard to get a good shot. None came, though, and
we headed off after the Lumberjacks cleared the puck for a change of their
own. However, I got tangled at centre with one of their defencemen, making me late. Frantically, I fought to get free and once I did, I put my head
down and rushed toward the bench. It was then, while I was on my way,
that something made me stop. Even though, I didn't know where the puck
was, I believed I could hear Tyler whispering, even amid the din of the
crowd, "Now, Scott, now." I looked up and saw Tahani "One-Axe" Kohono
with a skate already on the boards, ready to jump on to take my place. I
took another stride to the bench and my gaze shifted to Brendan. He had
done a doubletake, looking behind me, then past me, then behind me
again. His jaw was open. I took another stride and turned my eyes to
Tyler. He was staring at me, dead on. *Now, Scott. Now!*

I turned up ice, swinging my head around in time to see Tony Lacroix
snapping a pass toward me. I lasooed the feed with my blade, taking it on
my backhand then pushing it in front of me, just before I crossed into
Lumberjacks territory. Alone.

After two quick strides toward the goaltender, I began to glide, my
skates cutting a straight line through the ice. Then, as I prepared to make
my move, I pointed my toes in to slow. By first faking to my backhand, I
got the goalie to his knees, when I pulled the puck back to my forehand,

he was sprawled on his side. He stretched desperately over his head with his trapper like a man caught in deep, rapid-flowing water. But there was no rescue. I had released the puck. Roofing it just inside the crossbar. Flicking on the red light. Inciting loud cheers. Putting the Kildare Kougars into the Finals.

Leaping with my hands raised, I circled the goal and skated to my teammates. Once those on the ice congratulated me, I moved to the bench, knocking fists with half of the players there before Tyler Raycliffe, foot on boards, reached over and grabbed me by the front collar. I skittered, my skates bouncing off the ice, as he yanked me to him, his eyebrows furrowed and his eyes flared. His forehead was nearly touching mine when he yelled into my face: "That's it! That's it right there! That's why you're gonna be a pro!"

43

A re you worried?" Randy Delisle asked me.

"You mean about Tallard?"

"Yeah, him or one of their goons?"

It was the day before the Finals began and we were in the equipment room, where I was working on putting more of a curve on my sticks. "No, I mean, it's the Finals," I said. "I expect them to be playing hard and I know I'm gonna be finishing my checks." I stopped to compare my stick with one of Brendan's Bauers. (He and the other centres — Dion, Chaput and Mackilwraith — didn't curve their blades because that made it harder to steer and pass.) "But if they want to come after me that's fine, I'm ready. And I'm sure Brendan would love not getting all the attention out there."

When he asked his next question, Randy spoke slowly, like people do when they give a warning. "You've heard about The Bruise?"

I looked at him and nodded.

"I've seen him; he's a mean sonofagun."

Randy wasn't kidding. The OHL had banned Bruce Broussard for life after he started uttering threats and wheeling his stick around like a mad man following a game. Supposedly, he was upset at the other team's coach for not putting on his star player in the third period, that cost The Bruise ice time and a chance to do what he was becoming known for: ruining careers. Already, in only his first season, he had broken one guy's face in a fight, wrecked another's ankle and smashed a kid so hard into the glass he had a concussion that took months to get over. He got kicked out of the OHL just before the playoffs and Coldbury didn't waste any time in picking him up for their blueline.

"You know, with this Tallard thing and you fellas winning the league, they've been saying they got a score to settle with you lads," Randy said.

"Yeah, but they're the champs, too," I said and paused again to hold Brendan's stick up to mine to make sure the curve wasn't too pronounced. Satisfied, I tested my new blade by flicking a roll of tape into a corner, then said, "They're not going to do anything stupid."

"Okay, Scott. That's it for now." Randy shut off his tape recorder and turned to go. "By the way, congratulations on Raw-cha-cha. It's a good school."

In Game One of the Finals, it seemed like all of Kildare had found a way to get into Leroux Arena. People were standing in the aisles and the tops of heads were visible all the way to the back wall, bobbing like they were on a school bus as fans bounced on tiptoes to get a glimpse of the action. Banners held by little kids, with phrases such as "Kougars Rule" and "Give Coldbury the Chill," waved.

"This is it lads," Tyler said before the game began. "Hit 'em hard and go right after 'em. I believe in you." When he held his hand out, we all aped him. "Okay, on three. One, two, three . . ."

"Kougars!"

The whistle blew and our line moved into starting position. The puck dropped and so did Alain Tallard's gloves.

"C'mon, vite," he said to me. "Let's go." He threw off his helmet with its faceguard and held his fists up, waiting for me to do the same.

"C'mon, MacGregor! Take him!" I heard someone from the crowd shout. I was near the Chevaliers' bench and could hear them pounding their fists on top of the boards like old men urging a horse at the track. If I didn't meet his challenge, it would be a let down to my team; we would have looked weak and easy to intimidate. If I dropped my hands, stayed submissive, drew the penalty, I would have gotten booed, called a wuss. And, if I chose to skate away, to turn my back without care, it would have been a shock and some might have even understood it as a statement, but hockey players don't do that sort of thing.

It's part of the game, I told myself.

"C'mon," Tallard said again. And I did.

Launching my arms up, I threw my gloves in the air and flung my helmet to the ice. Tallard, two inches shorter than me, came with a fist that hit my shoulder. I retaliated with a punch that barely scraped him. He brought his hand up to my neck, but I batted it away and grabbed hold of his collar with my left hand, and began to deliver rights to his head. It wasn't long before he fell and buried his face in the ice. He held his hands over his head as I kept hitting him until the linesmen came to break us up. One official pulled me away and I pushed my sleeves up as I skated toward the penalty box. My teammates stood on the bench and banged their sticks delightfully on the boards. The fans cheered me and jeered Tallard. "Hey, you're a frog, not a turtle," someone called to the Quebecer.

Then Bruce "The Bruise" Broussard introduced himself. He skated over as I was heading into the box and said, "Next time, it's me." His voice was low and dull, like it came from under earth. He stood a head above me and had fiery red hair and a full beard. Before the door closed on me, he made sure to give another look with his small, blue eyes that looked as cold as the ocean. It was then, I know, that he saw fear on my face.

Tallard and I both received ten-minute penalties for fighting, but he was also assessed an instigating minor that gave us a two-minute power play. Just twenty seconds into the man-advantage, Dion Marcelle set up Brendan at the side of the net with a cross-ice pass for a 1-0 lead. Before Tallard and I got out, the Chevaliers were down by two after Skurilev skated through the defence on an end-to-end rush to score his league-high twelfth goal of the playoffs. Giguere slammed an open hand to the glass behind his bench and the crowd began to chant, "Coldbury sucks! Coldbury sucks!"

Giguere, needing offense and to avoid penalties, had to keep The Bruise on the bench for most of the game. After Skurilev's goal, Tyler kept a winger back at all times, aiming to cause reckless dump-ins and turnovers. The scheme worked as Chris Cooper faced only 16 shots and earned his second shutout of the playoffs as we claimed a 4-0 win, the Kougars' first against Coldbury in more than four years.

"Three more, ladies. Just three more," Brendan said after we walked into the locker room, elated.

"The Tremblay Trophy," Jesse Sullivan said contemplatively and with a grin, like a man ready to cross a finish line yards ahead of his competition. "I'm gonna hold it like this" — he put his hands in front of his chest as if he was waiting for a baby to be placed in them — "and just give it a kiss."

"Can wee dreenk vodka from eet?" Rushchenko asked.

"Yeah, but no orange juice," Cooper said, getting a laugh from Jesse and me.

"Hold your horses, lads," equipment manager Peter Jones said. "Don't get overconfident now. It's a long way from bein' over."

How dare he?, we all thought. Of course we were going to win. It was destiny. I mean, the whole business of us having to suffer through Lannie Leroux's tyranny and putting up with all that losing for three seasons just to build a strong team that got along despite everything and understood where we came from. The fortune of having obtained a talent like Skurilev, not to mention Dion's emergence after his own battle. If it wasn't biblical, it certainly was Hollywood. And we basked in the anticipation of the happy ending. Unfortunately, real life has a harsh way of rewriting scripts at the most inopportune times.

The Chevaliers proved to be as hard to conquer as a villain from any horror movie. While the first game was a battle of skill, Game Two was a contest of wits. Giguere changed much of his gameplan overnight, trying to play his top line against Skurilev, Dion and Kohono. However, Tyler, who had the last line change as the home coach, shied away from that matchup. He preferred to check Tallard, centre Sebastien Gendron and left winger Michel Theodore with Chaput's line or our line. So, throughout the duel, the two coaches jockeyed players on and off the bench in hopes of getting their way and staying ahead of each other. Giguere also implored his squad to stay patient as he scouted us, waiting for the one bad change or poor breakout that would make the difference. He put The Bruise on infrequently and he wasn't a factor, except for one check on Brendan that got us nervous. When our captain went down, the crowd hushed like it was saying a collective prayer, but he got up quickly and made it to the bench with ease.

"You okay?" I asked.

He nodded and said, "Yeah, he's got nothin'."

Tyler wanted to keep everyone focused and hollered, "Let's go! Let's go! No stupid plays!" then clapped his hands excitedly. Clyde Parker was intense, too. He was always chirping out instructions and quick scolds that were said and gone before we could take issue. One time he even yelled at me for not coming back on defence. "Don't cherrypick!" he shouted and when I turned around, he was already in someone else's ear.

Parker was more hyped than usual and that made him a nuisance, but Raycliffe didn't notice. His standoff with Giguere was taking all his concentration and with less than eight minutes remaining in the third — and the game in a scoreless tie — Tyler decided to make his play. He put Brendan and me on the ice, but sat Manny Rivers. Instead, he tapped Skurilev on the helmet, teaming his top three forwards against Coldbury's third line. Giguere reacted quickly, making a swift change to get Tallard's line on. He realized Tyler had taken the reins off and that we were looking for an all-out rush to the goal. By making the change, the Chevaliers not only negated our speed but they gained an advantage because of Skurilev's underwhelming defence. With his immense scoring ability, defence just did not have to be a priority for Skurilev. Usually, one of his linemates, either Dion or Tahani, was ordered to stay back, just in case. That wasn't so with Brendan and me on that rush. Coldbury took advantage of that by trapping Skurilev through the middle of the ice, then stealing the puck before he reached the blueline. Upon the turnover, Tallard promptly headed up ice and Gendron fed him right away as they began a two-on-one break against Jesse Sullivan.

Tallard passed back to Gendron as they crossed into our zone. As the closest backchecker to Tallard, I sprinted desperately after his blue jersey with the No. 13 crested on the back. Crossing into our end, I was intent on breaking up a pass to him. Gendron glided toward our goal, the puck stationed on the blade of his stick like an arrow in a crossbow. I was within two feet of Tallard when the puck was released. The pass floated over Sullivan's stick as Gendron targeted his teammate's blade at the side of the goal crease. Chris Cooper slid a pad over and Tallard lifted his blade a couple of inches off the ice to take a swing at the puck, but it was not there to hit. My aim was accomplished. Tallard did not receive the pass. I took it for him, committing a crucial error by pushing my stick out at a puck in front of my goal. I had lunged my blade and before I was aware of what I had done, it was too late to pull it back. The puck was past Cooper, whose glare I felt as I pushed my neck back and heaved in a sigh. With my eyes closed, I skated to the endboards and knocked my head against the glass while the red light flashed on my face like a spotlight.

The boos poured down from above, but they weren't enough to drown the celebratory hoots from the Coldbury players.

"Don't worry about it," Coop said before I skated back to the bench.

"We'll get it back," Jesse said when I passed him.

Although it did not remove my guilt, other teammates also offered understanding and forgiveness. Nevertheless, there was one on our side who did not want to vindicate me. I sat on the bench with my head buried and eyes closed when a voice began to whisper in my ear.

"You stink," it said. "That's the worst fuckin' play I've ever seen." The voice was echoing my thoughts, reinforcing everything I wanted to tear down. *You're shit. You're not good enough. You'll never get anywhere.* All of that was implied, and malice, too.

"The worst fuckin' play I've ever seen," it repeated, slower and with more bite.

I lowered my head more, I remember, and it seemed like it would have been easy to sink into where Clyde Parker was pushing me. Into despair, doubt, self-loathing. But I was stubborn, thankfully, and refused to fall for it.

My head snapped in his direction and I glowered at him. Then I stood. My fists were clenched and I was ready to lift them, but his eyes were gleaming now and they had me scared stiff. I don't know how long we were there, staring at each other, waiting for something to happen, but it was definitely long enough for someone to notice.

"Clyde!" Tyler yelled. Parker didn't take his eyes off me and Tyler yelled his name again, then came over and tugged him by the arm. "You missed a change! What the fuck's going on?"

Parker said nothin', and Tyler shifted his gaze between the two of us, his face confused and worried. He told me to sit down, then had Clyde go into the coach's office until the game was over. Clyde leered at him, then me, before walking away.

Meanwhile, on the ice, we pressured desperately for the tying goal, one that wouldn't come. Cooper was pulled for a sixth attacker with about a minute to play, but the Coldbury netminder stood tall and Tallard scored into an empty net as we lost, 2-0. The best-of-seven series was tied and heading to Coldbury for the next three, and there would be changes before we got there.

"What the hell was that all about?" we heard Raycliffe shout from his office. We could tell it wasn't his first argument with Parker, although it was the first one we were privy to.

"The kid fucked up!" Parker yelled. "I woulda benched him two games for that!"

"You're not the coach!"

"Damn right, I'm not."

There was an agonizing moment of silence before Raycliffe spoke again, more calmly. "Clyde, that's it," he said. "This isn't working. It hasn't worked from the beginning. Now, you can stick around 'til the end of the series if you want, come on the bus if you want, but I don't want you on the bench. Peter'll take care of the defence. Sit in the stands, watch from the press box, I don't give a fuck, but it's over."

We heard some stirring, but no more words after that. I lifted my eyes and saw all the guys doing the same thing, sitting at their stalls, heads down, listening with concern. After the silence lingered, they started to raise their heads, slowly, to look around.

"This sucks," Coop said.

And everyone agreed. Nothing — *nothing* — was easy. There was always something else to deal with, always another obstacle, and we were sick of it. Sick of the bullshit. Sick of worrying about what's going to happen next. Sick of the roller-coaster. We wanted off and too many of us seemed ready to jump right then, as we sat in our sweat, shaking as our bodies cooled off, our minds trying to convince us enough was enough. It was so real, that fedupwithitness, you could see it settling. And maybe that was good, because if you could see it, recognize it on our faces and in the slump of our shoulders, you could fight it, too.

Brendan kept a hand around his ribs, winced when he stood and spoke firmly. "Screw it, we don't need Clyde." He made sure everyone was paying attention then continued, "Or Tyler, or anyone else. We've gotten this far. We can win this ourselves."

Some guys — myself included — said yeah and let's go, and it almost seemed like we had sat in and pulled the bar of the coaster down ourselves. Others still looked skeptical and Brendan spoke louder to get through to them.

"We can beat them," he said. "With all the coaches in the world on our side and we can beat them with no one but us. It's all about what goes on out there. And that's where we're in charge." He paused again before speaking slower and more firmly. "Three more wins. That's it. Three more and it's over, alright."

He looked around, several of us responded by banging our sticks on the floor for applause. A bunch of guys were satisfied and hit the showers. Johnny Carruthers, however, did not move. He sat in the corner looking stunned.

Raycliffe called me into his office later and told me I had disappointed him, that no matter what anyone says, no matter how they say it, I have to keep my head. I shouldn't have gotten up, that could've caused more problems. And did, really. We missed a change at a key point and my mind obviously wasn't into the game afterwards. He said Clyde was wrong and he'd been told before to stop being too harsh on players. Now, he would no longer be with the team because of it, but I was wrong, too, for reacting.

I told him I was sorry and tried to explain, saying Clyde had never done that kind of stuff to me before; I wasn't expecting it, especially in front of everyone like that. Tyler said he agreed, that he didn't know what had gotten into him.

Clyde just didn't like me because I'd questioned him a lot and didn't buy into his style, I said. There were enough things I disagreed with him on that I could have run down a list — Johnny's suspension, the porno tape, his rough scrimmage —, but Tyler stopped me before I started. He said what was done was done and we were going to move on. And we left it at that.

One thing I should have told Tyler, though, was that when I glared into Clyde Parker's eyes and saw the gleam in them, and knew he saw the hurt and fear in mine, he looked like he had won.

44

An eighth of an inch. That's the width of a skate blade. I have thought about that a lot in the past few years.

An eighth of an inch. That's it. It's what we place our brawny bodies on. We place a lot of hope on them, too, and some prayers.

From the first time we put a skate on the ice, it's a battle for balance. Sure, practice makes it easier, but no one ever perfects it. Frozen water is like alien land to our feet, and we're never absolutely sure of how they might react to it. Put them in boots with a thin blade separating the body from the ice and it's chaos waiting to happen. The skates want to wander, to follow the grooves carved by those before. So you battle constantly to get them to go where you want. If you're good, you rein them in and move with a smooth, easy stride. You get to where you don't even have to think about it. Sometimes, you show off, skating backwards, spinning in a circle, doing dancer's leaps. It's easy, I think, to get to feel like you've mastered living on an eighth of an inch. And easy to forget, too, that it is merely an eighth of an inch.

That's the beauty of hockey and the danger of it, too. Violently, hockey players will stride. Careening off the boards, zipping from end to end, zig-zagging around the rink, chasing a puck like it's a shifty mouse. All the while, entrusting our health and our dreams and our goals to two tiny strips of metal.

In the heat of a game, I have come to believe, the body has no clue of what's happening to it. You get on the ice and something in your mind tells your blades where to go, and they go. The rest of you is just along for the ride. It's all instincts and reactions: you see the puck, go after it; you get it, shoot it.

Only thing is, if you play long enough, eventually, the body will rebel. At some point, it will refuse to be pushed anymore, it'll say, "Enough." It will quit. When it does, the mind goes with it.

And so, too, the blades.

45

In Coldbury, the championship series became entrenched. Both sides had to fight attrition on top of the opposition and having to play three games in four nights did not help. The grind punished our bodies; the bruises didn't have time to heal and the muscles stayed tight no matter how much stretching we did. Tony Lacroix took a puck off his right ankle in Game Three, which we won, and played with a slight sprain the rest of the series. In the fourth game, which we lost, Dmitri Rushchenko was slashed on the left hand, resulting in a broken middle finger he had to endure. Of course, the Chevaliers were just as banged up heading into Game Five, the last time hockey was the most important thing in my life.

After another intense sixty minutes, we headed into overtime, tied 2-2.

"Just keep grindin', lads," Tyler said. He had huddled us around the bench before the start of the extra period. "Watch the middle, they're tryin' to split us for a break."

Jean Giguere's instructions were likely similar, since we were trying to do the same thing. On every shift, I was to sprint to the blueline while Brendan or a defenceman aimed to find me between checkers for the breakaway. Each time, the play didn't materialize because of a bad pass or good read by the Chevaliers. But Coldbury was also ineffective and we remained deadlocked after the first overtime. After a warmup skate that left me sucking air, I joined the others at the bench. Tyler, sweating, but still breathing easily, had the gall to say, "Forget the pain, boys!" He urged us to stay focused and to not make *lazy* mistakes.

It was on the first shift of the second overtime, however, that what Tyler feared most happened: he lost a player to injury. And it was one of his veterans.

Johnny Carruthers took a loose puck in the neutral zone and sent a pass through the middle. Bruce Broussard and another Coldbury defender began to close on the play. The weariness I felt from that game, and the whole series, finally caught up to me. Pushing my overworked legs, I was desperate to reach the puck, but knew I couldn't. So I stretched my stick at it, trying to at least keep it from my foes. In so doing, I left myself open and The Bruise unleashed himself. He began to plough into me at full speed. When I saw him coming, I stopped my lunge and quickly stood upright in hopes of avoiding getting hit flush. Except for my right knee, I was unscathed.

The Bruise banged his knee on mine, sending me crumbling to the ice. The inevitable pain was slow to come, like an explosion after a bomb is dropped, but when it did my mind reacted like a crashing computer. I screamed uncontrollably and contorted my face, then rolled from side to side while clutching my knee. The referee blew the whistle right away, I think, and Guy and Tyler ran onto the ice while my teammates jostled with The Bruise.

"Keep it still! Keep it still!" Guy said. He held my right heel as I tried not to whimper.

Guy instructed Jesse and Brendan to help me off the ice before telling

Tyler: "We better get him to the hospital."

I balanced on my left leg, keeping my right skate blade from touching the ice, and flung my arms over the guys' necks. At the bench, they passed me off to Guy and Peter Jones, who were going to lead me to the ambulance stationed outside the arena. "I don't wanna go," I said between clenched teeth.

"You're goin'!" Guy yelled.

"It's not that bad."

He jerked his head forward to tell Peter to take me into the dressing room. They put me down on a bench and Guy told Peter he could return to the game for a few minutes. "Look, Scott, you might've wrecked that knee," Guy said. He kept his hands around my leg, inspecting it. "Now, there's no way you can go back out there."

I shook my head furiously. He was adamant as he applied an icepack. "Lemme stay 'til the end," I pleaded.

He sighed, scratched his head and said, "I'm gonna tell 'em to start 'er up and then I'm gonna tell Tyler we're goin' and not to expect you back and then I'm comin' back for ya. Got it?"

I gave in.

"Hopefully by then they would've finished this game." Guy undid my skates, but did not instruct me to take off any other equipment. "Alright, don't move that leg," he said and exited.

I squeezed my hands over my face and tried to forget the pain. When I couldn't, I strained to listen to any sounds coming from the rink, but all I could hear were the "oohs" and "aahs" from the crowd. That did nothing for me as I sat alone and cold in that room, worrying about lifelong dreams that appeared to be nullified in an instant.

Guy returned and grabbed my boots. "Let's go," he said. "They'll bring the rest of your things."

Peter was waiting to help me into the ambulance. "How ya feelin'?" he asked.

"Like crap," I answered.

I got in the back with Guy. "Take care, Scott," Peter said. The driver closed the rear door and Peter headed into the arena, but before the ambulance was put in gear he ran back out. Guy bounced up to open the door. "We won! We won!" Peter screamed. "Tahani scored!"

Guy high-fived me and we laughed.

Tahani "One-Axe" Kohono, I was told several times, took my place on Brendan's left wing and after only a couple of shifts together, got free for a breakaway after taking a pass from Jesse Sullivan. On a play similar to the goal he scored way back in our first game against Coldbury that season, Tahani deked to his left before tucking a backhander behind the goalie to bring us to within a victory of the COHL championship.

But while my teammates rejoiced, I was admitted to Coldbury General.

"Scott MacGregor, eh?" the doctor said. He raised his eyebrows to look at me sternly before returning to the chart. "You're the one who broke that Tallard boy's arm."

"Uh-huh."

"Shoulda gone to jail for that, I thought."

Oh, Christ, I thought. I can't wait to get outta this league.

"Well, you're lucky," he said, seemingly disappointed. "The ligament didn't snap." He held the X-rays up and squinted. "Looks like it came close though."

"So, what's wrong with it?"

"It's severely sprained," he said. "Keep ice on it tonight. Get fitted for a brace tomorrow. And stay off skates for a week. At least."

"But we gotta game in two days!"

"I know," he said, his lips pursed and eyes down like he was trying to hide a smile. "Look, if you play, you could snap it by just stretching for a puck. You do that, and you're looking at surgery. You'd be out six months, at best."

I was convinced he was just trying to scare me. He was probably the father of some kid on the Chevaliers trying to undermine me and my team. No way was I not going to play. He fitted me for crutches, which I really didn't need, gave me a cupful of Aspirins and put my X-rays in an envelope, telling me to give them to my physician in Kildare. He then, mercifully, let me leave.

My jersey and equipment still on, I exited to the waiting room, where I had left Guy alone. He wasn't when I returned.

"Scott, you poor boy. Are you all right?" Gordie Joseph's mother asked in her gravelly voice.

"Ah, yes, Mrs. Joseph," I said, perplexed by her presence. "I'll be fine."

"Uh-huh," Guy said with skepticism. Guy had been around many injured and proud young men on skates.

"Yeah, he said I was lucky."

"Uh-huh," Guy said. "Well, we'll see. Anyway, Mrs. Joseph is here to rescue us."

"It's my pleasure," she said. "It's a long drive in the car alone."

We hastily departed, especially since my uniform was drawing leers.

As her stationwagon warmed up, Mrs. Joseph apologized for not getting my belongings — "There was so much confusion, all of the bags were already on the bus and they all look the same" — then reached in her purse and handed me a keychain. "I'll give you these before I forget. Brendan figured if you were okay, you'd wanna stop into the rink to drop off your equipment for cleaning, so he's going to leave his car for you." She stopped to cough. "But I'd rather just take you straight home. You really should rest."

Rest seemed only a fantasy after spending three hours with an injured knee in rotting equipment and listening to Mrs. Joseph espouse on how proud she was of her son while blowing the smoke from her cigarettes toward my face. I admired the woman for going to extreme lengths to attend all of her boy's home and road games, not to mention practices, but it was clear she suffered from delusions. "Gordie's athletic talent comes from my side. My dad was an umpire down in Toronto back in the Fifties," she said before telling Guy, who began dozing off before we reached Ottawa, and me about Gordie's first time on skates. "He was named after Gordie Howe." She later thanked me for helping her son, even though I wasn't aware I had. "He's learned so much from you lads this year," she said before delivering a final absurdity that, had I allowed myself to laugh as hard as I wanted, would have likely caused me to snap the ligament in my knee right there. "His uncle says he's got a real shot at the NHL someday."

"Your son is quite a player," I said, because I felt I had to.

"He'll be so happy to hear that," she said as we entered Kildare's city limits. "So, straight to the Kowalczeks then?"

"Actually, I wouldn't mind stopping at the rink. I gotta make sure this stuff gets washed."

"Okay then. Be careful with that knee," she said. "Don't be a hero."

We pulled into the empty parking lot at 2 a.m. Even in the dark, the arena had the cruel look an April thaw gives to land sculpted for winter. The parking lot was muddy as puddles filled in potholes. Dead leaves once buried by snow now flew off the roof while icicles dripped like wine from an emptying bottle. The trees around the building were barren after the ice that clung to them melted and the blossoms had yet to come. The piles of snow that had flanked the entrance were also gone, revealing grime and dirt on the aluminium siding. Indeed, Leroux Arena was being exposed.

As I hobbled to the front door, crutches and shoulderpads in hand, Mrs. Joseph drove off and Guy was about to do the same as he refused to wait for his car to warm up. Fumbling for the key that opened the entry door, I pressed a hand against it and discovered it was ajar. They must've forgot to close it, I assumed, and walked to the dressing room, which was also unlocked. I limped in and immediately the hairs on my back began to stand.

Steam and light were coming from the showers, but everything else was black. It took a second for my eyes to adjust before I was able to move to my stall, seeing my things, left behind by Brendan, I put the shoulderpads and crutches down, squeezed my grandfather's cap, then proceeded to investigate the shower. "Hey, anyone here?"

A groan and whimper came.

As I got to the opening, warm steam blew into my eyes like a mother's protective hand. But I could still glimpse through it. Naked, Johnny Carruthers, his face away from me, lay limp under one of the many showers he had turned on as his blood diluted in the water, which enveloped it and washed it away.

46

My boots splashed water as I limped through the shower toward Johnny. My jersey and undershirt began to get wet and cling to my skin. An empty bottle of Jack Daniel's was beside him. I bent over to lift his head, which was bleeding from a fall.

"Johnny, you okay, man?" I asked, noticing swelling around his mouth.

He was obviously drunk and tried to shoo me away with one arm while putting the other over his eyes.

"C'mon, we gotta get you outta here," I said. I could see welts on his back, and when I tried to drag him by gripping around his armpits, he kicked his feet in defiance and I had to set him down. "C'mon, bud," I said and sat next to him because my bad leg kept me from kneeling. "You just had too much, tonight."

"Nooo!" he shrieked. His desperate green eyes turned to me; he was wounded, deeply. The kind of wound you can't see, smell, taste, touch, hear, but you can still sense because it can fill a heart and be pumped out from it beat by beat until it floods a soul.

Johnny grabbed my hair, pulled my head toward him and whispered in my ear. I said, "Oh, my God, Johnny," and everything became crystal. The whys — why is he so depressed; why is he so scared; why is he so self-destructive — all suddenly had vivid answers. One answer. One horrible, disgusting, despicable answer.

Tears began to roll out of him like a handful of dirt through fingers as he held his head in his hands and turned away from me. I was holding his shoulder and shaking him a little when I heard the locker-room door open.

A familiar voice called, "You here, boy."

Johnny yelped and started to bawl louder. I told him to shhh!, but it didn't matter; Clyde Parker was already coming for us. With each step, his black shadow filled in more and more of the tiled shower walls until he was there in the opening. He stood with his fists on his hips and snarled. His wild eyes met mine and, in them, I could see it: the anger, the humiliation, the sickness. Clyde Parker had done more than abuse my friend, he had taken his dignity, made him feel something less than human. Worse, it was clear Johnny wasn't the only one he had done it to nor was he intended to be the last, and I was a mere obstacle to this.

"MacGregor, you shit," Clyde said. "Let me take him home."

Johnny shrieked and went scurrying to the back corner of the showers.

"No way," I said.

"What did he tell you?" Clyde asked, his eyes narrowing. He was peering over me to look at Johnny, sending him into more hysterics.

"Enough that I'm not going to let you touch him."

"He's a stupid drunk!" Clyde threw a finger toward Johnny. "Aren't you, boy?"

"Get outta here, man," I said and picked up the empty whiskey bottle; Johnny kept crying.

"All right, I'm going," he said and turned to leave. I followed slowly.

He opened the door and exited. Relieved, I started back to the showers without waiting for the heavy door to close. It didn't. Parker flew back into the dressing room and came at me bent down like a football tackler. He got me around the waist and hoisted me into the wall. As the pain shot through my spine, I screamed and arched my back. He got himself balanced and delivered a punch to my stomach that slowed me, then continued after Johnny. But I recovered quickly enough to take out Clyde's feet by diving at him. His fat body flopped to the floor where the carpet and shower tile meet. Once I regained the whiskey bottle, I smacked it over his head as he tried to stand. He fell to a knee, paused to touch his head, then tried to punch me in the crotch, but I stopped him by throwing an elbow down on his spine. And he collapsed.

"C'mon, get up!" I screamed. I hopped a foot or two away from him and stood with fists up. "You sick fuck! C'mon, get up!"

He crawled after me, but couldn't get himself off the floor. That's when he must have seen the crutches. After picking up the nearest one, he wielded it at my stomach and caught me by surprise, I stumbled backward and he started to rise. But when he got to a knee, I seized the metal crutch from his hands then hammered it down on top of his shoulder. He wailed and the disgusting pleasure of punishing him seized me. There was evil in Clyde Parker, I was certain of it then. And I am certain of it now. He deserved this; yes, he did. For what he did, for what he had taken, he deserved it, and much more.

Still, I shouldn't have done it. I shouldn't have fallen to where he was. But there was evil in the room, then. Maybe it had strayed from Parker, maybe it was beaten out of him; in any case, it was there and it got a hold of me. And I lost myself to it.

After recocking the crutch, I gripped it over him like an axe. He dragged himself into a corner and held up a shaking hand in front of his turned-away face. "Please don't," I think I heard him murmur. But such hate I have never known. Like a strongman determined to tilt a circus arcade game, I brought the crutch up and down again and again on his body. When I was through, the only movements I noticed came from a spasm in his left leg.

47

J ohnny, being careful not to step on broken glass, refused to wear his own soaked and stained clothes, and I didn't have time to argue. I gave him the jeans and sweatshirt I had in my duffel bag, and found a towel for his bleeding head. My knuckles, which were almost healed from the fight with Tallard, began to smart again and my injured knee stung like shin splints when we hurried out the door. I hoped the blood on my jersey wasn't obvious, but not nearly as much as I hoped and prayed that the answer was "No" to Johnny's question of, "Is he dead?"

The time was 2:35 a.m. when I started Brendan's car; I knew what I had to do, but had less than a half-hour to do it.

We reached Kildare Inn in five minutes. Laughter and MuchMusic could be heard from outside Room 23. Banging on the door, I glimpsed at Johnny, just to see if he was okay, to see if what I was thinking was true. The poor kid stood behind me with his head down, shuddering. I made a promise to myself right then: No matter how uncomfortable I ever got to feel, no matter how badly I didn't want to deal with things, I was always going to, for Johnny. No matter what, I was going to see him through this. If it took the rest of my life.

Standing there scared and nervous, I banged again. "C'mon, open up guys! It's Scott."

The door flew open. "Holy sheet," Dmitri Rushchenko said when he looked at us. "What's happeneeng?"

After hustling Johnny into the Russians' room, I closed the door. "Need your help boys," I said and reached into my pocket. "You gotta let Johnny stay here tonight. Here's ten bucks for the corner store and get him a blanket, all right?"

"Sure," said Vlastimil Skurilev, who sat up in one of the two beds. Then I headed out.

"Where you going?" Dmitri asked.

"I'll explain later." I turned to face Johnny and said, "Take care, okay?" He nodded, but didn't look up.

Trying to ignore the pain in my knee, I hobbled back to the car. Before long, I was banging on another door. This time, I got a speedy reply and was let into the *Chronicle*. Randy Delisle hurried to greet me; I wasn't too late.

"I was just heading ho . . ." He paused to look at me. Blood on my shirt, uniform still on, soaking wet, maybe a black eye or cuts on my face. "My God, what happened to you?"

"Can I sit down?" I asked. "I gotta story for you."

"I bet you do." He peered around the dark office before saying, "A-ha. Let's go in here." I followed with my limp, causing him to recall, "Weren't you in the hospital tonight?"

I confirmed I was.

"This is going to be some story."

He sat across from me in a desk that appeared to belong to an account-ant. After getting a better look at me, Randy said, "Scott, are you sure you shouldn't be in the hospital? You look like a mess, son."

"Randy, really. I'd just prefer to get this over with," I said. My healthy leg had begun to shake.

"Okay, shoot." He pulled out a notebook from his vest pocket.

"Clyde Parker's a pervert."

"I knew that."

"No, I mean a real pervert," I said, but still got a "let's-get-to-the-point" look from him. I took a breath and came out with it. "A molester."

"What?"

"Look, I got back from the hospital in Coldbury and went to the dressing room and found Johnny Carruthers drunk and bleeding in the shower. And he told me something and then everything just fit in my head."

Randy looked stunned. He shook his head, put his pen down and leaned back in his chair. "What did Johnny tell you?"

"He said Clyde 'does things' to him."

"That's it?"

"Yeah, I know. But it's the way he said it. He just started bawling. I think he might've been trying to kill himself. He had all the showers on and was just layin' there in the water. When I first saw him I thought he was drowning. And then Clyde walked in and he just freaked."

"Clyde was there?"

I said yeah and wanted to move on fast, but the reporter wouldn't let me.

"Where's Clyde now?"

"We left him in the dressing room."

"What do you mean left him?"

"I don't think he's dead or anything."

"You don't think," Randy said and stood to pace. "Holy Christ, Scott."

"I know. It's bad."

He nodded repeatedly while holding a bent index finger to his chin. "Okay, quickly, tell me everything you know about Johnny, and about Clyde and this theory of yours." He retook his seat and readied a pen. And I told him.

Johnny was from out of town, a quiet kid who didn't mix in right away. Easy prey. He was depressed and anxious a lot, real nervous all the time, especially when people asked about Clyde. Maybe this is why Clyde'd left Saskatchewan, too; he'd have good reason to skip out if he suspected someone was onto him. No, I hadn't asked Johnny specifically about it, but from the way he acted and the way Clyde acted that night, it just seemed to fit. Mostly, though, it was my hunch.

"It's not a lot to go on," Randy said. "But I believe you."

And I had that one brief moment of glee, of relief. Then the door opened behind me.

With my back to it, I couldn't see who it was only that Randy's face turned bleak. "You forgot this," a harsh voice said. The man to whom it belonged threw the 50 Mission Cap into my lap before gripping my shoulder and announcing, "Scott MacGregor, you're under arrest."

48

J ohnny Carruthers never spent another night in Kildare. He was driven home the next day for what the paper called a "family emergency." For the remainder of that spring and summer, Johnny was coddled by his parents. They sought counseling for him and lavished him with gifts they couldn't afford but thought might take away his pain and their guilt. Johnny responded. And Minnesota State, and the chance to start a new life, followed. For a while, he looked like he would pull through. He played well enough to be named a third-team conference all-star in his second season. His confidence was growing and play was rapidly improving, so much so that people began to take note. But fate wouldn't let Johnny be.

He blew out his knee in his junior year and his hockey career — "The one thing that makes the pain almost tolerable," he once told me — was forever lost. From that point, Johnny began to truly spurn life. He accumulated addictions as if he were a collector of them. The drinking worsened, and after his junior year (he never graduated) he gained weight at a frightening rate because his workouts stopped and metabolism slowed.

Johnny had spent less than three years in Kildare, but a lifetime's worth of damage was done. Clyde Parker would become infamous because of it. It took time, but Johnny, with Randy Delisle's help, eventually revealed the truth to the world.

It had begun when Clyde was thirty and still out west, leading a life of small-business owner and volunteer coach. He pondered his life then and recognized it was a fragmented one broken by discord and abuses and failures that were heaped onto his husky frame like penalties. Somehow, because of that, he was able to justify what he did.

A pillar he was not, but neighbours in his boring Saskatchewan town were aware he had done well — coped well, really — with a harsh life, and they respected that. Trusted that. And allowed him to become the keeper of twenty-one young boys, all thirteen or fourteen or fifteen, all full of wild dreams and lasting hopes.

Gradually, the young boys in his charge began to fill Clyde's thoughts. He pictured them in the locker room, so close to him, naked, their bodies wet with sweat and scarred by fresh bruises. They didn't care that he was there, looking. Even more, they had respect for him and the way they spoke! "Yes, Coach"; "I'm sorry, Coach"; "Let me skate, Coach. Please." He could do anything he wanted. And slap him stupid if they wouldn't let him.

In his second season with the midgets, a small forward caught his eye. He was a quiet kid. They were all quiet kids. Quiet kids have more pride, they're slow to react because of it. That first one took guts, though. He was talented. (They had to be talented, too. Had to think they had a chance of getting somewhere.) The kid was going to juniors, no doubt about it, but he was insecure, didn't fit in well with the other guys. Wasn't terribly smart either, nor good looking. Just a good hockey player who wanted desperately to be better.

Clyde earned his trust. Gave him lots of ice; told his parents he had a real future, even got invited to their home; became friendly; spoiled the kid, giving him collectibles — autographed hockey cards and pucks — he had picked up. The kid loved Clyde, and so did the parents. Trust was there, like an ally.

Then things changed.

Clyde would berate the kid in practice for the slightest error, saying he expected more; tell the parents he was slacking off; come over less and less, then not at all, ending the gifts, maybe giving them to someone else; a benching would come, maybe for falling asleep on the bus or goofing around in practice, an example would be made of him. And the kid would be scared to death, wouldn't understand what was going on, why everything he wanted — had — was being ruined. He would want answers.

Then Clyde would have his way.

He would speak to the kid one-on-one, later at night, after practice, when everyone else was gone and not coming back. Hockey's a tough game, Clyde would say, not for wimps or pussies like you. The kid was going to be benched. For a long time. No way was a junior team going to take a wuss like him. He was a gutless piece of shit. That's what they were thinkin', anyway. But Clyde knew better, he saw the kid had talent. Lots of it. He didn't want to bench him, but what choice did he have? Really, what choice?

From behind, he would touch the kid's shoulder. Grip it, actually. Then muss his hair, pat him on the chest, then rub his hand there, stroke a tear away.

What choice did he have?

He kept his hands on the boy. The kid started to whimper and weep, and Clyde would put a finger to the lips. And keep the other hand where it was, rubbing and caressing. If he said a word to anyone, no one would believe him and he would be off the team. So, better to keep quiet. "Just do as I say and I'll get you back on the ice, kid. You're lucky, you know, that I'm doing this for you . . ."

And so it went, for nearly a dozen years and who knows how many boys. But eventually Clyde Parker had to mess up and when he did, his world turned awry. The boy who did it to him had gotten jumpy as soon as Clyde had him alone. When Clyde put a hand on him, the boy bolted; ran away so fast, Clyde didn't even get a chance to yell. Or make his play. The boy told his parents, who told the police, who didn't have anything, but still catalogued the complaint and mentioned it to the league. That brush was enough to convince Clyde he had better move, far off. He got pointed to the Kildare Kougars. "The owner's a riot," someone told him. "Knows nothing about hockey and will let you do whatever you want. You'll love it!"

So, Clyde Parker entered Kildare a predator reborn. He was as cautious as a spooked criminal with the first Kougar who billeted with him, even acting like a cordial host, befriending the boy, and taking good care of his appetite and well being. And although Clyde spied on the boy, he never touched him. Three seasons and three billets later, Johnny Carruthers arrived and Clyde Parker's inhibitions had long been lost.

Like I said, it would take time before all of this came out. Time in which Clyde Parker could gather himself, mount a defence, reflect. Time in which I had my own share of regret. For, five years ago, I was the criminal and Parker was the victim. He was in the hospital, I had put him there and that's all the law knew.

Officer John Franklin began to read me my rights that night after the fight. He spoke in the bellowing tone authority figures seem trained to have and I sat in the newspaper office shivering, my skin bubbling with goose pimples. Thankfully, Randy Delisle cut the cop off. "John, I think you should hear what he has to say."

Officer Franklin paused to look at Randy, who closed his eyes and nodded in return. The cop took a chair and gestured at me by pushing his open arms forward. I told him pretty much what I had told Randy — that I was certain Parker had sexually assaulted my friend, had probably been doing it to him for a while and had likely done it to others. That now that Clyde was off the team, Johnny might have felt he could blow the whistle on him, maybe threatened to do so and Clyde was going to do God knows what that night to stop him.

"You believe him?" the officer asked the reporter, who had filled in some of the blanks for me.

"It fits. Won't know more until we dig," Randy said.

The cop asked about Johnny — where he was and what kind of shape — and after I told him, he folded his arms and looked down, thinking. After a moment, he pushed up his hat and scratched his head. "Can we get Gary Curran on the phone?" he asked.

I cringed.

Randy got the number, the cop dialed and waited several moments before speaking. "Mr. Curran, it's Officer John Franklin from Kildare Police. I've got Scott MacGregor in custody; I believe he's one of your players." He paused to listen. "No, it's not a joke." Another pause. "No, we're at the newspaper office." And finally, "No, I'm being quite serious."

Gary arrived within minutes wearing a robe. "Are you insane?" he said as he whisked into the room, glaring at me.

"Hold on, Gary," Randy said. "You better listen to what he has to say."

Skeptically, Gary pulled up the last chair in the tiny office while I began to retell my account. When I was through, he patted me on the back.

"So, now what?" I said. That's when I noticed that the three men not only looked at me with admiration but each also held a countenance that seemed eager to say, *Thank God I'm not him*.

"Scott, I could run this story," said Randy, who leaned forward and clasped his hands together on the desk, "using everyone in here as anonymous sources, but I have to mention Clyde Parker and I have to mention abuse, sexual or not. If I do that, everyone in this town is gonna know that what he did, he did to that boy. You see what I'm sayin'?"

Slowly, I began to understand my predicament.

"What Randy's saying is that if we make this public now, there's a good chance Johnny's going to be worse off than he is already," Gary said. "He needs time to deal with it."

"So Clyde's gonna get away with it?" I said, frustrated and fatigued.

"No, he's not going to get away with it," officer Franklin said. "But, if this did happen, we need the victim or victims to come forward. We need real proof."

"You're just gonna cover it up, then?" I buried my head in my hands.

"It's not a coverup, son," Randy said. "This isn't Toronto or Ottawa. Everyone here knows their neighbour's business and that's the world Johnny's lived in for the past three years. If we let this out, everyone that boy knows will know his secret. And pretty soon after that, it'll be the entire country." He paused because he didn't get the desired response from me. "Look, you may have saved that boy's life tonight. At the very least, you gave him a fighting chance to have a life. Be proud of that. Understand that's more important than seeing Clyde Parker suffer for what he may have done."

I shrugged and looked away.

"In the mean time, we'll gather information on Clyde," officer Franklin said.

In the mean time, I realized someone would have to be held responsible for the incident that night. "So what happens to me?" I asked.

"Parker's in the hospital, in bad shape. And you put him there," officer Franklin said. "I'm sorry, Scott, but we have to be accountable for our actions, even though every one of us in here might have done the same. But I have no choice. I'm going to have to take you in."

"But it was self-defence! He came after me!"

"Scott, you did more than just defend yourself against him."

"You can't do this to me," I said. Tears formed and quickly streamed down my face like blood to clot a wound.

Desperate for help, I looked to Gary Curran. The general manager got up and turned to the wall. He put his chin to his chest and shook his head. "Scott, I'm sorry." And I knew the worst was coming. "You know the rules."

My arms crossed over my chest like a barricade and I kept my head down, trying hard to stop from outright bawling. Randy uttered an "Oh, no," and officer Franklin asked, "What?"

"Any player arrested is automatically off the team," Gary said decisively, like a man binding his own son.

"No!" I shouted and pulled my head to my chest, trying uselessly to keep back the pain.

Officer Franklin blew out a sigh, got up and said, "When you're ready, kid."

Randy pushed a button on the phone and said, "Pete, we may have to stop the presses." He then exited, touching my shoulder like I was a widow.

Gary said he would pay whatever he had to to keep me out of lock-up. The officer told me not to worry. "I'll lean on Parker to drop the charges, if he doesn't the worst it'll be is a suspended sentence," he said.

Before we left, Gary convinced the cop to give me privacy. I dialed and the other end rang and rang, and when an answer finally came, the tears burst hard, like they had been squished out by a fist. "Mom," I said.

"Scotty, what's wrong?" she said, waking up quickly.

"Mom, I've been arrested." I struggled to remove my wet jersey that stuck to me like an appendage. "And there's more."

49

Game Six could not start soon enough. Word had spread, but the town was still distracted by the game. I didn't want to face the questions or the leers when my beating of Clyde Parker became a popular issue. Of the Kougars, only Brendan knew the truth. He told the guys what they had heard or read was a mistake, but didn't elaborate. Their job was to concentrate on the game, he said, not to worry about me. I would be fine, and I would be watching.

Gary Curran escorted me into the press box, though some of its denizens were not pleased by that. "Is this wise, Gary?" asked the COHL president.

"He's staying," Curran answered, sternly.

"Have you got a leash for him?" the Coldbury general manager asked.

"Shut up," Curran snapped.

I took a seat at the far table, which overlooked centre ice. Co-owner Arnold Bramburger rapped me on the arm and said things'll work out. Then Randy Delisle walked in and sat his laptop beside me. He whispered, "How you doing?"

I lied and said I was okay.

"When this thing comes clean, what you have done will be lauded," he promised.

"That is if I haven't screwed up again by then, eh?"

"Hey, don't worry," he said. "You'll be fine — and you haven't screwed anything up."

I said thanks, then "O! Canada" began to play.

When the puck dropped, everyone forgot about me. During the nearly three hours of that game, I even had long lapses where I stopped thinking of my mess.

"C'mon, c'mon," I would say under my breath when I saw from above the open pass my former teammates couldn't from the ice. When they got a two-on-one, I would yell, "There it is!" before the rush began.

When Brendan scored to give the Kougars a 1-0 lead, I hopped wildly, despite my injury. Letting out a "Wooo-Hooo!" I returned an upturned thumb in his direction after he looked up to spot me. In the second period, Chris Cooper threw up his trapper then fell backward on his butt after snaring a breakaway shot by Alain Tallard. "'Atta boy, Coop!" I shouted.

I followed the puck like I was attached to it, touching Bramburger as I moved my body to the right when it went behind the goal-line at the south end, or if it was deep in the north end, I would strain my neck like a snared fish. On power plays, I looked like I was being bothered by flies because my head moved back and forth as rapidly as the puck did going from tape to tape. When the Chevaliers evened the score, I slammed my hand on the table, then rubbed my face with both hands and wished I didn't have to go through the same anxiety for a Game Seven. My heart raced and sweat coated me like a balm; my knee was fine, I knew it. I could play. Go a shift or two, that's all it would take. I could score that winning goal; I knew I could and the anguish hit me again. There had to be a way I could be part of this.

I looked down, surveyed everything, then, with four minutes gone in overtime, I stood. Dion Marcelle hopped off the bench with a curved stick. Tyler had put him on left wing, with Brendan and Skurilev. Those three had never been on the same line before. And they would never be again.

The Chevaliers rushed across the redline before Skurilev, backchecking of all things, lifted the stick of the puckcarrier for the turnover. He slipped a behind-the-back pass to Brendan, who swooped in to take the disc before darting ahead with only one Coldbury defenceman back. Crossing the blueline, Brendan cut to his right before sending a cross-ice pass back the other way. The puck floated millimetres above the surface and toward the top of the faceoff circle. I had seen him do that so often, I actually stood there expecting to take the pass. And when I sighted the blade in Dion's hands high in the air, I shivered. The puck barely touched the ice before Dion unleashed the stick on it, and slapped it into the back of the net.

Just like that, the Kildare Kougars were champions.

I raised my arms and yelled, "Yes! Yes!" Looking down, I saw the boys charging off the bench to pile on top of each other. The fans erupted in a din of hoots and claps. Hats were strewn on the ice, and people were hugging and handslapping each other like long-separated friends. Tyler Raycliffe wore a huge smile and raised a fist as he slid in his loafers to the celebration site.

And where was I?

Up there, away from all of it. It hit me again and I leaned over, gripping my hands together, trying desperately to be more happy than sad. When

Coop flung off his mask to pile on, I blurted a laugh that turned into a cry. I couldn't believe it. I wanted to get away and hide until I got myself together. First, though, I chose to dry the tears. I brushed my eyes repeatedly, first with the backs of my hands, then with the knuckles of my index fingers, finally with the top of my shirt, and when I was done, I opened them again to see the Kougars doing an odd thing. They had begun to unpile as aggressively as they had piled on and started to bang their sticks. This happened as a red carpet was being rolled out, causing even louder cheers. Next, Brendan and Dion signalled the others to form a circle near centre as the sticks continued to smack the ice like marching boots. Once the players were in formation, Brendan and Dion yelled above the crowd: "One! Two! Three! . . ."

"We want Scott!" the whole team shouted.

And the fans kept roaring.

The players began to chant, "Scotty! Scotty! Scotty!"

I lifted my head and let out an ecstatic howl. Then clapped my hands and pumped my fists, all as they called for me. Gary Curran came over to put his arm around me. He pulled me close and said, "Go on, get down there."

After hobbling down the press-box stairs as fast as I could, I struggled through the frenzied aisles and almost bowled over the Tremblay Trophy on my way to embrace my friends. Even some in the audience, not just my parents and acquaintances, had joined in chanting my name. I was able to wave to Mom and Dad before Brendan and Dion tackled me playfully to the ice, ruining my best suit. And the others — all grinning — followed, nearly stifling me as I struggled to breathe and to stop laughing. All the while, I aimed to keep the new brace on my knee out of harm's way. It took a while, but the mauling ceased and we separated. That's when Dion threw me the winning puck. "It's yours, man," he said.

I gave him an aw-shucks look and began to hand it back to him, but he insisted, "It belongs to you." I shook my head and Dion grabbed me by the shoulders as if to wake me up. "I used your stick!" he said and laughed loud.

"What?"

"After the third period, Tyler tells me I'm going on with Brendan and Vlastimil. So I say I want Scott's stick, so you could be out there with us, too, and Guy found me one. It's your stick that scored the goal, man!"

I looked at the puck, ogled it, more like, and felt a rush of happiness. I was so flabbergasted it probably seemed like I was hyperventilating. *My stick*, I thought. *It was my stick! Of course!* I looked at the puck and shook my head in disbelief, then began giggling. Dion gave me another big hug and Brendan, who had gone back to the boards briefly, skated over to us. "I thought we could use it on the bench for overtime," he said and handed me my grandfather's cap.

I waved it in the air as the silver-plated Tremblay Trophy, with its two thin, ornamental handles and gold top, was presented to Brendan, the captain. He raised it in front of me. And the enthralled citizens of Kildare saw the trophy in Brendan's hand eclipse the 50 Mission Cap in mine. Like it was taking its place.

Thus, on one mid-April Saturday night, the tiny town of Kildare, Ontario, felt like a champion, like the cradle of something great. Like Eden.

So, it gave itself a holiday. Folks ate and drank and applauded their Kougars. You would have expected to see prayer books in tow as they walked with smiles wherever they went and shook each other's hands exuberantly upon passing on the street. They, again, felt a part of something real and vital. Ottawa had the builders of the nation and Toronto had the employers of it, but Kildare had its team, not a bunch of overpriced millionaires who lived in the States and jumped from squad to squad every couple of years. No, Kildare had hockey. It owned it. As sure as the sweetness of sugar and cinnamon on a beavertail, Kildare had the essence of this country: Its game. In our group of immature and sometimes arrogant boys, most of whom found our selves in Kildare, the town lived. It saw itself a winner.

But what about us?

What else did that season give us? Indeed, what more did it take?

50

Rochester State didn't happen, of course. I got a call a week after the season ended saying they were revoking my scholarship. Turns out they had some discipline problems on their football and basketball teams, so a hockey player who had been arrested once and suspended twice in a season wasn't attractive to them at all. Even though Clyde Parker had dropped the charges, it was no use, the school had made up its mind.

I'm not going to lie, it was a real bummer. I had already started making plans, even bragging about it, promising Brendan and the guys I would e-mail my game stats, and that I wouldn't drink any cruddy American beer. Afterwards, I was pissed for a long time, hated a lot of things. Only lately have I been able to look back at what happened and see that things worked out okay for me. That any sacrifices were not only worth it, but had their own rewards, too.

Yes, Johnny Carruthers is struggling, but at least he's alive. The last time I saw him was a month ago in the hospital. It was actually a bit of a reunion. Jesse Sullivan, Chris Cooper and I stood around Johnny's bed trying not to notice the rope burns around his neck. Johnny never talks about Clyde Parker, and he doesn't have to. Clyde's marks are all over him.

In a plea bargain not long before Johnny's latest attempt, Clyde, who had been arrested in his Mississauga home, got a four-and-a-half-year prison term. He also was punished with injections that have chemically castrated him for two years. With good behaviour, he could be out too soon. Clyde Parker had gotten away with it, most agreed. And, again, Johnny was his victim. It still gets to me, the injustice of it. But I try not to think about it too much.

I honestly don't know what will happen with Johnny, but I told him I'll be there if he ever needs anything and he says he's grateful for that. He really is trying his best to go on. We all are. And, thankfully, there have been other get-togethers — joyous ones — to help us along.

Last year, Dmitri Rushchenko, recently retired — at age 22 — after reinjuring his shoulder in the minors, wedded Brigitte Chouinard in a huge party held at Lannie Leroux's mansion (and without Vlastimil Skurilev, a superstar who has chosen to leave his past as a vacant memory), and just last week Brendan threw a bash of his own after signing a million-dollar extension with Calgary. He never made it to B.U., because he impressed so many NHL scouts who had come to see the Russians that he got chosen in the fifth round. Today, he's considered one of the best young forwards in the game, along with Skurilev and Dion Marcelle.

Sometimes, when one of my ex-teammates is playing on TV, a commentator will note how extraordinary it is to have three players from the same Junior A team make it to the big league. And maybe, just maybe, there might be a fourth.

I went to the University of Toronto, where I studied English and played hockey. My knee healed fine and I was able to captain the Varsity Blues to a national title. In Toronto, I took up rollerblading and I have just finished my first season of professional roller hockey. I did so well, the Senators invited me to their NHL tryout.

So, who knows? Like Grandpa Joe taught me, just when things look the worst, in flies some force to steady life, maybe even grant a wish or two. I suppose it was that lesson I was pondering when I trekked to Kitchener not too long ago. Wearing a dark brown trenchcoat, a poppy on my lapel standing out like a lush sunset, I walked to the cemetery at Weber and Franklin. In front of the grave of Grandpa Joe's saviour and best friend, I donned the 50 Mission Cap. I had clutched it, grappled it, held it high, tossed it in anger, but never worn it. Before doing so, I punched my fist into it, working it in. I wanted to look like a soldier, like Grandpa Joe did.

And I worked it in to look like that.

Standing sharp, I gazed at Frank Masters' name and epitaph — "A brave soldier, loving husband and dear friend" — before stiffening my right arm, and bringing my hand to my temple. I whipped it down in a salute. And proudly walked on.

THE END

About the Author

Adrian Brijbassi was born in
New Amsterdam, Guyana, in
1971 and raised in Kitchener,
Ontario. He has a journalism
degree from Ryerson
Polytechnic University in
Toronto and currently lives in
New York. 50 Mission Cap is his first novel.

DATE DUE	RETURNED